Vengeance:

A Never Ending Nightmare

Vengeance:

A Never Ending Nightmare

Johnna B

www.urbanbooks.net

Urban Books, LLC
300 Farmingdale Road, NY-Route 109
Farmingdale, NY 11735

Vengeance: A Never Ending Nightmare

ISBN 13: 978-1-62286-541-3
ISBN 10: 1-62286-541-3

First Trade Paperback Printing November 2017
Printed in the United States of America

10 9 8 7 6 5 4 3 2 1

Distributed by Kensington Publishing Corp.
Submit orders to:
Customer Service
400 Hahn Road
Westminster, MD 21157-4627
Phone: 1-800-733-3000
Fax: 1-800-659-2436

Vengeance:

A Never Ending Nightmare

by

Johnna B

I am dedicating this book to myself. At one point in my life, I didn't think I would make it here. Actually, I didn't think I would want to make it to this point. But here I am happy, joyful, living, and loving life. I am so proud of myself, and no one can ever take this feeling away from me. I'm just now realizing it's not where I've been, but where I am going.

Are you watching my journey?

That was my first dedication, but now I have to add a new one for my mother, Dana Williams, whom I lost. I miss you so much, but I know you are still here with me. I feel you in my smiles; I feel you when I laugh. At times, I swear I feel like I'm being hugged. It hasn't been easy going on without you. I wish I could call you and sing to you one more time and hear you call me Stephanie King one last time. I'm still working on that killer squirrel movie we talked about. Sending you hugs and kisses. Loving you forever and always, my luv.

Chapter 1

Wish upon a star

Raina sat at the bar in the all-white linen outfit her boyfriend Tory had picked out for her. He said it made her look angelic. The clothing fit her short frame perfectly, hugging her in all the right places. Her multicolor pumps added dimension and matched her accessories.

Every time she went out with Tory, it was destined to end in disaster. She could hear her heartbeat over the music playing. Fun was a thing of the past, and she always felt like she was being watched. Raina watched everyone have a good time and wash all their sins away with their liquor of choice. A virgin margarita was on the menu for her. Tory didn't like for her to drink. He said he didn't want her looking like a drunken ho in the club with him.

All the young ladies danced on the dance floor, living their young lives to the fullest. Raina admired their skimpy outfits and six-inch pumps. She knew her beauty could rival that of any woman in the club. However, Tory never let her shine; he wanted to keep her self-esteem as low as possible. She could only imagine how they were feeling. Tory never allowed her to go on the dance floor. His reasoning was that only hoes shook their ass in public. She thought about her own life and how it had gone from shit to shitty. Tory knew the moment he offered her a place to live that she would be nothing without him. He had made it that way.

"Excuse me, Miss Lady, but can I join you?" a fine gentleman asked, interrupting her thoughts before he took it upon himself to take a seat.

He smiled at her, not taking notice of the horrified look on her face. Raina could have shit a brick right there on the spot. Her heart stopped beating for a second as she snuck a look at him out of the corner of her eye.

"I don't think that would be a good idea."

She looked around the club, making sure her psychotic boyfriend didn't see this man talking to her. She knew he would go bananas. Tory was a certified nutjob, and he took pride in his reputation for being a menace to society. He was someone who the murderers and thieves looked up to as a role model. She didn't feel like the headache that was sure to come. There was no telling what he would do once he caught wind of the interaction, no matter how small it was. She could have just said, "Excuse me," to a man, and that would have been considered flirting.

"Why not? You here with your man or something?" He smiled.

Raina took notice of how handsome he was, but she turned her head very quickly. She knew Tory was somewhere close. She couldn't see him, but she could feel him hovering somewhere close. She could just feel the evil in the air. His presence was so thick that it took her breath away sometimes. The mere thought of him sent chills up her spine.

"Yes, I'm here with—" Raina's sentence was stopped by the intense pain shooting through her head. "Wait, please, I wasn't doing anything!"

Her eyes were as big as saucers. Her pleas fell on deaf ears as she scratched at Tory's hands. He had grabbed a handful of her hair with a death grip. She could feel each and every strand as it was being pulled from her scalp.

Tory's grip got tighter as he bent down to whisper in her ear, "You want to disrespect me in public, bitch?"

He pulled her by her hair up into the air so that she was facing him, lifting her up literally about twenty inches off the ground. His six foot three inch, 220-pound frame needed her five foot three inch, 135 pound-frame to see his eyes up close and personal. Raina could see the rage flowing through them. His light brown eyes had turned so dark they almost looked black. She could see the fire behind them and she couldn't seem to tear her eyes away. It looked like the devil himself was staring back at her. She clawed at his hand for him to let her go.

"Yo, my man, that ain't necessary. She told me she had a man and that was it."

The look Tory gave the man made the dude take a few steps back. Tory wasn't the biggest or the baddest, but his aura was strong and thick, and you couldn't see past it.

"Nigga, was I talking to you? You need to mind yo' muthafuckin' business!" Tory said through gritted teeth. "You was talking to this nigga?"

Raina could see the flames burning in his eyes, and she knew she was in for a turbulent night. He held her in the air by her hair with one hand. She felt his other hand wrap around her side. She could feel her ribs cracking under his grip, he was squeezing so tight. Pain was shooting through her body at lightning speeds.

"No! I just told him I had a man and that was it. Please, you're hurting me!"

She knew he didn't care what she had said to the man; the problem was the fact that another man had the least bit of her attention. She could barely breathe the pain was so bad, but she knew not to shed one tear. That satisfaction she would never give him again.

"Bitch, I will finish you, do you understand me?"

Tory began to squeeze harder, and he laughed when he felt one of her ribs crumble underneath his grasp. The sneer that spread across his face gave him a weasel-like look. His teeth were clenched so tightly that a couple should have broken. She could see he was holding back what he really wanted to do to her. The security didn't even bother to approach. Tory brought on horrible problems, and they wanted no part of that.

"Yes." Raina nodded her head.

She would do anything at that point for him to let her go. Tory dropped her to the floor and walked away, but she knew he was far from done with her. Tory was sick in the head and got off on torturing her. She had been with him since she was fifteen. She was now going on twenty-two and ready to end her young life.

Tory had been there for her when her family left her for dead. Like a knight in shining armor, he came in and saved the day. But it seemed like she went from one nightmare to another. Two years into the relationship, he changed significantly, morphed right into the devil. The hitting was the least of her worries. His mind was far sicker than the average woman beater. The sight of blood and fear turned him on to the fullest. It was like the more she cried and bled, the harder his dick got. He would get so hard it would feel like he was trying to get into her chest cavity. The sight of blood in their bed was the norm. Whether it came from between her legs or from him scratching or biting her everywhere, blood was there.

"Let me help you up."

The man came back to see if he could help her. He felt bad for what had happened to her. If he had known she was Tory's woman, he would have never even approached her. He knew all about Tory and wanted no part of that nutjob.

"I'm okay. Just go away before he comes back."

Raina didn't even look at him; she just kept her head down and refused to let the tears fall. She waved him off, and he backed up and stepped away. Raina slowly stood up and could barely stand straight. The pain that was flowing through her midsection was almost unbearable. She could see Tory charging toward her like a raging bull so she stood up as straight as she could. She had learned not to show any pain if she could. She never wanted to feed his sickness. She stiffened her body and put a stern look on her face.

"Let's go. You done fucked up my night, out here embarrassing me by acting like a fuckin' ho. I should bust yo' muthafuckin' head open. You's a useless-ass bitch!"

Tory didn't even bother to look at her; he just kept walking as if he were talking to himself. But Raina knew he was talking to her. She reluctantly followed him out of the club. The valet brought the car around, and they began to walk toward the car.

"Where the fuck you think you going?" Tory stopped walking and mean-mugged her.

"To the car," Raina stuttered. His stare sent chills down her spine.

"Bitch, you done lost yo' mind! You ain't getting in my shit with yo' disrespectful ass! You walking home, and it bet' not take you more than fifteen minutes to get there." With that, Tory got in the car and drove off.

Raina looked around at all the people who were standing in line and looking at her with sympathy, like they felt sorry for her. She didn't blame them. Hell, she felt sorry for herself. By far, she was the hottest woman out there, but not one chick standing in that line was hating on her or laughing. No one wanted her life at all. Everyone knew how Tory's mind worked and they steered clear of his antics. Forget the glitz and glamour he portrayed to the world; it wasn't worth it.

"You want a ride? You shouldn't be walking this time of night by yourself." A nice young lady stepped out of the line.

Raina looked at the pretty young lady, who was dressed in a colorful, very short minidress, and wondered what her life was like. It didn't matter what her life was like because Raina would still trade places with the young lady in a heartbeat. She looked Raina in her eyes telling her that she knew what she was going through.

"No, thank you, I'm all right. We only live about fifteen minutes away. I need all these fifteen minutes to clear my head." Raina chuckled a little. "Thank you though."

She started on her walk to the inevitability of the rest of her life. She wanted to raise her head like she was full of pride, but that would be a major lie. Raina and Tory lived in a loft downtown not far from the club. She would gladly walk any day if it meant she could be away from Tory, even if only for a little bit. With each step, she could feel a pain shooting in her side. She knew that one of these days he would be the one to kill her and he would be the last thing she saw before she left the earth. He had broken her spirit long ago, but she knew there had to be something better for her out there in the world.

Raina often prayed that this was one of the trials God put you through before the good blessings rained down on you. Raina looked to the sky, and the stars seemed so far away. She dreamt of the day she would be far away. She imagined she was a star in the sky shining down on everything, not feeling any pain, just living a peaceful life. She wanted to be far away from this world, Tory, and anything that resembled him.

Luckily for her, the night wasn't that cold. The night breeze flowing all around her felt soft, and it lightly tickled her skin. Before she knew it, she was standing in front of her building. She rang the buzzer for Tory to let her up. He never gave her any keys; he said she didn't need them because she would never be without him. She rubbed her arms to fight off the cold that was starting to set in. Midwest weather was crazy. It could go from warm to breezy to just freezing in a matter of minutes. She rang the buzzer again and, still, she got no answer.

"How did I know he was gon' pull this bullshit?" Raina said to herself, knowing he was on some straight bullshit tonight.

"What the fuck you want?" Tory's voice boomed through the speaker.

Raina took a deep breath. "You know I want to get in." She danced on her feet. The night breeze had kicked in, in full effect. The linen she wore was so thin it felt like she had nothing on.

"Nah, sit out there and think about what you did, and when I'm ready to hear your apology, I'll let you in." He laughed.

"Please, it's cold out here! I'm sorry," she pleaded, even though she really had nothing to be sorry about. She had done nothing to deserve the treatment she was receiving.

"I told you when I'm ready I'll let you up." Tory laughed and left it at that.

Raina felt an overwhelming sadness and resentment take over her because she knew there was nothing she could do at this point. She hated him with every ounce of her being, and yet he was all she had and her lifeline. He never gave her money so she couldn't save any. She had no driver's license. He had everything with him that showed she was ever born so he could make her disappear at any time. He made sure she knew that every chance he got.

Raina plopped down on the dirty stairs and waited for him to open the door. She looked up to the sky, wishing on a fallen star that something in her life would change soon. This couldn't be her whole life story. Pain and misery surrounded her and it felt like the little life she had left was being sucked right out of her. Sometimes it seemed like her lungs weren't getting enough air, as if someone were trying to squeeze them until there was no air left, and oftentimes it was Tory. She couldn't help the suffocating feeling that came over her. Her last thought before she fell asleep was of herself floating in the sky with the stars.

The sun's rays shining down on Raina's eyes caused her to put her hands over them. When the realization set in that she was still outside and it was morning, she was furious. The door opened, and she had to catch herself from falling backward. She looked up, and there was a girl standing there with a smirk on her face.

"He said you can come up now." She laughed as she walked down the stairs.

With every click-clack from the girl's heels, Raina became more furious. The sound beat into her head like a drum. Raina stood up, and her anger came boiling out. If she couldn't get to Tory, this little bitch would do just fine.

The girl didn't have a chance in the world. Raina grabbed a hold of her hair and snatched her down to the ground with a force so strong she knocked the breath right out of the girl's lungs. She jumped on top of the girl and pounded her face in with no mercy. She could feel an excruciating pain in her side every time she swung her arms, but once her adrenaline took over, there was no going back. *How dare this bitch think this shit is funny?* Raina was outraged and showed it in every swing of her fist.

"You want to laugh at this bullshit?" Raina punched some more. "This shit funny to you, bitch? You can have him; take him!" she yelled with every punch. The girl swung wildly, trying to get Raina off of her, but it was in vain.

The girl's screams could be heard all the way upstairs, and this got Tory out of bed. He looked out the window and laughed. He could see that Raina was putting a hurting on the young girl. He'd told the dumb ass girl not to say anything to Raina, but he guessed she didn't listen, hence the situation that was taking place. He knew she would be furious, but he didn't give a fuck. She couldn't do anything to him, but this chick, he knew, had a snowball's chance in hell of coming out of this in one piece. He rushed and put on some clothes to get Raina off the girl before she killed her.

There was nobody outside yet; it was still a little early. Raina let all her pain and abuse out on this young lady who thought she was being cute. Raina showed her differently. There were only a few words spoken, but she said them with no sympathy at all. That smirk drove Raina over the edge. It was the same one Tory got after he'd done something to her, testing her and taunting her to fight back.

Raina felt herself being lifted in the air, but she still had a hold on her victim. She wasn't letting up anytime soon. She kept connecting with the girl's face, making it feel mushy under her knuckles.

"What the fuck you doing? Let her go!" Tory yelled as he yanked Raina off the girl. But she never let up on her grip. "Let her go, Ray!" Tory put a little more force behind his words. He was trying to keep from laughing. Raina had run ol' girl raggedy. There was blood everywhere, and the material from their clothes was scattered about.

"Bitch, is you crazy?" the girl said while spitting teeth out of her mouth.

There was so much blood running down the front of her shirt that it looked like someone had cut her throat. She tried to stand, but her body found the earth again. She was too dazed. Raina felt good as she admired her handiwork.

"Yeah, bitch, I'm crazy. What the fuck you thought? Coming out here like you did something because you fucked him. You fuckin' slut bucket! That ain't hard to do," Raina lashed out while trying to get to her again. She was nowhere near finished. Some of Tory had rubbed off on her, and she now knew she could get rid of him.

"Go upstairs, Raina, now!" Tory barked, pointing to the door. He was breathing hard like he was the one who'd just gotten done brawling on the streets.

"What, you don't want your apology now?" Raina stood defiantly.

"You better get up them fucking steps before I fuck you up out here," Tory said while looking at her like he was thinking, *bitch, test me if you want to.* He hadn't seen her like this before, and it was making his dick hard.

"Nigga, fuck you and that dizzy slut bitch!" Raina yelled as she stomped her way up the stairs. She paced back and forth, waiting for him to come into the apartment.

As soon as he walked in she started in on him. "You left me outside all night so you could fuck?" Somewhere along the timeline between leaving the club and the fight, she had found her courage.

"No, I left you outside because you were being disobedient."

Raina stood stunned. Once again, he never ceased to amaze her. He looked like a two-headed monster standing in front of her.

"You know what? You are a piece of shit!" she yelled as the tears rolled down her face.

Tory was in her face before she could blink. He snatched her by her neck and pulled her to his face.

"Go ahead, do it! Ain't nothing else you can do to me. Because of you, I have no heart or soul. Do it; I want you to."

For the first time, Tory could see the pain in her eyes, and they held no fear. She stared him straight in the eyes, waiting on him to finish her off. She was ready to go. This was no world for her live in.

"You lucky I have to go take care of some business. I'll deal with you when I come home tonight. And, bitch, you better be here! There's nowhere you can go without me finding you." He licked the tears off her face and dropped her like a rag doll. When he left out the door, Raina let out a scream that came from the depths of her soul.

Raina felt like there was nothing she could do because he had cameras all over the house; plus, Tory had connections all over Detroit, and she was afraid she'd be snatched up within minutes of her escape. She had found cameras while searching the apartment for anything to help her leave. When he had seen the footage of her searching the house, he almost beat her into a coma. But, luckily for her, she had found the lockbox with everything she needed. Now that she had everything she needed, she was waiting on opportunity to come knocking. She couldn't just run away. No, she needed him dead and gone.

Raina went to take a long hot shower; she had blood and dirt all over her. After her shower, she lay down to take a long-needed nap. When she woke up, she could see the moon and stars shining through her window.

"Damn! I can't believe I slept all day." Raina got up and went out onto her balcony. This was her favorite time of the day. Everything seemed so peaceful. The stars were shining down on her. This was the only time of the day she felt like the gods were smiling down on her. Tory was rarely home at night, so that was another reason for her to rejoice. Thoughts of her past and how she ended up with Tory took her down memory lane.

Chapter 2

Knight in Shining Armor

Seven Years Ago

Raina could hear her mother Raylene pleading with her boyfriend Carl not to leave. To Raina, her mother was beyond beautiful, but Raylene couldn't see it. She was so desperate to hold on to any man who showed her the least bit of attention.

"Please don't leave; you don't have to go!" Her mother was crying on her knees; it was totally pathetic in Raina's eyes. The thought of begging such a loser to stay was way beyond Raina's comprehension.

"I told you, you got too much going on in this damn house. All these fucking kids is about to drive me crazy. I ain't with all this shit." He jumped to his feet.

"What you mean my kids? You knew I had kids before we got together. Now all of sudden it's a problem with my kids?" she yelled. "What you want me to do, put my kids out?" She waited for his answer.

"I don't give a fuck what you do with 'em. It's too many; I can't take it." He crossed his arms over his chest.

"I only have two kids, you jackass!" She walked past him, went into the living room, and sat down on the couch. As she picked up her cigarette, she could see

her hands shaking. She looked up to see him walking toward the door.

"Where you going?" She had a worried look on her face. She couldn't afford for him to leave her. Raina and Kelly's father had left long ago. He wanted to take his daughters with him, but Raylene refused, hoping it would make him stay. She knew he wouldn't leave without his little princesses. But she never took into consideration that he hated her and her ways.

"What, you thought I was playing?" Carl headed for the door.

"Wait, please, okay? Okay? Can I at least keep Kelly?" she said, referring to her youngest daughter, who was six years old at the time.

"Yeah, man." He rubbed his hands down his face in frustration. Raylene breathed a sigh of relief. "I'll be back in an hour. Be ready to be out." He slammed the door on his way out.

Raylene looked up to the top of the stairs and could see her daughters standing there and looking down at her.

"So you just gon' leave me?" Raina asked with flowing tears of anger. She stood at the top of the stairs, feeling the hatred build up in her heart. Her nostrils flared, and her chest moved at a rapid speed like she was having a hard time breathing.

"You grown now." Raylene couldn't even look her oldest daughter in her eyes. She was so ashamed, but she was even more desperate. The thought of being alone was her worst fear. After her husband had left, she clung to anything that would hold her at night, or at least lie on top of her.

"You know, it's funny how all of sudden I grew up in the last hour. I could have sworn about an hour ago you said, 'You ain't grown, little girl. Get in there and clean

your room.'" Raina laughed and held Kelly's hand while they walked down the stairs. Raina had never in her life tried to step into a grown woman's shoes but, for some reason, she did feel grown up in that moment. Her heart turned cold, and her soul went black. This was no longer her mother standing in front of her. This stranger was a pathetic portion of a woman, and she no longer held a place in Raina's heart.

"Well, you know what I meant," Raylene stammered, so ashamed and embarrassed that she could barely look at her daughter. Raylene fidgeted with her lighter, trying to light another cigarette.

"Yeah, I know what you meant then, and I know what you mean now. Back then you meant I was your daughter; now I'm ass out. You don't give a flying fuck about what happens to me."

Raina was pissed, but mostly hurt, and she did not care how her mother took her words. She had never cursed at her mother or around her. Hell, she had never even rolled her eyes at her mother. No matter what Raylene did, Raina loved her unconditionally, even with all the men she had running in and out of the house. As long as she and Kelly were safe and her mother seemed a little happy, everything was okay.

"You better tone that shit down!" Raylene walked toward her daughter. No matter what was going on, there was no way her child was going to disrespect her, or so she thought. Raina had only just begun.

"Why? I'm grown now, ain't I? You about to leave me, ain't you? Then I think it's about time I start to toughen up," Raina said with a smirk. "I would say be more tough like you, but that would be a total lie." She still held tight to Kelly's hand. Raina was all she had in the world.

That last remark was like a dagger through the heart. "Go pack your clothes." Raylene looked to Kelly and, after a long pause, she turned her attention back to Raina. "Now you listen, little girl, I will fuck you up if you ever speak to me like that again!" She pointed her finger in Raina's face.

Raylene was shaking and really didn't know what she was doing. Never in her life had she thought about leaving her children. She always said that no man was worth leaving her kids; but, here she was, leaving her oldest for dead. It hurt her to her heart to look into her daughter's eyes. She could see they were filled with hatred and hurt. As she and the younger version of herself had a stare-down, she tried her best to stay strong.

"Well, we won't have to worry about that after tonight, now will we? You're about to run off into the sunset with a man who don't care about you enough to accept you as you are."

Raina was young, but she caught on quickly to the ways of the world. Her mother talked to her about boys and men. She and her sister also watched Raylene struggle with different men. She had watched Raylene go from beauty queen to downright desperate. Carl had taken her all the way down. He came in two years ago and told her she didn't have to work anymore. She jumped at that opportunity. After that, she had to stop getting her hair and nails done, and designer clothes went out the window. He sucked out all the self-esteem Raylene ever had in her.

"Go have a wonderful life with Chester the child molester. You want to know why all of a sudden there's too many kids in this house? Huh, Mommy?" Raina looked her square in the eyes. "Because I put a knife up to his neck when he thought he was about to get some from me the other night."

The shocked look on her mother's face was priceless, so she dug the knife deeper. She walked in closer. "Yeah, he came in breathing hard, all liquored up, rubbing all over my body, talking 'bout he couldn't wait to feel my sweet, warm, tight, little pussy. That is, until I pulled that knife so quickly that he looked like he was about to piss his pants. His little stuff shriveled right up." Raina laughed. "Thought he was getting ready to get it in. He was hella amped." She laughed some more. "Until I tried to carve a permanent smile on his face."

"You a fuckin' liar, you little bitch! That's why I'm leaving yo' little ho ass here! Carl would never do no shit like that! He been taking real good care of us." Raylene felt her soul shake with every word that Raina spoke. It can't be true, *she thought.*

"That may be why you're leaving your virgin daughter here, but that ain't why yo' man leaving me here. He started whispering sweet little nothings in my ear, talking 'bout it was time for me to start earning my keep around here."

Raina kept that little smirk on her face 'til Raylene slapped it off. It stung a little, but it didn't faze her; she came back even harder. She was riding off pure anger. Raylene didn't even get a chance to defend herself. Even if she could, she would not have been able to fend off the fury of Raina. She rained down punch after punch on her mother's face. Raylene was finally able to get a couple of punches in, but with Raina running on pure adrenaline, the only thing hurting on her was her heart.

The pain was indescribable to Raina. Her mother was about to leave her for a child molester. In her mind, she had the right to punish her mother. What kind of mother would leave her child for dead? At that point, Raylene had no motherly rights anymore. It hurt her to her soul that her mother would leave her for dead without so much as a second thought. But she wasn't leaving unpunished. To her, God wasn't acting fast enough. Raylene needed to get hers right then and there.

The only thing that saved her mother that night was Raina's little sister pulling on her, crying for her to stop. She got up, breathing hard and looking down at the woman before her. She wasn't even worth all the energy. She didn't know where she had gotten the strength to go at her mother. Raina couldn't even begin to describe the pain she was having. Before that night, Raina wouldn't have dreamed of putting her hands on her mother. She loved her mother to no end, and she would have been too scared of the repercussions. But things had changed in a matter of minutes, and her pain gave her superhuman powers. Thoughts of being left alone and for dead were scary, but the worst part about it was that Raylene was taking Kelly away. Since the day Kelly was brought home, she and Raina had been inseparable. Now she would be all alone.

"God is gon' get you for this, and I pray for that from the bottom of my broken heart. I wouldn't spit on you if you were on fire. Forget you ever had me, 'cause I'm gon' definitely forget I ever knew you." With that, Raina grabbed Kelly's hand and went to help her finish packing.

"I want to stay with you, Ray Ray," Kelly said in her cute little six-year-old voice. Kelly had never been without her big sister. Raina was more of a mother to her than Raylene was.

When Raina looked into her little sister's bright hazel-brown eyes, it crushed her because she knew her mother was going to take her away and they would probably never see each other again. "I know, sweetie, but you have to go with her." She let the tears fall down her cheeks. "I will look for you when I can." She pulled Kelly into her arms, and they cried until their mother came in and snatched Kelly away.

"No, Mommy, no! I want to stay with Ray Ray! Please don't take me away!" Kelly cried hysterically as she fought to get back to Raina.

"If that pervert touches my little sister, you and he will answer for it. That's a promise."

Raylene stopped and looked at her daughter through swollen eyelids and walked out the door without so much as a good-bye.

Raina lived in that apartment for two months before the owner showed up at the door demanding his rent money. She had been surviving off Ramen noodles and cans of corn. Luckily, her mother had all the other bills paid up.

Raina could hear someone banging on the door. She jumped out of bed pissed and marched toward the door. They banged on the door again.

"Hold on, here I come, dang!" she yelled as she got closer to the door. She snatched the door open and was completely embarrassed. There she stood in a wife beater, no bra, some boy shorts, and her hair every-where. She stood in front of the finest man she had ever seen in her life. He looked to be about six feet tall, and he was a perfect shade of hot cocoa with a reddish tint. He was thick: not skinny and not fat.

"Excuse me, is your mother home?" Tory stood there checking her out. She was a fine little thing, but he knew she couldn't have been more than sixteen. He was twen-ty-four and he wasn't trying to see jail anytime soon for something so petty. He had plenty of gushy on deck.

"No," she said with an attitude at the thought of her mother.

"Well, I don't know what to tell you, but y'all gotta get out. She ain't paid rent in two months, and I can't

have y'all just living here for free," he said halfway
sympathetically.

"That's okay. I'll get out, but can you give me a week
please?" She was trying not to cry in front of him. She
knew she had no money to give him, and he needed his
money.

"You'll get out? Where is your moms?" He looked
around into the empty apartment.

"When you find her, shoot the bitch!" Raina's hurt
turned into anger when she thought about the fact that
she was about to be out on the street.

"You don't mean that." He raised his eyebrows.

"How the fuck do you know what I mean? That dirty
bitch left me for dead, so fuck her! I'll be out. Can you
just give me a week?" She crossed her arms under her
breasts, pushing them up. She was stacked up real nice,
and Tory couldn't help taking in all her curves.

"How old are you?"

"Fifteen, why?" She put her hands on her hips. She
knew why he had asked that question. By the look in
his eyes, he wanted her, and she would surely take
advantage of that.

"What's your name, shorty?" He licked his lips. All
that mess he was thinking a few minutes ago went out
the window. The opportunity for him to mold her
into the perfect woman popped into his head. He didn't
know exactly where she would fit in, but he would find
a place.

"Raina." She put a bounce in her words.

"What?"

"Raina, like rain with an 'a' at the end," she said,
pronouncing each syllable for him.

"Nice, I like that. All right, look, I have to rent this place
out, but I got room in the basement of my house you can
sleep in for a while." He rubbed his hands together and
licked his lips while looking her up and down.

He had come in on a beautiful white horse and sold her a fairy tale of a prince saving the princess. They rode into the sunset to a destination she would have never imagined.

The cool breeze brought Raina out of memory lane. She couldn't believe how a little while turned into seven years. She let the breeze flow through her one more time before she went back in.

When Tory got to his front door, he could hear the TV up real loud and singing coming through. He took a deep breath because he didn't feel like hearing the same thing he had heard every night for seven years. He never understood how one person could watch the same movie over and over again and act like they had never seen it every time. But this was her happy time; this was the only time he could see how beautiful her smile was. No matter how badly he treated Raina, he did love her in his own sick way. He put his key in the door.

"'Is there a heart, is there a heart in the house tonight? Stand up, stand up, let me know, let me know that you understand,'" Raina sang along with her favorite movie, *The Five Heartbeats*. "'The whole world is an ashtray, Eddy Kane.'" She added her own ad-lib, mocking the movie.

"How can you watch the same thing over and over again? I don't get it," Tory asked as he walked in and put his keys down on the table.

"You know this is my shit." She snapped her fingers and continued to sing along with "Choir Boy." She took a quick glance at him and wondered how a man could be so beautiful on the outside but so ugly on the inside.

"Well, when your movie ends, come see about me." Tory walked to the back of the loft and into the bedroom.

Raina flopped down on the couch, pressed stop on the Blu-ray player, and stared at the blank screen in front

of her. *There has to be a better life for me out there.*
Almost to the brink of tears, she took a deep breath
and headed to the back of the loft to see what sickness
he had in store for her. As soon as she stepped into the
room and shut the door, Tory pounced on her.

"You been getting real flip at the lip today. What you
think, I won't fuck you up?" He pressed his face into hers
as he bit into her cheek and sucked.

"I'm not scared of you! Do what you gon' do." Raina
winced as she bit down on her own tongue so she wouldn't
cry out from the pain in her face. She tried to push him
off of her, but he was like a mountain over her.

"Oh, yeah? That's what I like! I don't want you to be
scared; I want you to fight back."

Tory ripped off her tank top and snatched her panties
down around her ankles, all while holding her by the
neck and pressing her against the wall. If she didn't know
what was about to come, she would've thought the scene
was sexy. Every woman likes to be roughed up in the bedroom a little, but she knew he was about to go all the way
into left field. He dug his fingers in her pussy, scratching
at the inside of her walls. She swung wildly at him, trying
to stop him because the pain was so bad. When she
looked down and saw the blood running down his hands,
she really tried to fight back, but she was no match for
him. She looked at his face and could see nothing but the
devil. He was actually smiling and laughing at the sight
of blood coming out of her. He was getting ready to get
down and dirty.

"Pray to me." He breathed the words heavily in her ears.

"Fuck you!" Raina yelled as she spit in his face. She
refused to participate in any more of his torture sessions.
She just wanted him to get it over with. This was his way
of telling her to get down on her knees in the praying
position and suck his dick.

"Bitch, you gon' pray to me." He wiped his face and licked the spit as he pushed her head toward his crotch.

Raina couldn't fight the tears anymore. She didn't understand why he wouldn't just kill her if he hated her so much.

"Oh, you too good to get on yo' knees?" Tory snatched her up by her hair and slung her onto the bed on her stomach. Before she could get up, he was on her back and pinning her down. She was so worn out she could barely fight anymore. He had totally drained her energy and will to fight.

"Stop, get off me!" Raina screamed at the top of her lungs.

But Tory never stopped. He loved this whole scene taking place. Tory sat up on the back of her legs and spit down the crack of her ass.

"What are you doing?" Raina couldn't see him because he was holding her down into the bed.

"Oh, I'ma show you what I'm doing, and then, bitch, you gon' learn to respect me." He gritted his teeth as he leaned down and whispered into her ear. Then, with a sinister smile spread across his face, he spit in his hand, rubbed it all over his dick, and rammed it into her ass.

"Oh, my God!" Raina screamed as she bucked and struggled under his weight.

Tory grunted and moaned with each stroke, not paying any attention to Raina's cries. She lay under him motionless as he continued ravaging her anus.

"Nigga, you know the deal, break bread!" a masked gunman shouted, breaking into the room and holding a .50-caliber Desert Eagle with a silencer attached to the end, pointing it toward Tory.

But he never stopped pumping into Raina's ass. "I know you niggas better get the fuck out of my crib!" Tory finally stopped pumping and turned toward the robbers, showing his bloody and shitty dick.

Raina quickly jumped up and scrambled for the covers and covered herself.

The gunman and his boys had been watching Tory for a while and watched him walk in the house like shit was sweet. They were about to show him the shitty side of the game. None of them cared about his reputation. Shit, money was money, and they didn't care where it came from.

"Ain't this a bitch? Fuck you niggas doing? You know who the fuck I am?" Tory was heated that he had gotten caught slipping. *How the fuck these niggas get in my shit? If I make it through this shit, I'm gon' torture the building owner.*

"Yeah, nigga, we know who the fuck you is: a dead-ass ma'fucka in the next five minutes if you don't get to talking right now!" another masked man stated while walking up to Tory, hitting him in the head with a gun equally as big as the first gunman's.

"Aw, fuck! Chill out, cuz!" Tory felt pain radiating all over his head.

Raina just sat there watching, hoping and praying that they would kill him. But she just knew her luck wasn't that good. She wasn't scared of death anymore. If this was her last night on earth, she wanted to see Tory die first. She hoped tonight would be the night she watched the life drain from his eyes. The masked man pushed Tory on the bed next to her.

"You muthafuckas may as well start shooting, 'cause I ain't telling you shit! Pussy-ass niggas!" Tory looked each and every one of them in the eyes. One gunman took aim.

"Wait, please!" Raina jumped in front of him, shielding him from the bullet that was sure to blow his whole top half off.

Tory smiled a little, thinking he had himself a loyal-ass bitch.

"Wait for what? Both you muthafuckas gon' to die. Which one goes first is up to you!" one of the gunmen spat.

"Just chill, baby, I got this." Tory pushed her off him. Raina looked at him and started laughing, then looked back to the gunman.

"Man, fuck this shit! Nigga, start talking before I start shooting!" The gunman took aim again.

"Wait, please!" Raina took a pause before her next words came out of her mouth. She didn't know how it would end. "Let me do it." She never broke eye contact with the gunman.

"Let you do what?" Tory and the gunman asked simultaneously.

Raina rose out of the bed and stood in front of the gunmen, naked as the day she was born. They could see the bruises all over her body. They could clearly see the blood that was beginning to dry on her thighs. There was a footprint on her thigh, fist marks on her chest, and bite marks damn near everywhere else. She watched them take in all her beauty and bruises. She was stacked up real nicely, but the bruises took away from her beauty.

"Let me kill him," she said seriously as the tears fell from her eyes. "I don't care if you kill me afterward; I just want to be the one to send him to hell." She looked Tory straight in the eyes.

"You scandalous-ass bitch! You set me up!" Tory yelled and lunged toward her, but she backed away.

One of the gunmen stopped Tory with a wave of the gun.

"I have never met these men a day in my life, but they seem to want the same thing I want: you dead."

Tory looked Raina deep in the eyes and could see she was dead serious.

"Now please, I don't want anything. I know the number to the safe, and I can give you the keys to the cars. I don't want anything but him dead." Raina pleaded her case as calmly as if she were negotiating a car deal. Tory looked at her; she knew what he was thinking. He didn't know she knew all that information. She had watched his every move whenever he allowed her to be around him.

"Damn, nigga, you must have really fucked ol' girl over! Ain't nothing like a woman scorned. But you know, she drives a hard bargain." The gunman handed her the gun, not worried about what she would do with it because he pulled another one from behind his back and pointed it at her.

"How you know she ain't lying?" Tory asked, praying she was. He didn't think he was that bad to make her want to dead him.

Raina pulled the trigger, blowing his whole leg off without a second thought. The backfire almost knocked her down, but she caught herself before she could fall backward. She had never in her life shot a gun. But Tory made sure she saw one almost every day as he forced it into her mouth or vagina as a scare tactic.

The scream that came out of Tory's mouth was nothing like any of them had ever heard. Raina relished the sound of his screaming; it was hers multiplied by ten. And he still hadn't felt as much pain as she had. He had tortured her for seven years straight, but no more. It was payback time.

"The safe number is nine left, eleven right, four left, and the keys to the cars are in the closet on the top shelf," Raina told the robbers, never taking her eyes off her target. She loved watching the tears run down Tory's face. She could see him screaming words, but she could barely hear him. The sound of the gun had deafened her for a minute. But the sight alone was enough to fulfill her desires to see him writhe in pain.

One of the gunmen ran to see if she was telling the truth. Raina got in a better stance and pulled the trigger again, shooting Tory in the neck, blowing his head completely off. The gunman watched on in excitement. If this were a movie, this shit would have been sexy. Raina didn't want to torture him; she just wanted him dead. It was as if she were having an out-of-body experience. The tingles that were running through her body felt orgasmic. She stood there thinking of everything he had ever done to her. Now it was over. She could leave and live her life.

"Yo, she wasn't lying, dog!" The second gunman ran back in with a trash bag full of money in one hand and keys to the cars in the other hand. "Jackpot!" They looked back at her as she dropped the gun and sat back down on the bed.

"How you know we ain't gon' kill you or do nothing bad to you?" He waited for her response.

"There is nothing you can do to me; I'm already dead. I know my life may end here tonight. But, like I told you before, I just wanted to be the one to end his life." Raina looked back at Tory's headless body. "There is no way in the world I was leaving this earth with him still here," she said with conviction in her voice.

Raina didn't know if Tory had made her stronger or more hateful. Either way, she knew she was going to be all right.

"Let's go, man," one of the gunmen said. He was ready to go.

"What we gon' do about her?" The other gunman looked at her for a while. He couldn't imagine what her life was like to make her want to kill her own man. The bruises on her body told a thousand stories though.

"Don't worry. He owned the whole building. No one lives here but us." Raina sat down on the bed, waiting to see what they were going to do. Either way, she was happy, even if only for a brief second.

"Just leave her, man. Let's get out of here."

"If I hear anything, I will come back for you," the gunman threatened.

"You have a nice day, sir." Raina half smiled at him.

Chapter 3

New Beginnings

For the next twenty-four hours, Raina sat and stared at Tory's body. The odor of his rotting corpse didn't seem to bother her. He was gone and never coming back. He could never hurt her again. Now all she had to do was figure out what her next move would be. She wasn't worried about being caught; no one knew who she was. Tory never told anyone her name. She had never taken an ID picture, and she had never been fingerprinted. When he let her move in with him, he took over her life and kept her as his little secret. On the rare occasions that he let her go out with him, she didn't need any identification because no one dared to ask Tory or anyone with him for ID. He never introduced her to anyone, and she wasn't allowed to talk to anyone. Tory didn't have a crew; he robbed and killed alone. His theory was that you couldn't tell on yourself.

Raina went to the safe hidden in the closet underneath the floor. She punched in the code, and the door popped open. She squatted down and stared at all the stacks and stacks of money. She knew he had two safes where he kept everything. Fear gripped her so tightly sometimes that she felt as though she couldn't breathe. The thought alone of escaping and being caught stopped her in her tracks every time she considered getting away.

After Raina cleaned out the safe, she started on her closet, taking every piece of clothing she had. She left nothing that could be traced back to her. Tory may have been an asshole, but he kept her cleaner than the Board of Health. She walked around, going through every nook and cranny of the loft, walking past Tory's lifeless body as if it were nothing. She finally had everything and was ready to leave.

There was one last thing to do. Raina went into Tory's little secret room and took all the surveillance material he had in there. She got all of her belongings out of the apartment and packed them up in the car, then walked back to the room where Tory lay and tossed all of the tapes in a pile next to him. She took a can of oil sheen off the dresser and found a lighter in his pocket. Looking around the room, Raina felt a sense of emancipation. Taking a deep breath, Raina aimed, sprayed the oil sheen, lit the lighter, and then set everything on fire with her handmade blowtorch. The chains had been broken, and the grip he had on her life was gone. She could now breathe.

"Die, bitch, and burn in hell!" Raina spat before walking out the door.

An hour later, Raina stood at the Greyhound station, staring at all the destinations where she could run. She had stopped in a back alley and taken out the belongings she was taking with her and set the car and rest of everything else on fire with her handmade blowtorch. She wanted to erase the fact that she was ever in Detroit because she knew she was never coming back. She thought her heart would beat out of her chest. She had gotten a few feet away when the car blew up, but she never lost a step in her stride. She ran as fast as she could to the nearest bus stop. With two suitcases and a duffle bag, she boarded the bus to the Greyhound station. She had never been anywhere beside Detroit, so it really didn't make any difference. She just wanted to get away.

Now, she closed her eyes, ran her fingers down the list, and counted to three. Wherever her fingers ended up, that's where she would go.

"One, two, three!" Raina opened her left eye and saw that her fingers were sitting on St. Louis, Missouri.

Raina watched the city of Detroit, Michigan disappear into the background through the window of the bus. All the bad memories were being left behind. All she wanted was a fresh start, to maybe find someone who would love and appreciate her. The eleven-hour, twenty-five-minute ride gave her enough time to get her mind right. She knew she had nowhere to live, but she had her life and her health. At that point, nothing else mattered.

As the St. Louis Arch came into view, a big smile spread across her face. Raina looked around the city and could see that it was beautiful in its own right. The big, tall buildings of downtown were a bit overwhelming, and she had heard about the crime rate in St. Louis. But she didn't care if it was run-down and a war zone. It was nothing like where she had come from.

She had more than enough money to go to an expensive hotel, but she opted for the Residential Inn. She had no ID, but money talks and bullshit walks. After tipping the customer service rep a few hundred bucks, she was in her two-bedroom suite. The suite had an upstairs and downstairs with a bedroom on each floor. There was a full kitchen and living room. The décor wasn't much on the eyes, but it was her new home for now. She had paid for the room for two months.

Raina looked around at the room and noticed the silence that filled the atmosphere. She felt a peace she hadn't felt in years. The tranquility of the situation brought her to tears. Finally, she cried a good, heart-wrenching cry. That day she cried from her soul and washed away all the bullshit that she endured. The tears cleansed her spirit. These were the tears she wasn't able to cry when she was with Tory or when her mother had left her destitute.

She cried for her little sister, whom she missed with all her heart. Everything wrong that had happened to her, she cried away. Flashes of Tory lying there dead came rushing to her mind. She still couldn't believe she had killed a man. She knew that she had done wrong and had no right to play God, but it was either him or her, and she chose the latter.

For two days, she stayed in her room, only ordering pizza and Chinese food. She was officially addicted to the Chinese food and Imo's Pizza. Finally, she decided to get out and get to know the city of St. Louis.

Raina stood looking into the floor-length mirror, studying her bruises. They were turning a light yellow, which meant they were going away. It had been about two weeks since Tory had actually punched her, but the new handprints around her neck were leaving slowly.

"Thank goodness," Raina said to herself. She was tired of piling makeup all over her arms, and it was too hot to be wearing long sleeves. St. Louis weather was like none other when it was hot. It was hot with a capital H, no in between. Raina picked an outfit out that suited the weather and she headed out the door to learn more about the place she now called home.

"Hey, Niki," Raina said as she walked up to the front desk. The girl who had first hooked her up with the room was there, and Raina needed her services again.

"Hey, Shay-D." Niki called her by the alias Raina had come up with. She wanted no one to know her real name yet.

"I need a car, and you know my situation," Raina said, referring to the no-ID problem. "Do you know anybody? Money is no problem." She knew the word "money" would make her ears perk up. She could tell Niki had put to good use the money she had given her before. Her hair was in a fresh wrap, her eyebrows were shaped with precision, and her nails were done. *Money can do wonders for a person,* Raina said to herself.

"Yeah, I know a guy who works at Enterprise. I take my lunch in twenty minutes. Don't worry about the fee for me. You just don't know how much you helped me out a couple of days ago with that big tip. So I got you." Niki knew how it was when you were running away from your past. She, too, had relocated to find a happiness she had never known.

"Hey, you know a store where I can get my personal things and cleaning supplies?" Raina hadn't been shopping in years since going with her mother. Tory had someone he hired to do all the shopping for them.

"Yeah, girl, Wally World is my favorite store!" Niki exclaimed with nothing but excitement.

"Wally World? That's really a store?" Raina frowned, thinking she would never go to such a place.

Niki laughed. "No, girl, Walmart. You never been there?" She gave her a questioning look.

"Yeah, it's been years though. I didn't know it was still open. Thanks."

Raina spent the next two hours getting her rental car. She opted for a black Challenger. She had wanted to get into one of those for forever. Luckily for her Tory had taught her to drive. She drove him around like his personal chauffeur, and she hated it. But now she was grateful for the lessons. She thought the car was so sexy and she couldn't wait to get out and about. After she set up her GPS, Walmart was next on her list.

She hit "Wally World" up something fierce. She had two buggies literally full of food and cleaning supplies, toiletries, movies, a few shirts, pajamas, and bedding material. The way her buggies were filled, you would have thought she was shopping for a new home, but in a sense she was. As she was walking down the food aisle, she felt a tap on her shoulder. She stood frozen in place, and her mind began to race. Who could possibly know her here? She turned on her heels slowly but breathed a sigh of relief when she saw it was a teenage girl with two small kids at her side.

"Yes, can I help you?" Raina looked her up and down then ran her eyes across the kids' faces. They weren't dirty, but you could tell they were in need.

"I'm sorry, I didn't mean to disturb you, but I have four hundred dollars' worth of food stamps I'm trying to sell so I can get some stuff for my kids and my house. I'll sell 'em to you for two hundred."

Raina could tell the girl was scared and just trying to provide for her kids. She really didn't need the discount, but she wanted to help the girl out. After damn near buying the whole Walmart out, she ended up giving the girl $500 to help her out, and she let her keep her food stamps. The girl immediately broke into tears. Not able to control herself, she gave Raina about a hundred hugs before she let her walk away.

Raina also got a prepaid cell phone while she was there, even though she had no one to talk to. She had always wanted a cell, though, and now that she had one to occupy her time, she knew it would take her forever to learn how to work the foreign technology.

Raina felt good about the deed she had done. She knew how it was to have no one in the world to help you out, to feel like no one cared if you took your last breath. She gave the girl the number to her room and told her to call if she needed anything else or if next month she had some stamps she wanted to get rid of.

Raina's next stop was the Quiktrip gas station. "Damn, it's like a club out this bitch!" People had their music going, and there were long lines to get to the gas pumps, but it was a beautiful Saturday afternoon. Everyone was out enjoying the day. She couldn't remember the last time the sun shone so bright. As she walked into the store, she looked on in amazement. The electricity of the city was overwhelming to her, or maybe it was just the fact she had never been on her own. She could hear a couple of girls talking about a soul food restaurant nearby.

"Excuse me, I'm not from here, and I have been fiending for some good soul food." Raina looked at the overweight girls and wondered why they were even talking about eating when it looked like they had already eaten a whole restaurant. She kept her thoughts from leaking out into her facial expression.

"Oh, Sweetie Pies is right down the street. When you leave out of here, just make a right onto West Florissant. It will be next to a club called the Fox Trap; you can't miss it," the heavyset lady explained. "It's right past the stoplight up the street on the left."

"I might have to use my GPS for this one. You called it Sweetie Pies, right?" Raina was storing it in her mental Rolodex.

"Yeah."

"Okay, thank you."

After driving past the restaurant three times and finally finding it, the smell of good food assaulted her nostrils and invaded her senses as soon as she walked through the door.

"Mm-mmm, it smells good in here!" Her stomach started growling immediately. She looked around the family-owned restaurant. It wasn't a hole in the wall, but it wasn't a five-star restaurant, either. The smell of the food made you look past any discrepancies.

"Man, I'm gonna put a killing on this food! I'm hungry as a mug," a young guy stated while getting in line behind her, talking on the phone.

Raina could smell his cologne. It was overpowering the smell of the food, and she would much rather smell him. She looked over her shoulder at him. *Yes, sir, you could get it.* She had only been with one man her whole life, and she was ready to sow her royal oats.

He was dark as night with teeth bright enough to light the city at night. Raina's eyes did a quick scan of his facial features. His thick eyebrows led to almond-shaped eyes with really long eyelashes, and his juicy lips were lined with a thin mustache. A dimple on each side of his cheeks completed the perfect smile.

"Am I too loud for you, beautiful?" He smiled at Raina, noticing the way she looked at him. He looked her up and down, liking what he saw.

"No, sir, not at all. I was just looking." Raina smiled back at him then turned around, giving him a full view of the lady lumps she had in the back. She knew she looked hot today in her black skinny-leg jeans and her baby blue camisole with a black leather half-vest that pushed her breasts up. Her four-inch wedge heels made her seem a little taller.

"Ay, I'll be down the way in a hot minute," he said before pressing END on the screen of his phone. "You are breathtaking, ma," he whispered in her ear. He could see her smile from behind.

Raina walked up as the line moved. "What would you suggest I get? I have never eaten here before." She turned toward him, looking him up and down. The man looked edible. She could always put a little chocolate on the menu. He looked so wonderful that she wanted to lick him to see if he was as sweet as he looked.

"You looking at me like what you want ain't on the menu." He laughed a little as he looked her in the eyes.

"My bad. I didn't mean to stare." Raina had never been in the presence of such a fine specimen. He had told her she was breathtaking to him, but here she was struggling to breathe. She blushed and tore her eyes away from him and focused on the menu.

"No problem on my end. You can look at me all you want if you let me eat this meal with you." He was smitten with her and hadn't even held a real conversation with her yet. Her smile did something to him; it was so innocent.

Raina loved his cockiness. She had never encountered anyone like him before. Tory was her first and only in everything, but now it was on to the next one. She was ready to experience life at its best. She looked at him one more time before she answered. "All right, but don't be trying to slip me no mickey," she teased him.

"You got jokes? That's cute. Why don't you go pick us out a table, and I'll surprise you. Is there anything you don't eat?" He laughed at her.

"No beans, no onions, no pork, and nothing slimy. Other than that, I'm good." Raina stepped out of line and went to find a seat.

He admired her from behind. She had a nice jiggle, and it made him smile to himself. He was quite the ladies' man and he needed to add her to his list. She could definitely be his top chick.

Raina watched, looking him up and down, licking her lips unconsciously as he approached the table. At this point, she didn't care how long they knew each other; she was ready to get her back beat out. Sex with Tory was always a chore, boring and torturous. She knew sex had to be better than what he was throwing out. There were too many kids in the world for sex to be that bad for everyone. She had only had one orgasm ever, and that was in the beginning when Tory faked like he cared about her pleasure.

"So what's your name, sweetheart?" he asked as he sat down.

"Shay-D. And yours?" Somewhere between Detroit and the St. Louis sign welcoming her, she had come up with that name. She figured that what she had done to Tory was shady, so she came up with that as reminder of what she had gone through.

"Skillet."

"You say what happened?" She frowned.

"Skillet." He laughed at her response. Usually the girl would smile and say, "Aw, that's a cute name."

"Your mother named you after something she cooked with?" She looked at him like he was crazy.

"No, my brother named me that." He laughed some more.

"Well, I hope you got a helluva name for him." She laughed. "I hope you don't expect me to call you that." She rolled her eyes as she took a sip of her water.

"Call me whatever you want to call me." He flashed his pearly whites.

"Where's the food at?" She looked around. From what she could see, people were walking from the line with their food, but he was empty-handed.

"It should be coming soon. What, you in a rush?" He smiled at her.

"No, I'm not, but my stomach is." She laughed while rubbing her stomach.

"You got a man?" Skillet studied her to see if she was lying.

"No," she answered, plain and simple, not caring to go into detail.

"Well, I'm single, if you wanted to know," he threw out.

"I didn't see a wedding ring. The rest doesn't really matter." Raina hunched her shoulders as she watched the waiters walk up with more food than she could ever eat. "Now why do you get special treatment?" she inquired as the food was placed in front of her. "Everyone else is carrying their food."

"What? Oh, the food? I couldn't carry everything I ordered, so I paid one the busboys to bring the food to us." He played down his connections. He didn't know her yet and he wanted to feel her out before she knew the benefits of being with him.

"Uhm hmm." She looked at him, trying figure out his intentions.

Skillet looked at her, liking her response to his statement about not having a girlfriend. He decided he wanted to get to know her a little better. "I can dig that. So what do you like to do?" he asked while he put a forkful of food in his mouth.

"I like to read, listen to music while I read, and watch movies. I'm really a homebody." While she was with Tory, she had become a hermit and she enjoyed being alone.

She looked at him to see if he was really paying attention. "What about you?"

"I don't know how to describe myself. I go with the flow. If you want to read, I can read. If you want to walk, I can go for a walk. Watch a movie, I can do that too. I'm not a difficult guy. I just like to be happy. You have any shorties?"

"No, sir. I just turned twenty-two. I don't want any just yet." Raina honestly didn't believe she could have any kids. She and Tory had sex almost every day without protection, and she never got pregnant. Then, with the damage she was sure he had caused, she felt it wasn't possible. "You have children?"

"Nah, not yet. I haven't found that special lady yet." Skillet paused to put some more food in his mouth. "Okay, one more question. What is a habit you have that no one would understand?" He liked to know a lot about the people he kept company with. It was a habit he had adopted when hanging around his peoples. They were very nosy, but he didn't blame them, considering the kind of work they did. He was hoping her bad habit wasn't that she didn't like to clean.

Raina laughed a little before she answered, knowing he would look at her like she was crazy. "Okay, I have to watch the same movie at least five nights out of the seven days a week."

"How can you watch the same movie that many times?" He chuckled at the thought. "I don't think there is a movie that good. What's the name of it? I wonder if I have it."

"*The Five Heartbeats,* and that's why it's my habit, not yours." She didn't take offense. She was used to Tory asking her the same question every time he came home and she was watching it.

"I can dig it," Skillet responded while putting some more food in his mouth.

They ate and talked for the next two hours until his cell phone went off.

"What up? A'ight." He hung up the phone. "I got to get going. It was nice meeting you. Can I see you again?" He looked at her, waiting for her response.

"Of course!" Raina picked up his cell phone to put her number in it, liking the fact that he didn't have a heart attack about her picking his phone up. "Call me when you not busy. Maybe we can pick up where we left off."

Raina handed him his phone back. They walked out of the restaurant together. They watched to see what kind of car the other one was getting into, both equally impressed with the other's choice of style as they parted ways.

Chapter 4

Forever?

When they first got together, it seemed like things were going good, but tragedy struck. He had been shot and robbed leaving her home one night. No one knew if he would make it, and his best friend had threatened to take her life if he didn't make it. Moochie, his best friend, felt like she had set Skillet up and he was determined to make her pay if she had anything to do with what had happened. But, luckily for her, Skillet made it through.

After him getting shot, things didn't seem like they were going to work out. And after the death of his best friend Moochie's big brother Kidd's girlfriend, Valencia, everything went haywire. Shay-D liked the girl who was killed a lot, and they were all starting to get close, but then, like a wrecking ball, her death almost broke their whole foundation. Her death almost took Kidd out, and Moochie tried his best to be there for his big brother while Skillet tried his best to be there for Moochie. Everyone was lost. It was like a domino effect because everyone looked to Kidd for guidance, but he was no good to any of them. But Shay and Skillet were going strong and raising a baby girl together.

"Hey, babe, what you doing in here?" Skillet walked in and grabbed his baby out of her hands, waking her back up. He started making baby noises with Kayla.

"Why you gotta come in here causing a damn ruckus? I been trying to get her to go to sleep for almost an hour. She's a stubborn little thing." Shay let out an exaggerated breath.

"I wonder where she gets that from?" he asked with a little sarcasm. "Kidd and Moochie about to swing through for a minute and get down on *Madden*. What you cooking? I'm hungry as shit right now." Skillet blew bubbles into Kayla's stomach, and she giggled with delight.

Skillet knew the best thing he had ever done was listen to Kidd. His life was lovely now. He had a beautiful woman and daughter, money wasn't a problem, and he was happy. Kidd had put him down when he was younger, just on the strength that he was Moochie's best friend. Kidd would do anything for Moochie because he was his little brother, so after a little persuasion on Moochie's part, Skillet was in and never looked back after that. Kidd took him under his wing. If he was going to do what they did, he had to do it right.

After Kidd had gotten out of the game, he insisted that they all get out. In the beginning, Kidd had started a savings account. It was a safe in the bottom of his basement, but they called it a savings account. Everyone had to put 25 percent of their earnings in it every week. Kidd had no plans on staying in the game; he wanted them to get in and get out. When it was time to get out, Skillet walked away with almost $350,000 after only two years of slanging. He gave $50,000 of it to Devin, Kidd's lawyer, who dabble in a little of everything to invest. He hadn't had to touch his money really since then. When Kidd traded in his drugs for guns, he pulled Skillet in every now and then to help out. It paid pretty well, too.

Life hadn't always been grand for him. His mother loved him to death, but there was only so much she could do. In a sense, Kidd had raised him. He had been listening to Kidd's advice since he was ten years old and nothing had changed.

"Well, when she is fat and full, I'll tend to you and your pack of wolves," Shay-D said, bringing him back to the here and now.

Shay loved her life. She didn't have to work, and she was thankful for that. Tory had never let her go to school and learn how to do anything. All Skillet wanted was some fire head and a good meal. The rest would come easy. They were like best friends. He kept her laughing, and she now knew there was such a thing as good love. The way Tory had raised her was to worship her man, forsaking all others. She lived by that still, even though Tory had never appreciated it. She did anything Skillet asked her to do with no questions asked, and it'd been like that since that day in Sweetie Pies. He never asked too much of her, even though she felt she could never give enough.

The baby had finally fallen asleep. Shay put Kayla in the Hello Kitty–decorated crib and snuck out of the room. Then she went to their bedroom and her Blu-ray/ DVD player to do what she did almost every night. She could hear that company had already arrived, so she went out to greet them.

"All right, now if y'all get any louder and wake my baby up, you niggas gon' take turns holding a joystick and a baby," Shay told them as she slapped Kidd in the back of the head before heading for the kitchen.

"What I get hit for? I wasn't even talking. And what the hell you got on?" He was laughing at her outfit for the night.

"What? Don't hate on SpongeBob. That's my cat; he go hard." She modeled her pajamas, which had SpongeBob SquarePants all over them, and her oversized house shoes to match.

"Dude, you betta leave my woman alone! That shit is sexy!" Skillet winked at Shay-D.

"Tell 'em, babe." She flicked her tongue out and flipped him off. "What's up, Moochie? You antisocial tonight?" Shay looked him up and down.

"Nah, sis, it ain't like that. I'm focused, ready to take yo' man's money. Some new J's coming out this Saturday, and I want 'em, all expenses paid by Fat Man over here." He slapped Skillet on his protruding stomach.

Thirty minutes later, Shay had the chicken and the macaroni baking, the green beans boiling, and the Kool-Aid getting cold. Back in her room, she shut the door and pressed play on her movie. After about twenty minutes, the boys could hear Eddy Kane so clear, he could have been sitting next to them. She had surround sound added to her entertainment center for this reason alone.

"Damn, this is a flashback like a mug," Kidd said in a sad tone, remembering how his deceased woman used to watch that movie a lot too. He was doing a lot better now. His heart still hadn't mended, but he felt like he could go on. If it weren't for his family, he didn't think he would have made it. Watching her die the way he did had done something to him mentally. He was real messed up after all they had been through. She came back to him only to be snatched away in such a horrible fashion.

"Right? Vee used to blast this shit day and night." Moochie smiled at the thought of the sister he had loved and lost in such a short time. "Man, I wish I could break the shit or hide it, but I know she got backup DVDs to the backup DVDs. I ain't never in my life watched a movie so much. I know the words better than the fuckin' actors."

They heard the music go low. Shay-D was having an interesting conversation on the phone. "So you calling my phone to say what?" Shay-D said into her phone. She was a little disturbed by what the caller had just said.

"That me and Skillet is trying to make things work, but you fucking up the groove, acting all clingy and shit. Let him go; he wants to be with me," the female caller said.

"Is this a joke or some shit? 'Cause if it isn't, bitch, you bold as a muthafucka!" Shay had to be sure this was real before she went on with the conversation. *This shit can't be real. Things like this only happen in movies.*

"No, it ain't no fucking joke, bitch! He said you wouldn't listen, so I'm telling you now, and maybe you'll get the hint."

The caller got a little too loud for Shay-D's liking. "First of all, you calling me on some grown woman–type shit, so act like it. Ain't no need for the cursing; at least, not yet." Shay got up and took a deep breath before she blew her lid. She walked into the living room and sat on the dining room table right in front of Skillet, blocking his view of the TV. He started to say something, but the look in her eyes said not to move. It was a mixture of hurt, anger, and kill mode.

"Okay, so you calling my phone to tell me you fucking my man and that he wants to be with you?" She was looking Skillet dead in the eyes, seeing a little fear flash through them. He looked like he wanted to throw up. Kidd and Moochie tried to get up and leave, but she signaled them to sit back down. "He might need a witness," Shay took the phone from her mouth to say.

"What the fuck you doing? Who that is?" His words got jumbled as he reached for the phone.

Shay palmed him in the forehead, fighting everything in her not to cry. Just the thought of him touching this woman made her want to kill somebody. "It can't get any simpler," she said with a little sarcasm.

"Okay, dig this here: I have entertained yo' dumb ass a little too long, so I'm gon' break it down like this. You hoes don't know how to be side hoes no more. Bitch, I'm the wife, so know this: when you sucking his dick, that's all you are, a dick sucker. What nigga ain't gon' sell you a dream to get some head? Know for sure that I'm going nowhere; I'm permanent. And what the fuck are you calling me for anyway?"

The girl tried to get a word in.

"Shut the fuck up, bitch! You done got me started with this bullshit, calling my fuckin' phone. What was we supposed to talk about? Was we supposed to exchange sex stories? Who he spending the most money on? How vicious his head game is? What?" She was now yelling, which was out of her character. She hated to be yelled at, so she normally didn't yell at people. "You still there?"

"Yeah, ain't shit changed. I'm just letting you vent." This girl was relentless.

Shay had to laugh a little. "This nigga got you too souped up. It's good, though. But check it: if you call my phone again, it's gon' get real ugly. I'm really gon' step out of my square. And just so you know, if you ever see me, don't make it known who you are, 'cause they won't find your body." Shay hung up and looked at Skillet again. He had a dumb expression on his face.

"Y'all can leave now; I ain't that mad no more." She was fighting everything in her soul not to claw his eyes out. She felt like her whole world got turned upside down in a matter of minutes.

Skillet looked at his friends with an expression that said, "Nigga, you bet' not leave."

They didn't budge. This bitch had flipped the script all the way. They had expected some fists and objects to be thrown, but she was a little too calm for them. She turned from them back to Skillet and walked to the middle of the room. No longer was she the scared little girl willing to put up with the bullshit.

"So this bitch fucking yo' brains out to the point where she in your phone and getting numbers and shit?" Shay was crushed. She knew he wasn't innocent, but he had bitches calling her phone?

"I don't even know who that was," Skillet tried to explain, but it only made it worse.

"Damn! So it's that many, Skillet?" She knew that stung him. She had never called him by his street name. She had refused, and after a little persuading, she learned his name was Kaylin. She liked that much better.

"I didn't mean it like that," he tried to explain.

"I'm sure the fuck you didn't! Just leave." Shay was hurt beyond words and the tears running down her face showed it.

He reached out to touch her.

She jumped back like his hand was a snake's head. She hadn't been in this situation in a long time, but it was all too familiar. She was shaking so badly that it looked like she was about to have a panic attack. "After all the shit I been through in my life, you want to pull this shit? Get the fuck out!" She pointed to the door.

"I ain't going no-fuckin'-where! This my shit!" Skillet stood up too.

Kidd and Moochie just sat and watched the show. Their loyalty wouldn't let them budge, not that they would put their hands on her. They were there to make sure they didn't do anything stupid that either one of them would regret.

"I just need you to leave. Give me some time. I don't want to look at you right now. Every time I look at you, I see this faceless woman fucking you." That part made her sick to her stomach, and that's when she went from hot to a full-on blazing fire.

"Get out!" she yelled as she pulled the sixty-inch big screen down to the floor. "Get out!" Next, the table went flying, making everyone jump over the couches. "Get the fuck out!" she yelled as she ran to Kayla's room and slammed the door. She heard her baby crying, and she needed to get to her. She needed the distraction, anything to get her away from Skillet.

Shay had put on a good show for the little chick. She would have never given her the satisfaction of knowing that she had gotten to her. She wasn't even mad that he cheated. She figured all men did that. But this bitch violated and called her phone, talking out of the side of her neck. Then he claimed he didn't even know who it was, which raised the question of how many there were.

In the living room, Skillet was beside himself. He didn't know what to do.

"Come to my crib for a day or two and let her cool off," Moochie offered.

"Man, what the fuck just happened? This dizzy bitch done called my wife on some bullshit." He punched the air, imagining it was the girl's head. Skillet was irate. He couldn't believe she did that shit. He knew exactly who it was and he hoped to God he didn't see her anytime soon.

"Who was it?" Moochie couldn't even imagine what Skillet was going through. For one, his woman, Sena, had a few screws loose and was not to be fucked with. He would have to literally sleep with both eyes open fucking with her. People outside of their circle didn't know how crazy she was. She probably would have tried to make him take her to ol' girl's house. This whole little scene would have been multiplied by ten. He had to shake his head at the thought. He was a stone-cold killer, but he knew that it was nothing compared to his better half. She got orgasms just thinking about drama. She was the kind of girl you could choke slam while you fuck her. But he wouldn't trade her in for all the gold in the world.

"Man, this bitch whose name ain't even worth remembering! I sold her a dream to hit, and that was it." He threw his hands up in the air. He rubbed his head in frustration. "What's gon' happen now? I don't know what I will do if she leaves me and takes my daughter away." Skillet looked up into his friends' eyes.

"Man, she said give her some time. Don't think like that; she loves you." Kidd was trying to comfort his friend, but he didn't really know if there was any coming back from that. He had never been in the situation. He and his late wifey Valencia were soul mates and he truly never thought about cheating on her, not even once. He believed their hearts had been matched together by the gods and he would give anything to have her back. Before Vee, there was no one in his life important enough to cause this kind of drama.

Skillet went into the bedroom to get some of his clothes, enough to last a few days. Behind the door he let his tears fall. The thought of Shay leaving was enough to make him stop breathing. He felt bad after he cheated; it had only happened a couple of times. Shay did everything for him, and not once had she ever told him no. She knew what to give him even before he asked for it. She was his world and, if she left him over this, there was going to be hell to pay. He left the house feeling defeated.

When Sena walked into her living room and saw Skillet on the couch, she smacked him dead in the middle of his forehead with all her might. He jumped up, ready for war.

"Nigga, I wish yo' cheating ass would!" She looked at him with an expression that said, "Nigga, try me if you want to." She would have used everything in that room as a weapon.

"What the fuck you do that shit for, Sena? Damn!" Skillet was hotter than fish grease. He wanted to yoke her ass up but he knew he was already in a fucked-up situation and he didn't want to add to it. He knew he should have gone to a hotel instead of taking Moochie's offer. Sena was crazier than a bag full of cats, and he didn't feel like her antics. He softly rubbed the burning spot in the middle of his forehead. He was pissed off that she had smacked him that hard and he wanted to pick her up by her forehead.

"Why the fuck you sticking yo' dirty dick in any hole you can find?" Sena walked into the kitchen, not bothering to wait for his answer. He walked in after her, and she regarded him through slit eyes as he walked in.

"Come on, man, don't do me like that. I told her I was sorry," he said, as if "sorry" were enough.

"Sorry? You niggas kill me with that 'I'm sorry' shit. 'I'm sorry' don't wash the pussy juice off; 'sorry' don't erase the thoughts of you and another woman fucking and sucking, and 'sorry' don't mend a broken heart. They only words and the only thing you sorry about is the fact that yo' ass got caught." She rolled her eyes and turned her back to him, looking in the oven to make sure Moochie's food wasn't burning. It had been in there awhile, but Moochie was still sleeping. He and Skillet had been up all night playing the game and arguing.

"I know." Skillet looked down at the floor. He already felt like shit and Sena wasn't making it any better.

Moochie walked in and could see he should have stayed in the bed, given the way Sena was looking at him.

"Hmm, what you looking stupid for?" Sena asked Moochie. He was looking like he was about to sneak back out of the room. She looked him up and down. *Look at you standing there stuck on stupid! I will fuck you up,* Sena thought as she watched him walk in.

"I ain't even did nothing! You looking at me like you about to gut a nigga!" Moochie's voice went up a few octaves as he hunched his shoulders. He completely understood what her look was saying. He knew her look was basically saying, "I will fuck you up; I wish you would."

"Yeah, I bet! Dirty dicks flock together." Sena waved her hand at him.

Moochie looked at Skillet and shook his head. He knew this was going to have a trickle-down effect on everyone. He hadn't even done anything but, now, thanks to Skillet, he was labeled as "ain't worth a shit either."

"Don't put me in that shit! I don't have nothing to do with what the next man does." Moochie sat down at the table to eat. The smell of food lingered in the air, so he knew Sena had cooked. The smell was what made him get up in the first place.

"Yeah, whatever! Why would I expect you to say anything else? You and that bitch bet' not neva tell nobody but God." Sena set his plate down in front of him. "'Cause you know I done fixed it to where I know if it's been messed with." She paraphrased some lines from the movie *The Color Purple.*

"Where my food?" Skillet looked at Moochie's plate, and his stomach started to growl.

"On the stove. You didn't think I was gon' to cook and fix your plate for you? That's something your wife or your woman is supposed to do, and I am neither, sucka!" She walked out of the kitchen to leave Skillet and Moochie to talk.

"Man, how the fuck you deal with her crazy ass?" Skillet asked as he got up to fix his plate. "She smacked the shit out my ass this morning. I wanted to pick her up by her head. I was so fucking pissed." He laughed. "It was one of them hits Kidd used to do to us to wake us up in the morning."

"Damn!" Moochie said, reminiscing on the beatdowns Kidd used to put on them. "But hey, I love it." Moochie laughed, because he knew that, as long as Skillet was there, Sena was going to fuck with him. It was always funny watching Sena in action. Her filter was null and void. You never knew what she was going to say.

Chapter 5

Come Back to Me

Four days later, Shay woke up to someone knocking at her door. She didn't want to answer it; she thought it might have been Skillet. He had been calling nonstop, all day every day, ever since he left. So much for him giving her space. She got up and went to the door and could see Sena, Moochie's better half and her only friend, standing on the other side.

"Hey, honey bunny," Sena greeted her as she opened the door. She immediately put her hand up to her nose. The smell coming out of the house was so rank that it made her eyes water. She had to take a step back to keep from throwing up.

"Hey, what's up?" Shay tried to rub her hair down as she stepped aside, clearly embarrassed.

"I came to get you out of this funky-ass house. There is no way you'll be able to free your mind if you're lying around everything that reminds you of Fat Boy." They shared a laugh. Sena had decided to give Shay a couple of days to get her mind right, but she could clearly see that wasn't such a good idea. Her poor friend had fallen apart.

"Girl, I don't feel like going nowhere." Shay wished Skillet had come home. Even though she never answered his calls she expected him to show up groveling at her feet for forgiveness. She, for the thousandth time, wished it was him standing in front of her instead of Sena. Sena was always welcome, but she needed Skillet back in the worst way.

"What time of the day is it?" Without looking at a clock, Sena sniffed the air. "Wait a minute, first of all, what the fuck is that smell?" She followed the smell to the kitchen, where she found the spoiled chicken and macaroni in the oven. "Look at you! This ain't you, ma. You are looking like a ho who came up short with her pimp's money. And you smelling like someone rubbed you down with a bunch of onions." Sena pulled the two pans out of the oven and threw them in the trash can.

Sena didn't mean to sound harsh, but she had a point to get across and didn't know any other way to say what she had to say. Ever since her best friend Valencia was killed, all she had was Moochie, and they had a tough love type of relationship. "I bet all you do is feed and change Kayla, then roll back over, smelling like you from Ethiopia or some shit. Where she at anyway? I hope she doesn't smell like you. Go take a shower, and I'll get her ready. Either you, me, and her are going by choice, or its gon' be a kidnapping in progress," Sena rambled on as she made her way to Shay and Skillet's bedroom.

Sena knew the baby was in her own room. It looked like Shay hadn't left the room in months. How could someone fall apart in less than a week? Sena had to find this information out. If it had been her, she would have made Moochie show her where the girl lived and skull-dragged the bitch up and down the street, then fucked him up for putting her in the situation. She always told him that as long as he kept his hoes in check, they wouldn't have any problems. But she was just talking shit, because if a bitch looked too long, Sena was going all the way off. That was just one of her personality defects. She loved Moochie to death, but she would fuck him up, no second thoughts about it.

As Shay got ready, Sena took it upon herself to call in a cleaning crew. She had never seen their house look like this. She knew her girl was going through it and she had to help her. Moochie had come home and told her what had taken place. It wasn't hard to believe; Skillet had whorish tendencies. She wanted to make sure that her friend made it through. Shay had really helped ease her heart after Valencia was killed.

Shay was in her room when she heard a knock at the door. Her heart started beating a thousand miles a minute. She just knew it was Skillet coming home to make everything okay. She checked herself in the mirror before she walked out of the room only to find, much to her disappointment, Sena standing in the doorway talking to some women with cleaning supplies in their hands.

"What's going on?" Shay asked as she walked up, trying to hide the disappointment in her eyes.

"Oh, I called Merry Maids to help you out while we go out for a little while," Sena said it like it was nothing to invite a bunch of strangers into her home.

"Uh-uh, I don't trust these people. I don't know them to be leaving them in my house," Shay said defiantly while looking the homely Spanish ladies up and down.

"Uhhh, excuse you, did we just meet? It don't matter what language they speak. Everybody speak that native tongue of 'bitch, I'll kick yo' ass if anything come up missing,' don't they?" Sena looked to the four Spanish girls standing in front of her.

"*Sí, sí!*" They all nodded their heads together.

The more time Shay spent around Sena, the more she could see that the chemicals in her brain were a little imbalanced.

"Let's go, girl." While holding Kayla on her left, she pulled Shay out the door. "I have been fiending for some Waffle House for three days. I can taste it now: T-bone steak with cheese eggs, cheesy hash browns, and some Texas toast, mm-mmm, yes!" Sena was all dreamy-eyed over the thought of getting to her favorite restaurant. She didn't care how much money they had; she was a Waffle House diehard fan.

"I should have known," Shay said as she watched the busy street pass her by. She noticed the sun wasn't shining. There were clouds in the sky, and it looked like rain was coming. She wished she was sitting on her balcony, just letting the rain fall down on her to hide the many tears she had been shedding.

"So what are we gon' do?" Sena asked, never taking her eyes off the road.

"About what?" Shay took her eyes off the gray skies to look at her friend.

"Skillet," Sena replied with a look that clearly said, "duh!"

"I don't know. I mean, I been through so much shit in my life. I finally found happiness, then he goes and pulls this shit. I just don't know if I'm built for this shit."

"What the hell you mean? I love you like a sister, but you got to be out yo' rabbit-ass mind to let some slut take yo' position. Look, I know it hurts, and I know hurt is only a mere fraction of what you're feeling, but you got a good man. He just slipped up. Don't toss him away for one mistake." She could see the tears running down Shay's face. "No, no, there will be no crying today. We gon' have us a fuck 'em girl party! We'll pack up my li'l rugrat Deonna and your li'l rugrat Kayla and leave them with my sometiming-ass nanny at my house then get out and have a good time tonight. "Gas tank on E, but all drinks on me," Sena sang.

"You's about a stupid whore!" Shay couldn't help but laugh at her friend. "I don't really feel like going nowhere."

She wanted to lie and sulk, listen to depressing music, and wish upon her stars.

"I know you all depressed and shit. I'm not telling you to get over it. I'm just saying get past it, 'cause you ain't gon' leave. No need in holding on to unnecessary anger."

"How you know I ain't gon' leave him?" Shay looked at Sena with much attitude.

"Whoa, li'l momma, save all that shit for the enemy. You not leaving that man; you can barely function without him. He has been gone for five minutes and your shit fell to pieces. You sitting around playing a role when all you had to do was answer your phone and he would have been home. Instead, he at my house cock blockin' like a muthafucka! Why you think I'm coming with so much force? His ass gots to go, plain and simple. I can't even get me none 'cause they acting like they teenagers, having sleepovers every night, playing that damn game all night long. Like really, that's all y'all can think of doing with your free time? If I get woke up out of my sleep to somebody yelling, 'This some bullshit,' one more time, I'ma come out swinging on everything breathing."

Sena felt like she was living in a house full of teenagers. "Girl, he gon' have some stories to tell yo' ass. Don't think he just been over there chillin'. I have been fucking with him the whole time." She laughed about the things she had been doing to him. She would walk in on him in the shower, flush the toilet, and then run out of the bathroom real fast. She and Moochie would share a good ol' laugh at Skillet's expense.

"Okay, I get it. But for now I'm free, so let's get it." A lot of what Sena had said made a lot of sense. Maybe after a few drinks, her mind would be free. After shopping and eating, then dropping the babies off, Shay found herself with Sena at St. Louis Bar and Grill having drink after drink.

"You know what? I would fuck the shit out of Busta Rhymes. I mean, *Halloween: Resurrection* Busta, not this nigga who look like he ate Busta," Sena stated matter-of-factly while bobbing her head to "Make It Clap."

Shay almost spit her drink out. "What the hell? Where did that come from?" Shay laughed so hard she had tears running down her face. To say they were drunk would be to say the least.

"Girl, shit, he looks like he got that elephant dick, like he'll rough a bitch up, put her in a headlock while hitting it from the back." Sena fanned herself.

"I know, right?" Shay said while giving Sena a high five. "He does look like he got that deal!"

"Hold on a minute." Sena went to answer her phone, which was vibrating in her purse. After fumbling with it for a minute, she missed her call, but she knew he would call right back. Her phone started vibrating again. "Hey. Yeah. Uh-huh. Hell nah! Huhhh, okay!" That's all Shay-D got out of the conversation.

"Who was that? And what the hell kind of convo was that?" Shay-D scrunched up her face.

"Girl, that was Moochie. I was just rushing him off the phone." Sena waved her off while signaling for the bartender to come over.

"You didn't tell him I was with you did you?" Shay wasn't ready to face Skillet just yet. She missed him like crazy, but she couldn't look him in the eyes right now because they would only tell more lies.

"How the hell else is we supposed to get home?" Sena gave her a dumb look.

"A cab, Uber, bus, Metrolink, call a ride, I don't know, anything but them." Shay knew Skillet was coming with Moochie. She had mixed emotions about the whole scenario that was about to play out. The butterflies in her stomach let her know she wasn't ready to let him go. She hadn't seen him in days and couldn't wait to lay eyes on her man, but she was also still hurt and wanted to smack the taste out of his mouth. She had been yearning for his touch. She had sprayed his side of the bed with his cologne to get her through the nights. But the sheets weren't hugging her back or making her feel good between her legs. She needed her man back like a diabetic needs insulin.

"Whatever! Why in the hell would I pay for a ride when I can get one for free?" Sena waved her hand at Shay again.

"Ay, ay, let me get a Jäger bomb. This white boy hipped me to this shit. Man, I was on my ass after two of these," Sena expressed drunkenly to the waitress. "And you need to quit it with that funny talk. You know yo' cooch is jumping for joy." She slapped Shay on the thigh.

Sometimes Shay couldn't stand Sena, but she loved her always. "Well, let me get two of those things she just ordered." Shay figured she was going to need to be a little bit drunker for the night's events.

Shay-D was having a good time when suddenly it seemed like every woman in the place stopped breathing and stared at the entrance. She looked over and saw Moochie and Skillet walking in. The sight of him made her clit jump. She missed Skillet like crazy and wanted to run and jump on him. She stared on in amazement until her concentration was broken.

"Ain't this about a bitch? See, these hoes don't know I will go berserk in this muthafucka," Sena said, watching a group of girls surrounding Moochie and Skillet. She had to admit her man was fine as a mutha. His dreads were freshly done and hanging down his back. It looked like he had just left the barber shop, the way his facial hair was cut to precision. The V-neck black Polo tee he wore perfectly showed off his well-defined upper torso. His

Polo jeans showed off a print you couldn't help but look at. Moochie wasn't flashy, but he smelled like money. His baby face was covered in a honey-colored tone, and it looked lickable. Yeah, he was the shit, but these chicks needed to know that he was all hers or they would have to learn the hard way.

"Be easy, Sena." Shay tried to calm her friend down but knew it was no use. Sena's elevator had stopped going to the top floor long ago, and with that "get stupid" juice in her system, things could go very wrong.

"I'm good, but if this muthafucka don't disperse his little fan club, it's gon' get real ugly around this bitch. I got my 'get stupid' juice in me, too," Sena said, reading Shay's mind. She took the last of her drink to the head.

Shay could see Skillet was looking for her. She turned her head so he wouldn't catch her watching him. She wasn't as crazy as Sena, but she too was watching to make sure nobody got too touchy. She wouldn't hesitate to give it to a chick real quick, but she would fuck him up first. If the bitch got out of line, then she too would feel her wrath.

"I'll be right back." Sena walked away like a woman on a mission.

Shay tried to grab Sena before she walked away, but it was too late. She followed her friend to make sure no crazy shit was about to jump off. The closer Shay got to Skillet, the more she wanted to turn and run away. He looked so good. It looked like he had just gotten a fresh haircut and left the Ralph Lauren runway. Her heart and mind were at war, but the heart was winning. Her heart felt empty without him while her mind was screaming, *fuck him!*

"Um, can I join this little fan club?" Sena asked as she walked up to the group.

Moochie looked up, admiring his woman in her Victoria's Secret sweat suit. It was tight in all the right places and made her look curvier than usual. He smiled and started to walk toward Sena, but one of the groupies pulled him by the hand.

"Where you going? We were just getting started." She licked her lips.

"I'm sorry for the misunderstanding, but this is my wife." Moochie tried to keep walking, but she never released her grip.

"That's no problem. She can watch," the groupie said, sizing Sena up, thinking she could embarrass her. She was looking at Sena with her long hair flowing down her back and her five foot five inch slim frame, figuring that, since Sena resembled a white girl and she herself was a stacked-up black chick, it was no problem. Wrong.

"You see, I been trying to act civilized 'cause he say I don't know how to act in public. But scum-ass bitches like you won't let me be great." Sena gritted her teeth as she grabbed a hold of the groupie's wrist and pushed her back.

"Bitch, you got me fucked up!" the girl yelled as she tried to run up on Sena.

Sena simply laughed at her. She knew she wasn't the toughest girl in the world, but she also knew there was no such thing as a fair fight. Her strong belief was using anything that was around and within arm's reach.

"Baby girl, it would be in your best interest to walk away," Moochie said as he put his arm up to keep ol' girl at arm's length. Sena was standing there as calm as a summer breeze, but he knew better. The bitch wasn't wrapped too tight, and it didn't take much to flip her switch from off to on. She was liable to pull a Taser or gun out of her pussy before anyone knew what happened.

"Nah, you betta get yo' bitch in check, 'cause she got the right one today!"

Moochie was really trying to keep this bitch from visiting the hospital. He knew Sena was ready to tear into her ass. There was only so much he could do. Sena didn't talk shit, so you never knew when it was coming. He kept his eyes trained on her as he pulled her away. Sena blew her a kiss as she wrapped her arms around Moochie's waist.

"Go play on the highway, bitch!" Sena yelled over her shoulder.

Shay breathed a sigh of relief when she felt the situation was dying down. She looked to Skillet but quickly moved to stand in front of ol' girl who was about to hit Sena in the back of the head. "Whoa, li'l momma, this ain't what you want," Shay whispered, trying to keep a drunken Sena from hearing the conversation. Lord knows she didn't want Sena coming back over there. Sena was a nut sober, but with that "Strong Man" juice she had been drinking, there was no telling what would jump off.

The girl sized Shay up, then looked to Skillet, who was scowling at her. She thought better of what she was about to do. He looked like he would shoot her where she stood and her thoughts were right on point. He wouldn't hesitate to fuck anybody up over his. He grabbed Shay by the hand and pulled her toward the bar, where Moochie and Sena were sitting.

"What's up, Bonnie and Clyde?" Skillet joked as they walked up.

Sena was standing in between Moochie's legs while he sat on a barstool. She raised her swimming head from Moochie's chest to address Skillet.

"You getting the fuck out of my house so I can get some dick, that's what the fuck is up!" She was dead serious. Since their little pajama party started, she hadn't been getting any good loving, and that was indeed a no-no.

"Damn, just like that, huh? You putting me out?"

Moochie threw his head back in laughter. He wanted to say he was surprised that she said that, but he wasn't. He was just happy to see Sena living again. It took him almost a year to get her back to herself. After Valencia was killed, it crushed her. She cried for months, hardly ever ate, and the smiles he loved came few and far between. The only ray of sunshine was their daughter, and he kept her while Sena was healing. It didn't make it any better that his brother was going through the same thing, at the same time, and over the same person. He never really got to mourn the woman he called his sister, but it was okay as long as he was helping his family.

"Hey, it is what it is." She hunched her shoulders, barely able to stand on her own two feet.

"Don't worry, you don't need her funky couch anymore. You can use your own couch." Shay laughed.

"Couch? That's where you want me?" Skillet pulled Shay into his arms and put his nose into the nape of her neck.

She smelled so good and she was cotton soft. He rubbed on her ass through her leggings, causing friction in her panties and inside his jeans. He didn't want to let her go. He had missed her so much. It felt like it was their first time seeing each other all over again.

"I want you where you belong." Shay looked him in the eyes as she put her arms around him.

"And where is that?"

"With me."

"Until the reaper comes knocking, that's where I will be." Skillet gave her a kiss so passionate that her knees almost gave out.

"Aw, ain't that cute," Moochie teased them. "You had my man over there suffering. I thought I was gon' have to give dude CPR a few times. Plus, I think if Sena would have come in and seen him sleeping in our guest room one more night, she probably would have cut him or put him out!"

Even Skillet had to laugh at that one. Sena had been giving him the evil eye every time she saw him. "Man, get the fuck out of here!" he tried to defend himself. But he knew Moochie was telling the truth. He was totally distraught about being away from his family, and sleeping with one eye open wasn't good for him, either. "Dude, is we partying or sitting on old shit?"

When Sena and Moochie got home, she attacked him at the front door. She was drunk, horny, and she wanted some rough sex. She didn't want to make love this round; she wanted him to pull her hair, smack it from the back, and get in real deep.

"You been missing yo' dick?" Moochie asked as she kissed him all over his face and neck.

"Yesss," she hissed in between kisses.

"Show me how much you missed this dick. Talk to him," Moochie said with sexy bedroom eyes.

He didn't need to say anything else. Sena went down into a squat and unzipped his pants to release her chocolate dream bar. She slowly licked each side to lubricate it, and then slid him all the way into her mouth, making him squeeze his eyes shut. She was sucking him so good he began to pump into her mouth.

"Ummm," he moaned, loving the way her warm mouth felt wrapped around his dick. She also moaned while she sucked on him. She loved the way he tasted. "Come here."

Moochie pulled her up so they were face to face. He stuck his tongue back into her mouth as he led her to the middle of the living room. He turned her around and bent her over, making her touch her toes. He pulled his shirt over his head and pulled her pants down, then positioned her a little better so that her legs were spread out. It was his turn to return the favor. He got down on his knees and spread her ass cheeks. He licked her slowly and deliberately, making sure he got all the juices that were dripping down.

"Ohhh yesss!" Moochie's tongue was driving Sena crazy as it went up and down her pussy and ass crack.

Feeling her legs starting to vibrate, Moochie knew she was about to cum. He stood up, knowing she liked to be fucked hard while she came. He slid his hard rod into her, making her scream out. He pumped hard, hitting her spot, making her orgasm feel ten times stronger.

"Oh shit, oh shit, oh shit!" It felt like her legs were about to give out.

Moochie was deep-stroking her into oblivion. He held her up while he pumped harder and faster, bringing on an orgasm that made him dig his nails into her ass cheeks. She felt his dick swelling inside of her, so she began to squeeze her pussy muscles around him, intensifying his orgasm. "I'm cumming, baby," he said with his teeth clenched shut.

Sena stood up hurriedly, got down on her knees, and slid him into her mouth so she could suck the nut out of him. She slid him down her throat and began to rotate her tongue around his shaft while she jacked him off at the same time. He grabbed the back of her head and came so hard he thought he was seeing stars. She didn't let go until she was sure she had gotten it all out. When she was done, she stood up and grabbed him by the hand.

"I hope you got your white flag, 'cause I'm nowhere near finished with you yet."

"Bring it!"

Chapter 6

Kill Them All

Sonny Jackson sat at the head of his uncle's ten-foot-long black marble table surrounded by six of his most trusted and dangerous killers. They had been sent on a mission but came back empty-handed, and he wasn't happy about that at all. The brothers' mission had been ongoing for a year and some change. He stared at them with his piercing emerald green eyes. He wasn't someone who you would fear on sight, but once you heard his name roll around in your head, fear would grip you tight. He wasn't a killer, but his family was one of the most dangerous cartels in St. Louis, and he rode the Jackson name train to the fullest. The only reason he was in the position he was in was because his uncle, Mr. Jackson, was killed. Other than that, his uncle would have never let him run a candy store, let alone his drug empire.

"You muthafuckers telling me you can't find these two fucks nowhere!" Sonny yelled at the supposed killers. "How the fuck is that?" He paused to let them answer the question and to catch his breath.

The girl on her knees under the table was giving him some award-winning head. She was doing tricks with her tongue that should have been impossible. But he never took into account how small his dick really was. She had his small penis all the way in her mouth, comfortably sucking away. It did nothing to irritate her gag reflex.

"These two cockroaches crawled under a rug or some shit," his right-hand man, Chuck, chimed in. He had the total opposite of Sonny's boy band looks. He was a hulk of a man, standing six feet four inches, with a shaved head and a beard that reached the middle of his chest. He looked like he could have been an extra on the show *Sons of Anarchy*. His beard was white and sprinkled with a little black here and there. It looked like it had all kinds of nasty shit embedded in it. His hands looked like they could wear a size twelve in shoes.

"Man, we have looked everywhere. No one has seen them. I heard since ol' boy's girl got whacked, he been on some brown recluse shit," the young killer named Tyron tried to explain. He was a short, chubby guy who, at first glance, looked no more than fourteen. But once you got up close on him, you could see the years in his eyes.

"Fuck that! I don't want your fucking excuses!" Sonny pounded his fist on the table, making everyone jump, including the girl under it. "Do I need to find someone else for the job?" No one answered. Everyone was a little distracted by the slurping sounds coming from under the table. "You sons of a bitches said you were the best. It's been a year and still nothing! You have 'til the end of this week, or you better start relocating your families." He pushed the girl's head out of his lap, adjusted his dick in his pants, and walked out, leaving them sitting there and staring at the naked girl on the floor.

"You think that was a wise thing to do? To threaten them like that?" Chuck asked Sonny when they were out earshot. He knew Sonny wasn't a killer; that's what he was there for and he needed him around for the benefits, so keeping him safe was top priority.

"At this point, I don't give a fuck no more. My uncle was murdered in cold blood by two niggers and because of some slut bitch. They will pay for the wrong they have done to my family." Sonny didn't care if his uncle was as wrong as two left feet. No one had the right to kill him. Sonny had always looked up to his uncle Ronald Jackson, a.k.a. Mr. Jackson. He was Sonny's mother's only brother. But he thought of Mr. Jackson as much more than just an uncle. Even though Mr. Jackson thought he was no more than a fuck-up, he never gave up on making him proud.

"You know I'm riding with you no matter what. I just want you to be sure."

Sonny stopped and looked Chuck square in the eye. "If I'm wrong, that's what you're here for." With that, Sonny continued his strut to his waiting driver.

Kidd sat in his basement, reliving old times with his deceased girlfriend, Valencia. He looked around at all the pictures they had taken with each other. Some days he could still feel her heartbeat next to his, her breath on his skin, and her touch on his face. He felt horrible for praying to God to let him go be with her. He knew that would crush his little brother, but he couldn't help the way his heart felt. It took some people a lifetime to find the kind of love they shared. He didn't think he was going to ever be able to let it go. He could still remember the first time he told her he loved her. It was the first time she'd ever heard someone say he loved her, and it was her first time ever making love. He reminisced on their time together.

"Man, you cheating like a muthafucka!" Kidd yelled. Valencia was beating him again in Madden. *"I can't play*

with this bullshit-ass controller; the shit is bedazzled. Who bedazzles a fuckin' PlayStation 3 controller?" he huffed as he tossed the controller on the couch.

"Hey, you break, you buy, no dolla." Valencia put on an Asian accent. "And don't be a sore loser, babe, I told you I could play. You doubted my skills, but ya girl comes through every time. And don't blame the bling; my shit is fire." She laughed at him as she got off the couch to get them something to drink.

Kidd admired her legs as she stood up in the little shorts she had cut from some sweatpants. She had no bra on, and her breasts sat perfectly in the air. He was totally in awe of her radiance. She was like the Eighth Wonder of the World. There was no explanation for this woman. He couldn't explain the move she put on his heart, but she stole it the first time he saw her. With all the bad shit he'd done in his life, he couldn't figure out how God could place something so beautiful and pure into his life. He thanked God every day for her and he promised that, if he could keep her, he would change his life all the way around. He would give up everything; all he needed was her.

"Whatever! If I hadn't taught you them new moves, you would be nothing!" he yelled over his shoulder.

"Yeah, all right, let that be the reason," Vee said as she eased her arms around Kidd's neck.

Kidd took the drinks out of her hands. She climbed over the back of the couch to land on his lap and, facing him, she put her arms around his neck. He put the drinks down on the table and put his arms around her waist, rubbing her lower back. The look in their eyes said, "I love you."

"You know what?" Kidd asked as he held her a little tighter.

"What's that?" She kissed him on the lips.

"Do that again. One more time and make it good."

Vee leaned down to his mouth and placed a long, wet, passionate kiss on his lips that had sparks flying everywhere. She didn't know where she'd gotten her kissing skills from, but they were there, and she was glad she could add something, even if it was just a kiss. "Now was that better?" She wiped the sides of his mouth like there was something there.

"Yes, ma'am." His eyes were still closed.

"Now what was it you were going to say?"

"I love you." Kidd looked her right in the eyes.

She stopped breathing for a full thirty seconds before she could respond. He awaited her response patiently. "Say that again." She could feel her heart flutter as the tears began falling down her face. She never thought those words would have hit her like they did. They sounded so foreign that she didn't know how to respond. Love was something she sang about and read about, but something that wasn't supposed to be real.

"I love you, Valencia Ball."

She had never heard that sentence from anyone besides Sena. "No one has ever told me that before. I'm sorry I can't say it back, because I don't know what love feels like." She pulled her eyes away from his gaze, too embarrassed to look him in the eyes.

"I didn't say it for you to say it back. I said it 'cause that's the way I feel. You'll know it when it hits you, and I'll be right here waiting patiently for you say it on your own." He wiped the tears from her face and kissed the tears that replaced the ones he wiped away. He wondered what kind of life she had led to never have felt love before. She was the most amazing woman he had *ever met. He wanted to announce to the world that he loved her the first time he met her, so he couldn't fathom the fact that no one had ever told her they loved her. It didn't matter, though, because that would just make another first for her that he would gladly participate in.*

"If it means anything, you are all I think about. When I see you or even think about you, I get butterflies in my stomach. You make me smile just being around you. Your touch sends tingles all over my body. I don't know what I'm feeling, but I do know that you consume my every thought and my heart, Wanya Brown."

In Kidd's mind, she had just told him she loved him because that was what love felt like and it was the same way he felt about her. His name rolling off her tongue sounded like angels whispering in his ear. He pulled her face back to his and gripped her ass firmly as he stood with her holding on to him. She clasped her ankles together around his waist as he carried her to the bed. Slowly and gently he laid her down.

"I love you," he said again as tears ran down the sides of her face.

Kidd kissed her tears away and continued kissing down her face and neck. He slid his hands under her back, unsnapped her bra, and allowed it to slowly fall. Gently, he took her breast into his mouth and made circles with his tongue around her chocolate-colored nipple. Hungrily, he took both nipples into his mouth, smashing them together.

Vee rubbed the back of his head as her eyes rolled around in her head. She had no idea there was such a feeling, and she couldn't describe it if her life depended on it. She couldn't believe this was finally happening.

Kidd made his way farther down and sat up so he could get her panties off. As he pulled at her panties, she raised her hips so he could get them off. He admired her body and rubbed his hands all over her one more time. Her body glistened under the moonlight, making it look like she had on body glitter. He felt like a boy doing it for the first time. His excitement was at an all-time high. He wanted to make sure that, after today, she would be his forever. He stood up and slid out of his pants and boxers. When he looked at her face, he had to hold back the laugh that was trying to break free. She looked at his dick like it was a machete. She had never seen anything like it in all her life.

"What a way to break me in!" Valencia nodded toward his thick and juicy pole hanging down his leg.

"Don't worry; we'll be gentle."

Kidd pulled her to edge of the bed and got down on his knees. He rubbed his hands up and down her pussy, smearing the juices all over. He had had dreams of this day for so long, and he couldn't actually believe it was happening. He was going to take his time and make this special for her. He licked at her cat, slowly sucking it all the way into his mouth, kissing it as if it was her actual face.

"Oooooh, sssss, mmmm!" Vee moaned and scratched the bed before grabbing the back of his head. She had never felt this good in all her life.

Kidd stuck one finger in her as he sucked. She flinched, but relaxed. "You want me to stop?" He hoped not.

"No, I'm ready. I want to feel you inside of me," Vee panted as she looked down at him.

Kidd rose up and crawled on top of her as she scooted back in the bed. He could see the fear in her eyes. "You sure you ready?" he asked again to be sure.

"Yes. I know you'll take care of me." She pulled his face into hers. She could feel him rubbing the head of his manhood up and down her slit.

Slowly, Kidd went in inch by inch. She was so tight it felt like something was cutting off the circulation in his dick. Vee felt like she was being ripped apart. Her nails were planted firmly in his back.

"You all right?" He pulled his face away from hers to look at her. "Breathe," he coached her, noticing she wasn't breathing.

"I can't!" She didn't want to move; it hurt so badly. He was too big to be her first.

"You want me to stop?' He was hoping she said no but he would do what she asked of him. He didn't want to pull out. He could live in her pussy, it felt so good. She shook her head no. "I need you to breathe, baby." Again, she shook head her no. Kidd went in deeper until he filled her all the way up. He rested in that position until she got used to it. Her legs loosened up, and he began moving in and out.

"Ummm, shhh." Vee couldn't get any words out. The moment was just too good to be true. Kidd felt so good that she never wanted the moment to end. She felt him lifting her legs in the air and he put them in the crook of his arms as he started doing push-ups inside of her.

"Damn, you feel sooooo good, ma." She was so tight. It was unbelievable every time he went out. It was like something was sucking him right back in. He let go of her legs and stroked her slowly. "I love you," he said as he looked into her tear-filled eyes. "Why are you crying?" he asked as he wiped the tears off her face.

"I'm so happy. It just doesn't feel real. I didn't think this would ever happen," Vee explained as she caressed the sides of his face.

"Well, it's happening and I ain't going anywhere."

Kidd put on a good façade for everyone around him because he was the leader and he had to be strong, but his heart hurt so badly, and he didn't know how long he would be able to live like that. He hoped to one day find love again, but he knew he would never be able to replace Valencia. Everything around him reminded him of her. When he felt a breeze, he imagined that it was her hands running across his face. The people around him were in love and happy, so he didn't burden them with his pain, but he prayed to God that he, too, would be happy again someday.

Chapter 7

Bonnie and Clyde Style

"Man, what's taking you so long!" Moochie yelled into the phone. He had been waiting on Sena to come downstairs for almost fifteen minutes. He didn't know why he was even wasting his breath. This was a ritual. He could see why Kidd would get so mad at him for taking forever, but he never paid Kidd any attention because even if you were on time, you were still late when it came to Kidd. But Sena was ridiculous. She was never on time; she called it putting on the finishing touches. His brother Kidd would always tell him this was his punishment for always keeping everybody else waiting.

"Babe, you can't rush beauty!" Sena shot back at him while applying her last coat of Victoria's Secret lip gloss. She loved her lip gloss. It was like her cell phone, and she would never get caught without it. She had four of every flavor. It wasn't expensive, but it still was her favorite.

"Yeah, well, bring yo' beautiful ass on." Moochie hung up, but before he could put the phone down, it was ringing again.

He hoped it wasn't her calling him back because he had hung up on her. She was the type of chick who would call back just so she could be the one to hang up. She was crazy as hell, but he wouldn't change a thing about her. She was all his, and he loved the shit out of her. He knew in a battle she would go hard for him. He had almost lost her before. She had left and taken his heart with her. He was heartbroken. But she came back, and they had been conjoined at the hips ever since.

"What's the business?" Moochie asked.

He gripped the phone between his shoulder and cheek while he put the finishing touches on his freshly rolled blunt. It was a habit he had picked up with all of the stress that he had been under. For so long he had been dealing with Sena and Kidd, trying to help them mend their broken hearts. It was very stressful and heartbreaking having to watch the two most important people in his life go through so much pain. Kidd wasn't happy about it, but he understood. His brother needed something to help him deal with everything that had been happening, and as long as it was just weed, he was good.

"Starvin' like muthafucka! Where y'all at, man? I been waiting on y'all for a long-ass time," Kidd said while crunching on a bowl of Fruity Pebbles. He knew he would need a snack. He was ready to get his grub on but, knowing his brother, it would be awhile before he would eat some real food. He knew to tack on an extra thirty minutes for Moochie and another for Sena. She was way worse than Moochie. Every time he asked them to go somewhere, he found himself regretting that he even bothered to ask.

"Man, you know how—" Moochie's sentence was cut short when he felt the cold steel press to the side of his head. A tingly feeling went down his spine. He didn't even have to look at it; he knew what it was. He himself had pressed that same kind of steel to plenty of men's heads. For the first time in a long time, fear gripped his heart like a vise.

Skip couldn't believe his luck. He had been driving past when he saw Moochie sitting in his car. Skip was a low-level drug dealer trying to get in good with the Jackson family. He was hood rich but he knew that, once he put in work for the family, he would be out of the hood in no time. He didn't know why Sonny wanted the brothers dead so badly and, frankly, he didn't care. Money was his motive.

"What's wrong?" Kidd could sense that something wasn't right. "Moochie, what's going on?" he yelled into the phone when he got no response. Kidd could hear voices, but they seemed far away and jumbled.

"Whoa, partna, be easy with that heat." Moochie tried to look up, but his face was pushed back by the pistol.

He looked in the rearview mirror and could see Sena stop in mid-step at the door, and he could also hear Kidd on the phone going into a full Code Blue yelling. He didn't know what was going on, but he did know that he had gotten caught slipping and he was pissed to the highest level about it.

"What the fuck?" Sena said as she checked her inner thigh to make sure she had her .380 strapped there. She wanted to panic but knew she had no time. Normally, on a family outing, she wouldn't have brought it because she knew Moochie or Kidd had something on them; but something told her she would need it. She was glad she had followed her gut instinct, because if she had to go all the way back into the house, Moochie probably would be dead by the time she came back down. Moochie had made it a point to make sure she could shoot first then ask questions later in case some shit went haywire. Now it was her time to show up and show out.

Sena took a deep breath, and as she was walking out the door, her phone rang, almost making her jump out of her skin. But she had to keep her composure. The phone ringing had caught both men's attention, but she pretended not to see them. She put on her best hip-swaying strut to deliver a little distraction if possible. Her heart was beating so hard that it felt like King Kong was trying to break through her chest cavity

"What's up, girl?" Sena said to a yelling Kidd, trying to play it off.

"What the fuck is going on!" Kidd was hysterical.

"Girl, not shit, had a li'l setback, but I'm on my way now." She laughed a little, keeping her eyes straight, trying not to look out the corner of her eyes. The click-clacking of her heels and the bounce in her walk held the gunman's attention as he took a quick look at her. The sway of her hips had him in a daze for a second. Her intention was to take his mind off the situation for a second, long enough for her to come up with a plan. She could feel the men watching her. Her mind was racing a mile a second. She had to get Moochie out of harm's way immediately.

"Where you at? Where is Moochie?" Kidd could tell she was talking in codes.

"I'm on my way to my car, and I'm about to pick him up. Then we on our way," Sena said as she hit the alarm on her car. She prayed the gunman didn't get on some "no witness" type shit and start spraying. But she didn't care if he did; she was going down with her man. Never would she be able to sit and watch him get killed. Her car was parked right in front of Moochie's. She could feel both men staring a hole in her, but she never broke stride and she kept on going to her car. *God, please let this work. Please don't take him away from me,* she prayed.

"Is he all right? How many are there?" Kidd needed the details. He hated the feeling of helplessness. He was all the way across town, and there was really nothing he could do. He prayed that whatever Sena had up her sleeve worked because Moochie's life was basically in Sena's hands. There was no way in the world he was outliving his little brother, too.

"One, and he about to be," she said as she slid into her car. She could see the gunman trying to hide the gun behind Moochie's head. That gun being put to her man's head had her blood boiling. Every muscle in Sena's body was on fire, and she couldn't wait to empty her clip in him. She could hear them exchange words as she pulled the silencer out of the compartment under the stick shift. To the naked eye, it would never be seen. It popped out after she pressed the lighter in.

"Damn, this has been longest two minutes of my life!" Sena breathed in deeply.

Moochie sat nervously looking at Sena. He didn't know what she was up to but he hoped she would get away safe. He watched her get in her car and then the engine came to life. He took a deep breath, thankful she had made it to her car. He didn't know what he would do if she got hurt. He saw her reverse lights come on, and everything after that seemed like it happened in slow motion.

"Mr. Jackson says hi, bit—"

The gunman couldn't finish his sentence for fear of being run over by the car that was backing into Moochie's car at full speed. Skip dove to the ground, landing on his stomach and dropping the gun.

Sena's car had crashed into Moochie's car, pushing it back a few feet. When she was on the side of the gunman, she jumped out firing, landing all twelve rounds into his upper back while he tried to crawl to his gun. She looked over at Moochie to see if he was all right. There was blood everywhere, but he was signaling her to get in the car. Sena ran and jumped into her car, and they both sped off. She wanted to run to him to help with any injuries, but there was no time.

Sena was so shaken up that she could barely drive. She talked a good game and had no problem proving her love, but she had never taken a man's life. Little did she know it wouldn't be the last.

How she made it to Kidd's house, only God knew. She felt like she was having an out-of-body experience. She heard her door being snatched open and she could hear Moochie's voice in the distance. Then she felt her body being lifted into the air. That's the last thing she felt before everything went black.

"Man, muthafuckas straight tried to body me!" Moochie fumed as he paced back and forth.

"Who?" Kidd asked.

Before Moochie could answer, the door swung open, Shay ran past them so quick it looked like she was running for her life.

"What the fuck happened, man?" Skillet questioned. All he got on the phone was to get to Kidd's house ASAP and bring Shay so she could look after Sena.

"Man, Mr. Jackson's people came for my head!" Moochie yelled as he pounded on the side of his aching head.

Once he got Sena settled into the guest room, he cleaned up a little. Sena had really done a number on his whip, but he didn't give a fuck. She did what she thought she had to do. His nose was broken, and there was blood everywhere, but he'd live. He just hoped Sena would be all right. She didn't look too good when he had carried her into the house. She had passed out and looked so lifeless. If he never saw her look like that again, it would still be too soon.

"How you know it was them?" Skillet and Kidd asked in unison. Everyone was confused because Mr. Jackson had died the same day Valencia died, trying to avenge his daughter's death. But all he did was get himself and his other daughter killed.

"Because right before he was about to pull the trigger . . ."

Moochie paused. He was still shaken about how close he had come to losing his life. No matter how many lives a person takes and how many times you say you ain't scared to die, when the time comes, you ain't ready to die just yet. "He said, 'Mr. Jackson says hi.'"

"Ain't he dead?" Skillet looked to the brothers.

"My point exactly!" Moochie exclaimed. He couldn't seem to stop yelling.

"Nobody knew it was us, so what they coming at us for?" Kidd asked.

"I don't know, but they sure as fuck are coming!" Moochie gritted his teeth.

"You sure nobody knew?" Skillet waited for a response.

"Yeah, I'm sure. The only people who knew about what happened that day are either dead or in this room."

"So now we got to be looking over our shoulder every time we leave the house 'cause we don't know who coming for us?" Moochie looked to his big brother for a good answer. If anybody knew what to do in this situation, it would be Kidd. Moochie would follow Kidd through hell's gates if that's where he said they had to go.

"Yeah, until I can find out what's going on. He was very well connected, so I'm gon' have to really dig deep to see if I can come up with any answers," Kidd said as he looked through his phone, trying to think of someone he knew who could give him some info. He ran across an old friend's number, someone he hadn't talked to in about a year.

"Where's the body?" Skillet asked, wondering how they were going to avoid the shit storm that was sure to come.

"Moochie called me and told me what happened. By the time I got there, it was police everywhere. They were asking questions. I paid this li'l chick to say she saw three men running from the scene, that it was three masked

86   Johnna B

men who robbed him and ran off with his car. I'm gon'
have ol' boy's car towed when I feel like the coast is clear.
I already called Rick with the tow truck and told him to
go and get the car tonight," Kidd explained.

"And they bought that?" Skillet asked.

"Yeah, they had no choice. Shit, nobody saw anything,
and she was the only one to say she saw something." He
rubbed his head in frustration. The thought of almost
losing his little brother wasn't sitting well with him at all.

"I hope that shit holds up," Skillet said, worried for his
friends.

"Shit, me too, but until something else is said, that's the
story. Both cars are being fixed and painted right now."
Kidd always moved fast and made sure to have a backup
plan for the backup plan.

"So what happened to Sena?" Skillet questioned.

Moochie ran down the story, and Kidd told of his
encounter on the other end of the phone with her, and
Skillet was amazed.

"Damn, shorty gangsta?" he asked with amazement.

"Man, damn right! My baby came through, but it
fucked with her. She passed out when we got here. I
guess it finally sank in what she did and she couldn't take
it." Moochie wanted to cry. He never wanted to involve
Sena in this life. He was out, so they were supposed to
be relaxing and living life to the fullest. Now the shit was
about to hit the fan, and he wanted her nowhere near it
when it started flying. He knew it was about to be on; this
would not go unpunished. There was no way in the world
somebody was gon' come for his head, miss, and not get
punished.

*"Vee, wait, don't leave!" Sena yelled as she ran after
her deceased best friend. "Please, I need you. Don't leave
me again!" Sena finally caught up to Vee and grabbed
her by the arm.*

"Sena, baby, you gotta let me go." Vee rubbed her face tenderly.

Sena looked at her friend. She was still as beautiful as the last time she had seen her. Sena never cried so hard in her life as she had when Vee had died, not even at her own mother's funeral. It felt as if her heart had been ripped out and stomped on. Sena would have traded in everything she had to have her friend back.

"I can't do this without you. It's too hard!" Sena cried. She never knew pain could get this bad. She missed Valencia so much; sometimes she wished she could have gone with her. Some days the pain got so bad that Sena didn't know if she would be able to make it through.

"Yes, you can, baby. You've got a beautiful family who needs you. Just know that I always got your back, even from up here." Vee stepped away from Sena.

Sena could see blood start to run down the side of Valencia's head, turning her beautiful white gown into a crimson red. "No, not yet, please don't go!" she cried. She dove for Vee, but she was already gone.

"Sena, are you okay?" Shay-D shook Sena to wake her up. She had been watching Sena sleep for a while, and it looked like she was having a bad dream. She was crying in her sleep and sweating profusely while tossing and turning. The crying turned into yelling, and that's when Shay really tried to wake her up. She hoped her friend would come out of it okay, whatever it was that she was going through.

"Vee?" Sena's eyes were so blurry she couldn't see that it was Shay in front of her. Something in her mind had snapped. She grabbed Shay and pulled her into a tight hug.

Shay didn't know what to do or say, so she just let Sena continue to squeeze her.

"I knew you wouldn't leave me again! Don't ever do that again! Please don't leave me again."

The guys had run to the room to see what was going on. Shay looked up at them with questioning eyes. She had no idea what to do. What they saw tore them apart, especially Kidd, because he knew how Sena felt. He too cried for her in his dreams. Valencia was his soul mate and would forever have his heart. Moochie ran to Sena's side of the bed to try to get her to let go of Shay. But Sena wouldn't let go, too afraid that, if she did, her friend would disappear.

"No, don't take her away again!" Sena kicked and screamed as loud as her lungs would allow as Skillet pulled a crying Shay-D away.

"Baby, calm down," was all Moochie could come up with. His heart broke into a million pieces all over again. He had been through this with her before when Valencia was first killed. She would wake up in the middle of the night screaming Vee's name.

"Please, Vee, don't leave me! Kidd, go get her. Don't let her leave! Don't you miss her too? Tell her not to leave again."

Kidd had to step out of the room to keep from crying in front of her. What was left of his heart went out to her, but he couldn't take it anymore; he had to leave. There was nothing he could do for her. How could he help someone get over something he wasn't over? His heart hurt every time he thought of Valencia. *Poor Sena.* He would pray for her sanity. But he had to get out of there quickly before he couldn't see straight anymore.

"Is it bad that I'm jealous of a ghost?" Shay asked Skillet while they lay in bed together. After three hours of Sena crying, Shay and Skillet finally left when Sena finally fell asleep. Moochie gave her something to help her sleep.

"What you jealous for?" Skillet answered. He was just happy she was talking to him again. She made it seem like he was coming home to a warm, loving environment, but she showed him that it was cold on his side of the bed. She hadn't said more than three sentences to him the past week. She barely even looked at him. All she did was play with their daughter with that *Your Child Can Read* program. And all he could do was watch from the sidelines. Shay said she wanted him home, but it was just to torture him; at least, that's what he thought. But he didn't care as long as he was near his family.

"I don't know. I never had anyone feel that way for me. I have never had a best friend. I have a sister somewhere, but she's much younger than me, and I haven't seen her since I was fifteen," Shay expressed as she ran her hands up and down Skillet's stomach.

"Damn, so I'm just shit on a stick, huh?" He laughed. He'd only had one true best friend, and that was Moochie. Kidd was like the big brother he never had. It was sad what Sena was going through. The thought of Moochie or Kidd being killed tore at his heartstrings. No matter what line of business they were in, what had happened earlier was too close to home.

"No, I didn't mean it like that. It's just different when you have a close friend you can run to. I thought me and Sena were getting there, but seeing how she is still heartbroken over Vee, I don't think she will ever have room for me," Shay said sadly. She would never try to take Vee's place. She knew that that was impossible to do. She just wanted a place somewhere in Sena's heart.

"Believe me, Sena loves you; maybe not as much as she loves Vee, but that's because they grew up together. They were like sisters for more than half their lives. But she does love you. Do you know how many times she threatened to cut my shit off if I hurt you again? I was glad to come home. I just knew I was gon' wake up with her crazy ass standing over me with a twelve-inch blade ready to take action." They both laughed. "So don't trip."

"You know, I wonder where my sister is." Shay looked up at him.

"Do you have a way to find her? 'Cause you know I got peoples. Just get me a little info, and I got it covered."

"Thanks, but I wouldn't know where to look. I haven't seen her or my mother in a little over eight years, hell almost 9 now. I was fifteen when they left. They took off and never looked back." She stared at the ceiling as thoughts of her family resurfaced.

"All I need is a name and birthday and an old address," Skillet assured her.

"Okay, I'll think about it."

Chapter 8

Unbreakable

Sena finally woke up from a long slumber. She had been asleep for almost three days. She looked around the room as she sat up in the bed. Flashbacks of what she did came flooding into her mind. She tried to shake the thoughts, but they wouldn't go away. It had been a few days, and everything was still a little fuzzy. They must have given her some strong medicine. She could remember bits and pieces of Moochie helping her to the bathroom, washing her up, and trying to feed her. She didn't know her mind had flipped out.

No matter how bad it may have been, she would have done it again in a heartbeat. Moochie was her life, and she never wanted to find out what life would be like without him. She couldn't even remember life before him. The thought of losing someone else scared her to death. All she had was Moochie and Deonna. At the thought of her precious baby, she jumped out of bed and ran to her room, only to find the nursery empty. She could hear voices coming from the living room. When she rounded the corner, she found Moochie and their daughter playing in the living room. He was lying on his back, raising her up and down, and every time she came down he would kiss her. She could watch them play together forever. These were the moments she lived for, and no one was going to take them away. She'd go to hell and back for her family. She laughed as she watched him sit up real quick after Deonna dropped slobber over his face and into his mouth.

"That's what you get! I told you about turning her upside down." Sena laughed some more as she walked into the room and sat down next to them.

"Aw, it's nothing. Daddy's baby girl can do whatever she wants, can't she?" He lifted her into the air again while talking baby talk to her.

"All right, next time it's gon' be more than a little spit." Sena grabbed Deonna out of his hands.

Moochie got up to go the bathroom. He had to piss like crazy, but he couldn't get the baby to go to sleep or stay in the playpen long enough for him sneak out. She would have a fit if he tried to leave her. Now that Sena was there, she wouldn't be paying him any attention anytime soon.

When Moochie got back from bathroom, Sena was laying Deonna down in the playpen because she had fallen asleep. He admired her beauty and he was glad she had come out of the funk she was in. He had missed her presence; even though her body was there, her mind wasn't. Knowing how much she loved Valencia, he let her mourn all over again. Sena loved Vee with every ounce of herself, and he also knew it killed her every time she thought about the fact that she wasn't there for her friend. It fucked with his mind to know he had only been about five seconds away from saving her life. His mind was always full of all the what-ifs: what if he had turned the corner a few seconds earlier; what if he had gotten there too late to save either of them; what if, what if, what if? He also thought about the fact that his brother never said anything to him afterward about the situation. He wondered if his brother blamed him.

"How the hell you get her to sleep so fast? I been trying for two hours to get her to sleep," Moochie whispered, not wanting to wake Deonna back up.

"It's all in a mother's touch." Sena winked and smiled at him as she walked up to him.

"Are you all right?" Moochie pulled her close to him and ran his fingers through her hair, taking in all her beauty. He loved that yellow woman standing in front of him to death.

"Yeah, I'm all right." She looked down.

"No, I mean really, are you all right? Talk to me, ma. You scared the shit out of me!" Moochie pressed his forehead against hers as he wrapped his arms around her waist.

"I am okay; I'll be all right. I've never done anything like that before, so it kind of shocked me." Sena shook her head as she pulled her forehead away from his to look him in the eyes.

"So you don't hate me?" Moochie looked like he was about to cry.

"Hate you? For what?" she asked, surprised by his question. She'd thought what she had done showed how much she loved him.

"For putting you in that situation. If it weren't for me, it would have never happened." He felt horrible for what he had put her through. Even though she said it was all right, he felt it wasn't.

Sena pulled his face into hers. "You didn't put me in nothing. I did what I had to do." She kissed him on the lips. "And I would do it again. No second thoughts about it."

Moochie pressed his face into the nape of her neck and inhaled her scent. He just stood there holding her, never wanting to let go. He didn't know what he would do without her, and he never wanted to find out. If it weren't for her, he would not be alive, and for that alone he would forever be grateful and true to her.

"Come on, now, you 'bout to start something." Sena felt his hands starting to roam all over her body, and she backed up out of his embrace, only to have him pull her back into his arms.

"Don't pull away from me; you fucking up my moment." Moochie took a big grip of her ass. "What, you didn't miss me?" He licked around her neck, making her panties fill with juices. Just when things started heating up, the baby woke back up.

"A mother's touch only gets me five minutes?" Moochie smacked her on the ass and went to get the baby.

"Nah, go rest. I know she been driving you crazy." Sena chuckled as she went to pick the baby up.

"You hurry up and get her back to sleep. You lookin' kinda good in them there shorts you got on." Moochie admired her butt as she bent over the playpen. "Yeah, just like that, that's exactly how I want it." He grabbed his crotch and went to the bedroom.

As Sena sat down and looked at her beautiful daughter, she wondered how she didn't wake up in a prison hospital. That would be the first thing she'd ask him in the morning. But for tonight she was going to get the baby back to sleep and get what she had been missing. After twenty minutes of rocking and humming and some Teddy Grahams, Deonna finally fell back asleep.

Sena walked into the bedroom to find Moochie knocked out in the middle of the bed buck-naked. *He must have been more tired than he thought.* But she didn't care about that. It'd been way too long since she'd gotten some loving. She was about to wake his ass all the way up. She stripped out of her pajamas and climbed onto the bed, slowly pulling the sheets off of him. She admired his body. He was a perfect specimen of a man, and she loved him to death. The excitement that was building inside of her was overwhelming. Wrapping her small hand around his shaft, she brought it to attention instantly. Slowly, she slid his manhood into and down her throat, waking him up in the process. Up and down she moved her head. It felt like she hadn't tasted him in forever. The taste of him was doing something to her, something she wasn't able to control. She was going crazy on his rock-hard phallus, doing tricks with her tongue and throat that should have been illegal in forty-nine states.

"Ah shit, ssss!" It had only been a few days since he felt that feeling, but it felt like it was the first time. Sena knew just what to do, which was why since the day they had met he hadn't been with any other woman. He could feel his nuts tingling, and he tried to pull her up so he wouldn't bust yet.

But Sena knew what she was doing. She wanted to get that one out of the way so they could go all night long. She didn't want to stop until one of them raised the white flag, and the way she was feeling, it wouldn't be her. Her pussy was so wet and ready it was throbbing. She could feel her heartbeat in every part of her body. Moochie's body stiffened, so she knew he was about to shoot his load. Grabbing the back of her head, he began to pump into her mouth. She could feel his love seed spilling down her throat, and she sucked up every drop. The taste of him was like no other.

After his body loosened up and she got him back stiff as a board, she rose up, crawled up to his face, and stuck her tongue in his mouth. Sliding down slowly onto his shaft, she could feel his nails digging into her ass cheeks. Both sighed when she finally reached the bottom. She sat there for a few seconds to adjust to his size then she rode him until he fell asleep, snoring loudly as a lawnmower.

"Man, please, the Eagles is going all the way this year," Sena argued with Skillet. They were all out to eat at Houlihan's. This was an ongoing argument between them: sports. Sena thought she knew everything there was to know about football.

"Man, get out of here! So they gon' beat Green Bay?" He twisted up his face. "I don't care how good Mike Vick is, he still need his team to help!" Skillet couldn't believe the words that were coming out of her mouth.

"I got to agree with her, my dude. I think Vick doing his thang this year. He got a lot to prove. With all the money they gave him, he got to get them far," Moochie said.

"Man, that's some bullshit, dude! Get yo' head out of her ass and see the sunshine! He can't win it by himself. And yeah, they gave him hella money, but they ain't give the rest of the team shit! He get it in, but his team sucks donkey dick, plain and simple!" As far as Skillet was concerned, the conversation was over.

"He has his own mind. It just so happens that great minds think alike," Sena pointed out.

"Fuck you, nigga, I'm stating facts!" Moochie defended himself.

"Damn, baby, you gon' let them double team me? What are you here for if you ain't got my back?" Skillet joked with Shay.

"You know I got you, baby. Um, but can we talk about more pressing issues like my baby turning two in a couple of days?" Shay was ready to go all out, but she knew they couldn't have a big party since their family only consisted of eight people. But they'd make do.

"Really, Shay? It ain't too much we can do with a two-year-old." Moochie laughed at her.

"You laughing at me? Shit, Sena has been planning Deonna's party since she was six months old," Shay joked.

"Hey, hey now, don't go throwing me under the bus," Sena warned, trying to avoid the questioning look Moochie was giving her. But Shay wasn't lying; she had a party planned at Disney World. She figured she would tell him after she paid for it all.

"I can only imagine." Moochie looked at Sena, but he didn't care. Sena could have told him the party was going to be in Jerusalem and he would have made sure they had first-class treatment the whole way.

Shay had stopped paying them any attention. Something had caught her eye. She watched a couple and their daughter sitting across the room. She couldn't see the couple, but she could see the little girl. She looked to be about thirteen or fourteen years old. The little girl resembled her little sister Kelly so much that she couldn't take her eyes off of her. It didn't hurt that Kelly had always looked like a younger version of Shay.

"Ay, you a'ight?" Skillet asked.

"Huh? Yeah, I thought I saw somebody I knew." But Shay knew it couldn't have been Kelly. She had left her back in Detroit eight years ago. The girl sat there looking timid like she didn't really want to be there and she played with her food as if she didn't want it. Shay hadn't seen her smile once the whole time she watched her, and she never really looked up at all. She must have felt Shay watching her, because she looked up and looked Shay right in the eyes. Shay almost jumped out of her skin. It was her sister.

"Oh, my God!" When Shay saw those bright hazel-brown eyes, she knew it was Kelly. She could never erase the memory of her sister's crying eyes pleading for her to keep her with her. *What is she doing in St. Louis?*

Shay's body felt like it was floating toward Kelly. She could hear Skillet calling her name, but she couldn't turn around for fear that Kelly would disappear. She watched Kelly watch her. She had missed her sister dearly. As she got closer, she heard her mother's voice, and it made her stomach do a thousand flips.

"Kelly?" Shay asked, looking at the girl she hoped was her little sister.

Her mother heard her voice and looked up to see the daughter she had left for dead.

"Yeah, and who are you?" Kelly asked, looking at the beautiful woman standing in front of her, wondering how she knew her.

Tears started running down Shay's face. It broke her heart to know her own sister didn't remember. She didn't even acknowledge her mother or her boyfriend. "It's me, Ray . . . Ray," Shay stuttered, hoping the nickname that Kelly had given her would ring some bells. Now that she was up close on Kelly, she really felt her heart skip beats. She was so beautiful and Shay couldn't believe she was looking at her little sister in person and not in her dreams. She studied her thick eyebrows, skin tone, and long, off-black hair.

"Ray Ray?" Kelly said as she got up to get a closer look. She hadn't seen her big sister in years but she knew she missed her. This woman standing in front of her could easily be a picture of her in the future. Her heart rate sped up at the possibility. She hadn't been the same since her mother took her away. She never forgave her mother and barely talked to her at all. She got close to Shay and touched her face. She felt something in her heart she hadn't felt since she was a toddler. She hugged Shay tightly and dug her face into her neck to inhale her scent. "I knew you would find me!" Kelly cried into Shay's chest.

"I told you I would!" Shay cried and grabbed Kelly's face so she could get a good look at her. "Oh, my God, you are so beautiful and grown!" In a matter of minutes, they were reunited and had totally blocked out the rest of the world.

"It's time to go."

Shay heard the voice of her mother's boyfriend, Carl, and she felt a rush of anger. She looked up and acknowledged him. The sight of him made her skin crawl, and her anger for him showed clearly on her face. "Well, if isn't Chester the Molester." She laughed at him. "What's up? How you been? You tried to screw any babies lately?"

"That's not necessary, Raina," her mother spoke.

Shay looked at her and laughed. By now, everyone Shay had come with was standing behind her, trying to see what was going on. They could see that this was her family; they looked just alike. Shay never talked about her family, so this was all new to them. Shay-D was a spitting image of her mother and Kelly was the same. Everyone was totally confused. They had no idea she had changed her name.

"What's up, Raylene? What brings you two lowlifes to St. Louis?" Shay looked to the older version of herself. She could tell her mother had had a hard life, but she had no sympathy for her.

"Hello, daughter." The comment had stung Raylene a little, but she deserved it. Raylene couldn't believe how beautiful her daughter had grown to be. It was like traveling back in time to when they were all together. She wanted to hug her but thought better of it. She had missed her daughter. No matter how things had ended, she was still her daughter.

Too bad Shay didn't see it that way. "Daughter?" She looked at her mother as if something in the air stank. "Look, I didn't come over here to see you. I came to see my sister." She looked back at Kelly, who just stood there staring at her.

Kelly was in shock, taking in her big sister's presence. She never wanted to be away from her again. She felt like the little girl running behind her big sister, wanting to do everything she did. She thought about Shay every day, the way they used to play and the way she had taken care of her. But the older she got the memories faded as she gave up the notion of ever seeing her sister again.

"I said let's go!" Carl's voice boomed through the restaurant as he snatched Raylene out of her seat.

Shay watched the scene unfold and shook her head. She could see her people ready to move. Things hadn't changed a bit. She wondered if he had been putting his hands on Kelly; and, if so, she would deal with him accordingly.

"This is not my problem; y'all chill. She likes this kind of shit," Shay said, never taking her eyes off Raylene.

"That's your momma?" Sena reasoned, not knowing the whole situation.

"Didn't I tell you I don't have a mother?"

Carl reached for Kelly, but Shay snatched her back. "I wish the fuck you would!" She looked at him defiantly. "Not in front of me you won't!" She had been waiting for the moment she would get to fuck him up.

"Can I go with Raina for a while, Mommy?"

Raylene looked to Carl, but she knew he would say no just to be ornery. She really wanted her daughters to be together again. She knew Kelly never forgave her for leaving Shay behind.

"You think yo' shit don't stink, bitch? You still ain't shit! You're just as stuck-up as you used to be, with ya fancy friends and clothes. That don't mean shit! You still ain't gon' ever be shit!" Carl spat.

Skillet tried to jump across the table on him. "Nigga, I will fuck you up!" he yelled as he lunged for Carl.

But Moochie grabbed him. Carl damn near had a heart attack at the sight of Skillet coming for him. He fell over his chair trying to get away.

"You done lost yo' fuckin' mind talking to my woman like that!" Skillet was outraged and ready to empty his clip in Carl right there on the spot.

"Chill, man, we in public. Look!" Moochie pointed out all the witnesses who were watching the whole scene in awe.

"I'ma see you, nigga, and you better run for yo' fucking life," Skillet said before he walked away. He had to get away before he went to jail. He didn't play about his woman. Anybody could get it, and he meant anybody!

Kelly held on to Shay's hand tightly like she was scared to death.

"I'll bring her back when we're finished." Shay pulled Kelly with her. It was the summer, and there was no school, so that meant she could keep her as long she wanted. By the end of the summer, Shay decided, Kelly would be with her permanently. Raylene could agree to disagree, or the situation could get real ugly. Shay had been selfishly kept away from her sister for far too long.

"How long will that be?" Raylene asked.

"When we finished!"

With that, they left Raylene and a scared-shitless Carl sitting at the table. Raylene watched her daughter and wanted desperately to go with her, but she knew Raina would never forgive her. How could she? She had literally left her child for dead and didn't look back. But she was happy to see her doing well.

Later that night, Shay sat watching Kelly and Kayla sleeping together on a pallet. Even though Shay told Kelly she didn't have to sleep on the floor, she insisted on sleeping with Kayla in the nursery. They latched on to each other instantly. Kelly fell all the way in love with Kayla and vice versa. Their hair was everywhere, sprawled all over the floor. Toys were stretched from the living room to the nursery. Kelly let Kayla play in her hair, but when Kelly took down Kayla's braids, Shay was hot about it, since she had just gotten them done. But she got over it.

"Are you coming to bed?" Skillet asked as he walked into the nursery.

"Yeah, babe, I'm just still in shock. This is my sister." She looked up to him with tears in her eyes. "I would have never guessed this would be happening."

"I know. You said you was gon' find her, and you did. I'm happy for you. But I need some loving. You not too tired for me, are you?" He pulled her up into his arms and poked his bottom lip out. He was happy for her, but he wasn't used to falling asleep alone. It was almost two in the morning, and she needed to bring her ass to bed.

"Never!" Shay winked at him and took one last look at the sleeping duo on the floor.

Chapter 9

It Ain't Over

Kidd sat watching everyone around him having fun. He had pulled a few strings at the community center and paid to make the pool private while his niece's party was going on. It was Kayla's birthday, and Shay thought it would be better if the family could be alone today. He watched his nieces playing in the one-foot kiddie pool. Everyone around him seemed to be happy and at peace for the moment. He, on the other hand, was missing Vee. He'd imagined this being their life: kids, having parties, and family gatherings. He tried his best to move on with his life, but his heart wouldn't let him.

When he got out of the killing game and met Valencia, he thought his life was just beginning, until the day she was snatched out of his life. He was grateful that his little brother was able to save his life some days, and other days he wished he had just let him die with her. He often wondered if this was his punishment for all the lives he had taken. If so, this was the worst punishment God could have ever put him through.

"Yaaaaaayyyy, thank you!" Kayla yelled, breaking his train of thought when she finally noticed all the gifts he brought. She was busy splashing and playing in the water. She didn't see him when he had walked in pulling two wagons full of clothes and toys.

"These kids ain't gon' be worth a damn with y'all three punks around," Shay said, slapping Kidd in the back of the head.

"What's up, Shay, what I do?" Kidd questioned. But he knew what she was talking about. It was like a competition of who could buy the best gifts. No one could outdo Kidd, since he definitely had the most money, and he had no one to spend it on but the kids.

"Y'all so tough but melt when it comes to these two girls. Shit, Moochie's gift is being built right now in their backyard." Sena threw in her two cents.

"Damn, what he get?" Kidd was going to try to outdo him.

"Don't tell him nothing!" Skillet interjected. "I can't have both these fools outdoing me." Skillet was glad his daughter had two uncles who loved her as much as he did. He looked around and was very happy with his life. He watched his mother playing with the kids in the pool. Kelly was jumping off the diving board, and he had his family sitting right beside him. It couldn't get any better than that.

Moochie looked up to see Lil Tony signaling them to come over to a table where he had just sat down. He tapped both Kidd and Skillet on their arms and signaled for them to follow him. They followed suit. Everyone was anxious to hear what he had to say.

"So that was Skip from the west side who tried to get at you, and it was Mr. Jackson's nephew Sonny who put the hit out. It's not out in the streets for anybody to shoot on sight, but he got a few men on the job," Lil Tony explained to Kidd, Moochie, and Skillet.

"So we still don't know who the hired men are?" Moochie asked.

"Not yet, but I'm working on it," Tony assured them.

"I'm not into sitting around and waiting for someone to come put a bullet in my head. We need answers like yesterday." Kidd was trying to be patient with Lil Tony, but he wasn't making it easy. He paid him good money to get information, not to try.

"Right," Moochie agreed.

"It's not that much info out there. The only reason I found out the little I did is 'cause one of the niggas got aired out. Give me 'til the morning; I'll come up with some info for you." Lil Tony did not want to get on those brothers' bad sides. He had been around long enough to know that if you fucked with them, ten times out of ten, you would lose your life, and it depended on what you did to determine how you lost it. He knew if anything happened to either of them, there would be hell to pay.

Kidd's eyes rolled around in his head as he received the best head he had gotten in a long time. He hadn't been in the mood for sex, but the build-up in his nuts was starting to fuck with him. He felt like he needed to release. The stress of everything that was going on was starting to work on his nerves. He almost lost control of the car she was sucking him so good. He had met the little chick a week ago in Saks Fifth Avenue. She was the first woman he had noticed in a long time. Ol' girl was beautiful with pretty, short, curly sandy-brown hair. She wasn't really thick, but she was well put together. He approached her, and the rest was history.

Celeste couldn't believe her luck. She had just been talking to her cousin Sonny about Kidd and Moochie and then she ran into one of them at the mall. She was at the mall to do a little boosting, but she got the surprise of her life. When she saw Kidd, she saw dollar signs dancing in front of her eyes. She knew if she could bring Sonny one of the brothers, he would compensate her greatly. So she set her plan in motion and was now enjoying giving him some sloppy, wet head in his car. He was indeed the biggest she had ever encountered. It was just too bad she wouldn't get to sample the goods.

She looked up for a short second to see where they were. She had told Kidd where she wanted to go and she already had Sonny's people waiting. *Two more blocks,* she thought. She wanted to make him nut before they got to their destination. Thoughts of Sonny yelling at her ran through her head. She could clearly hear him saying, *"Don't fuck this up, Celeste!"*

Kidd was in heaven, but he suddenly got a bad feeling in the pit of his stomach. He looked around as he drove, but he didn't see anything out of the ordinary. He looked back down at the bobbing head in his lap. He was glad he had invested in those presidential-tinted windows, and it didn't hurt they were bulletproof, either. He felt his nuts tingling, and he grabbed the back of her head. She went down farther on him, making the head of his dick touch the middle of her esophagus. He lost it and closed his eyes long enough not to see the minivan rolling up on the side of the car.

Right before he could bust his nut he saw what was about to go down: he had been set up. Celeste felt his body stiffen, so she knew it was time to get the hell out of there. She sat up, snatched the door open, and tried to jump out of the moving car. Kidd peeped what was happening and snatched her by her hair.

"Nah, bitch, you gon' die with me!" Kidd yelled.

But Celeste wasn't even trying to hear that. "Let me go!" she yelled as she scratched and clawed at his hands. "Let me go!"

"You set me up, bitch!" Kidd kept a death grip on her hair as he banged her head into the dashboard. She swung wildly as she hung halfway out the open car door trying her best to keep her legs from dragging on the ground

Celeste prayed that Sonny's men wouldn't start shooting before she got away. She had one last trick up her sleeve. She needed to stop Kidd from bashing her head in. She swung her arm one good time at his dick.

"Aww!" Kidd screamed as he let Celeste go for a split second. Before he was able to grab hold of her again, she was out the door. He kept a little memento from her: a big plug of her hair. He threw it on the floor and watched as she landed on her side and rolled a few feet before she was picked up by two men in another van.

Celeste knew she had to get away quickly because bullets had no name on them and she wanted to be able to spend that $50,000 her cousin had promised her. She thought she had it all figured out. She never gave him her real information. The only thing he knew was where he had picked her up from. But she wasn't worried. Who was he going to tell from the grave?

Kidd's instincts had kicked in. He pressed the alarm under his armpit to let Moochie know something was wrong. He wished he had time to call Moochie, but he had to concentrate on the road. Celeste thought she had gotten away with something, but he had a trick for all of them. She would get hers. Even if he didn't make it out, he knew his brother would find and torture her.

They had been on high alert because the hit out on them and Moochie made Kidd give him all of the girl's info before he picked her up. Even if it was the wrong info, Moochie had a way of finding people who didn't want to be found. That was Moochie's job: finding people and making them disappear. Moochie trusted no one outside his circle. Everyone was suspect until proven otherwise.

As he reached for his gun under his armrest, an onslaught of bullets bounced off his side windows. He stepped on the gas and pushed the gas pedal down to the floor. Kidd knew they would never catch him in his Aston Martin. He also knew that only the sides and rear window were bulletproof. He couldn't let them get in front of him, or he would surely be dead. He was scared shitless as he watched what seemed like a thousand bullets hit his windows from both sides.

"Where the fuck is the no-good-ass police when you need 'em?" Kidd banged his fist on the steering wheel, and then he heard his tire blow out. He guessed they finally figured out they weren't getting anywhere with the windows.

His car started to spin in a circle. Bullets came through his front windshield, ripping into his flesh. He could hear sirens coming near as his car started flipping. It flipped three times before he was thrown from the small, two-door car. His body felt like it was rolling forever. He could hear someone yelling in the background. He prayed that God would forgive him for all his sins before he died. He smiled inwardly at the thought of being with Valencia again, yet he knew he wasn't ready to die yet. But it wouldn't be his choice.

"Ay, babe, bring me some Kool-Aid!" Moochie yelled out to Sena.

"So am I not in here cooking? You can't leave that game for two minutes?" she yelled back.

"I'm on the Internet. Ain't no pause. Come on, man, you gon' get a nigga killed!" Moochie yelled as he got hit by a stray bullet.

"Damn shame my man's mistress is a video game." Moochie was addicted to the game *Call of Duty*. He could sit there for hours shooting and cursing people out on his headset.

"Come get my phone for me." Moochie could feel it vibrating, but he couldn't hear the ringtone. If he would have heard the ringtone, he would have known it was Kidd's alarm sounding. He hated when his phone rang while he was playing the game so, out of habit, he threw it on the other end of the couch so he could kill in peace.

"Look, nigga, leave me alone." Sena snatched the phone off the couch. When she looked at it, she was confused. No one was calling. The screen just read EMERGENCY.

"Emergency?" she said out loud.

"What'chu say?" Moochie had to be sure he'd heard her right.

"Emergency," she repeated.

Moochie snatched his phone from her and looked at the screen. His heart fell to the bottom of his feet. Kidd was in trouble once again, and he wasn't there with him. "Come on, we got to go!" he yelled, scaring the hell out Sena.

Sena slipped on her house shoes, went to turn the food off, and ran behind him. "What's wrong?" she was finally able to ask once they were in the car.

"Kidd pressed his emergency button. We only press that when something is really wrong." Moochie sounded worried. He didn't know what he would do if he lost his brother.

"Maybe it was a mistake," she tried to reason.

"Nah, it's a certain way that you push it to make it go off. You have to hold it down for ten seconds before it will sound." Moochie prayed she was right, but he knew better. His brother was in trouble, and he hoped he got there in time. "Read me the direction that's coming across the screen."

Once they got to their destination, Moochie felt like he had to throw up. There was yellow tape blocking off the street, and he could see Kidd's car turned over on its roof.

His knees went weak, and everything around him started spinning. His legs didn't seem to want to move. Sena had to hold him up. He hadn't even gotten to his brother. His thoughts alone were fucking him up. He finally got his legs to cooperate. He ran to where the police were standing.

"Excuse me, sir, that's my brother's car. Can you tell me what happened?" Moochie asked, not really wanting to know the truth. He felt it in his gut that his brother was gone.

"You said you're the victim's brother?"

At the sound of the word "victim," Moochie thought he would have a heart attack. "Yes, sir. Where is he?" He looked around frantically, thankful that he didn't see the coroner's van anywhere.

"There was a shooting that took place. Someone shot his car up pretty bad. He is in that ambulance right there."

Moochie looked over to see the ambulance pulling off. He took off toward his car. He could hear the cop saying something, but that was the furthest thing from his mind. He had to get to his brother. Sena jumped in the driver's seat, knowing he wouldn't be able to drive in the condition he was in.

"I can't lose my brother. I can't lose my brother." Moochie kept repeating that over and over again.

Sena had flashbacks of when Valencia had died. She knew how he was feeling and she hated that there would be absolutely nothing she could do to make him feel better if his brother didn't make it. She had had to come out of her comatose state on her own. No matter what Moochie did, it did nothing to soothe her broken heart. Kidd said that she helped him through it, but all she did was be there, and really that's all she could do.

"He's gon' be all right, baby." Sena reached for his hand, but he snatched it away.

"How do you know? Was you there or something? Didn't you see his car? It was about a thousand bullet holes in it. And why the fuck is you driving so slow? Come on, get there!"

Sena just shut up because she knew there was nothing she could say. Her feelings were hurt a little. She was only trying to comfort him. But she knew all too well that when you lose someone very close to you, there are no soothing words that will help.

When they finally got to the hospital, Moochie took off before she could get parked. While she parked, she made a phone a call.

"Hey, girl, where is Skillet?" Sena asked Shay.

"He right here. What's wrong?" Shay asked. She could tell that Sena was crying.

"Something happened to Kidd today." Sena started crying even harder as the words came out of her mouth.

"What!" Shay yelled

"Yeah, we at SLU and I need y'all to come down. I don't think I'll be able to handle Moochie on my own. He is already flipping out, and we don't even know what happened."

"Okay, we on the way."

"What's wrong?" Skillet asked, looking at her. He could tell she didn't want to say it. His stomach had already started doing somersaults. He knew it was Sena on the phone, and he prayed nothing had happened to Moochie.

"It's Kidd. Something happened to him," Shay said just above a whisper.

"What happened? Where they at?" he asked as he got up and started looking for something to put on.

"They are at SLU. I think it's bad. She said Moochie was flipping out."

"What the fuck you still sitting down for? Let's go."

Shay almost jumped out of her skin at the sound of his voice booming through the house. Shay did as she was told, knowing that this was a sensitive situation. Luckily, both couples' kids were over at Skillet's mother's house for the weekend. She said she had missed her grandkids and wanted to have Grandma time with them.

When they got to the hospital, they found Moochie pacing back and forth. When Moochie saw Skillet, he damn near tackled him when he got to him. Moochie gave Skillet a hug so tight it felt like he was trying to squeeze the life out of him. He was so heartbroken over his brother. He had just found out that Kidd was in a vegetative state and would never come out of it, and it was going to be his choice whether Kidd lived or died.

Tears instantly stung Skillet's eyes. He knew it had to be bad. The last time he had seen Moochie cry was at his mother's funeral. "What's going on? Is he gon' be all right?" Skillet asked.

"It's bad."

Once Moochie gave Skillet the rundown on what had happened, Skillet was devastated. He couldn't believe his big brother was about to die.

Shay sat with Sena. Neither one knew what to do. Both women knew how much Kidd meant to the duo.

"What's gon' happen now?" Shay asked, afraid of what was to come. She knew some shit was about to go down. There was about to be an atomic bomb dropped on St. Louis, and she prayed they would make it out alive.

"Shit, you better be ready to soldier up. They gon' need us. Whether it be just for support or to get dirty, you just be prepared," Sena said, watching Moochie pace back and forth talking to himself. She knew he was going through something like an out-of-body experience, but when he came back, he was going to tear the City of St. Louis down brick by brick until he found all the guilty parties. She would ride with him to the depths of hell if she had to. She didn't know how far Shay would go for her man, but there was no question what she would do. The loyalty she had to him was unwavering.

Shay sat watching everything around her, thinking. Was she ready to get dirty for her man? She had just gotten used to having her little sister around, and she didn't want to put her in harm's way. Kelly had gone to Skillet's mom's house too. She didn't want to be without Kelly yet. Was she willing to do what Sena had done for Moochie? She watched as the two men shed silent tears for someone they both loved dearly. She hated to see him so hurt and broken.

"I'll be ready when he needs me," Shay stated while she locked eyes with Skillet.

"You better!"

Chapter 10

Vengeance

"You did a good job, Celeste," Sonny said as he handed her an envelope full of money.

"Thanks. Such a waste. He could've been a keeper if he weren't such a snake," Celeste stated matter-of-factly while she counted her money. She didn't even know the whole story. No one knew except for the people who were dead and Moochie and Kidd.

"Well, he's a dead keeper now. One down, one more to go. This one will be a tough one, though; he's the killer of the two." Sonny was secretly horrified that it was Kidd dead and not Moochie.

Sonny didn't believe she could pull it off when she came to him with the plan, but he appeased her so she could feel like she was a part of something. Now he had started a war with the ghost of vengeance. He knew what Moochie could and would do now that his brother was gone. Celeste had inadvertently let a beast out on the streets. But he would never tell her that. He knew they would be looking for her. There was nothing he could do about that. She knew what she was getting herself into. She chose to step into a man's shoes, and that was not his problem.

"Let me get out of here. I'm about to go tear the mall down." Celeste fanned herself with the fresh, crisp hundred-dollar bills. She couldn't wait to start spending. She had nothing going for herself but her looks. She lived off her family and its name, so that meant the only finger she had to lift was the middle finger to tell the world, "Fuck you," if you didn't do things her way.

"I wouldn't be out and about just yet. His peoples are probably tearing this city down looking for you," Sonny warned her.

"How they looking for me? They don't even know my name or know who I am," she reasoned. She thought she had one up on everybody and that she was untouchable because of who her family was.

"Don't be so fucking dumb! That man you helped kill earlier is no joke; listen to me! Now you wanted to get in this. I can't make you do nothing; I can only warn you." He knew she wouldn't listen to him but, at that point, he really didn't give a fuck anymore.

"Well, what the fuck I got you for if you can't protect me? I thought this family was supposed to be untouchable," Celeste mocked.

"Spoken like a full-blooded Jackson; but you see how that turned out. I'm just letting you know what you have gotten yourself into." Sonny tried to get through her thick skull.

"Yeah, I can take care of myself." Celeste snatched her Alexander McQueen tote off the floor and left.

Sonny just shook his head because he knew she wouldn't listen to him. He figured it was the nigga side in her that was hardheaded. She was a beautiful, perfect mixture of white and black, the color of mocha coffee. His aunt had a thing for black men, which he would never understand. In the meantime, he knew where he would be: at home behind the locked fence where he could see anyone coming from a hundred miles away.

***

Moochie sat at Kidd's bedside, crying his heart out. He couldn't imagine life without his brother with him. Kidd was not just his brother. He was his father, hero, and teacher rolled up into one person. How could he pull the plug on his brother? This was a choice that would not be easy. He knew his brother wouldn't want to live like this, but the selfish part of him wasn't ready to let go just yet. Kidd would live long enough to hear him say he had gotten the bastards who were responsible for this.

The beeping of the machines was a constant reminder of what his brother had gone through. He was shot four times in the chest, his right lung was gone, and he was breathing on a ventilator. When he was thrown from the car, he hit a tree, and it crushed his skull, leaving him brain dead. But he was still alive. Moochie knew Kidd would never leave him without letting him say good-bye. He picked up his phone and dialed a number.

"Hey, I need you to do something for me," he said to Sena over the phone. He knew he had been treating her real shitty lately and he was sorry for it. He would apologize later but, right now, he needed her to get some shit done. Normally he would do it himself, but he wasn't ready to leave Kidd yet. He also knew he couldn't go looking just yet because if he did, he would not get any answer. He would shoot and kill anything moving.

When Sena got the phone call from Moochie, she was ecstatic. She hadn't seen him in three days. He had been at the hospital day and night with his brother. Moochie had told her not to come to the hospital because he wanted some alone time with Kidd. She respected his wishes, but she had missed him like crazy and wanted to be there for him like he was for her. She wanted to hold him in her arms to let him know that he still had a reason to live, that giving up was not an option. She wondered what he wanted her to do, but it really didn't matter what it was. She would jump off the Rocky Mountains if he asked her to.

When she had talked to Shay, she said Skillet had locked himself in the basement and had barely said two words to her. Shay didn't know what to do with herself either. All Sena could suggest was to give him time.

Sena got to the hospital to find Moochie asleep in a cot next to Kidd's bed. She walked over to Kidd's bed and admired his strength. She knew he was hanging on for his little brother's sake. Kidd would not leave until Moochie could handle it. She looked at him and had an instant flashback of when her best friend was brought to the hospital after almost being beaten to death. It hurt her to her soul to know she never got to say good-bye. The hospital smell, all the machines, and the coldness were making her stomach do flips. The room was almost silent except for the sound of the machines working, and there was a little light shining over Kidd's head.

She pulled up a seat so she could talk to Kidd before she woke Moochie up. "Hey, honey, I hope you can hear me," she whispered. "I am so sorry that this happened to you. I wanted to ask how you doing, but I guess I can see that it's not too good. You gon' have to give me some kind of guidance on how to get him through this. You know him better than he knows himself." The tears started falling. "I don't know if I can do it. This is all too familiar for me. You know?" She paused for a minute to regroup.

"I know how I felt when Vee was taken away from me, and if I can take any of that pain away from him, I would. If I could block him from ever feeling pain again, I would.

But how do you help someone heal when you are still in your own healing process?" She took in a deep breath and then exhaled slowly. "But don't you worry; he is in good hands. I will be there for him no matter what. We will get through this together. I wish I could hear your voice one more time, some kind of quick, clever remark about me. You tell my sister I love her and I miss her. I know you two couldn't wait to be back together." Sena knew Kidd was there in body, but his spirit had long since gone to be with the love of his life. She kissed him on the cheek then got up and went over to where Moochie was lying down.

Sena kneeled down in front of Moochie and rubbed her hands through his messy dreads. He looked to be at peace. She didn't know that he wasn't sleeping. He was lying there in turmoil. He hadn't been to sleep in days, and he was on high alert to everything around him. Sleep didn't come to him too often. Visions of the crime scene and his brother bandaged from head to toe ran rapidly through his head on a constant basis. He said no words; he just pulled Sena onto the cot with him and buried his face in her chest. He held on to her for dear life. His foundation had been shaken to its core. Life as he once knew it was over and would never be the same. Sena and Deonna would be the only good things left in his life.

Sena felt so helpless. She prayed he would come out of this okay.

"How can I do it, Sena?" Moochie asked after about ten minutes of silence.

"I don't know, baby. I know it's not going to be easy. But you gotta put yourself in his shoes. You know him better than you know anyone else. Would you want to live that way?"

***

Shay walked into the basement where Skillet was and lost her breath due to all the weed smoke coming from it. It seemed like he had been chain-smoking. He didn't usually smoke. She started to say something, but she knew he was stressed out to the max.

"Babe, you gon' come up to eat or do you want me to bring you something down?" she called from the doorway.

"Nah, I'm good," Skillet stated flatly. He just sat there staring at nothing. The TV wasn't on, but Tupac's "Hail Mary" was coming out of the speakers almost in a whisper. He could imagine Kidd rapping this song very animatedly. Tupac was Kidd's favorite rapper.

"Can you just please eat something for me? A sandwich maybe?" He had hardly eaten since he heard about Kidd.

"Look, I know you trying to be helpful, but don't. Not right now, anyway. When I need you, I'll let you know." Skillet could see he had hurt her feelings. She looked like she was about to cry.

"Okay, I won't bother you anymore." Shay turned and slammed the door.

She had to get out of the house. She called Sena but got no answer. Then she went to see Kayla for a while. She finally let Kelly go see their mother a day or two ago because for some reason Kelly begged to see her. Grudgingly, she let her go, mainly just because of everything that was going on. Skillet didn't want Kayla to come home with all this going on. His mother had long ago retired, so she had no problem with keeping the babies. She even still had Deonna. She had only had them for four days but, to Shay, it felt like an eternity.

"Hey, Momma Rogers, how you doing?" Shay asked as she walked into the home.

"Hey, baby, you just missed Sena. She came by a little while ago to see Deonna. She looked just like you with those puffy, red, swollen eyes."

Shay didn't think she looked that bad. She had been crying the whole way over though. "I called her but didn't get an answer," she said as she picked up Kayla.

"Chile, Moochie called her, and she went running out of here like her ass was on fire."

Momma Rogers was a little bitty feisty thing. Skillet looked nothing like her though. He looked just like his father, who had passed away many years ago. But she still held her beauty intact. She was aging beautifully. She could have been the poster woman for black don't crack.

"Did she say what he wanted?" Shay asked anxiously. She felt anxious and left out with no one talking to her.

"No, baby, she just said she had to go." Momma Rogers shrugged her shoulders and busied herself with picking up the toys that the girls had spread everywhere.

"I don't know what to do about all this." Shay sounded defeated. She looked around at all the pictures and couldn't believe how much Kayla looked like Kaylin when he was a baby. She picked up a picture of Kayla and then held up a picture of Kaylin and just stared.

"It's scary, ain't it? The male genes in this family are very strong. He is also identical to his father. For a long time after my husband passed away, I couldn't even look at that boy without breaking down." Momma Rogers took a glance at the pictures also.

"Look, I'll tell you like I told her. Stand by your man. I know these two knuckleheads. They're young and don't know how to handle their emotions right now. I was so happy when Kidd stepped in and started helping with my baby. Even though he wasn't that much older than him, for some reason, my son wouldn't do anything unless Kidd said it was okay. I didn't mind that 'cause he hadn't got my son into any trouble. Now I know they were out doing something. I ain't no fool to think I got this house and everything else by it falling off a tree. My son was happy and doing better than he had ever been doing though so I was okay with that. Kidd had become a father figure and didn't even know it. He did a good job, if I might say so myself."

Momma Rogers wasn't foolish enough to believe they lived the lives of angels. She couldn't have picked a better set of sons if she had handpicked them herself. "Everything around them is moving way too fast, but the pain is at a standstill and not going anywhere anytime soon. I know firsthand what these boys mean to each other. They are losing a big brother. It's like watching your hero die. So if he wants to be alone and all of sudden needs you there, you be there, no questions asked."

Shay let Momma Rogers's words sink in. "Thank you. I really needed that."

"Anytime, honey. Now you don't worry 'bout nothing over here. You go be with him."

"But—"

"I know he doesn't want you around right now. Just be on standby. I told you these boys don't know what they want right now. But don't abandon him."

"Okay. I'm going to see my little sister right now. I haven't seen her in a few days. Can you call him? He won't eat for me. I just want him to eat a sandwich or something."

"Girl, didn't you hear a thing I said? There is nothing none of us can do for the pain he is in. Food ain't gon' help. He will be all right. Lord knows my child ain't missin' no meals. Now, you try to crowd him, and you'll make him do something he doesn't want to do."

Shay thought about everything Skillet's mother had told her. It all made sense, but she really wanted to be there for him. The fact that he didn't want to be around her made her feel unneeded.

She took a deep breath as she got into the car and went to go see her sister. She didn't feel like the drama that was about to happen, but she had promised Kelly she was coming to get her.

Shay knocked on the door of her mother's house, but no one answered. She checked her watch. It was a little after eight at night, so she knew someone was there. She knocked again, only harder.

"Who is it?" she heard Carl yell from the other side of the door.

"Raina," she replied dryly. It felt weird saying that name. She hadn't said it in so long. She still hadn't told anyone her story, but she knew it would be coming soon. Everyone was distracted at the moment with everything that was going on with Kidd.

Carl swung the door open. He was wearing nothing but a pair of boxers and some ankle socks, looking like the creepy pervert he was. She cringed from the sight and wanted to throw up. His chest hair looked like taco meat, and he looked sweaty. He resembled an eighties porn star with hamburger meat all over his body, and he had a little nappy afro that was very unkempt.

"See something you like?" Carl asked.

"You wish, fuckin' perv!" Shay pushed past him. "Where's Raylene?" She looked around the semi-clean apartment.

"The fuck if I know. She been gone for hours," Carl lied as he grabbed his crotch, looking at her up and down.

"Well, where is Kelly?" Shay crossed her arms over her chest. She could see something in his eyes that he wasn't saying.

"She in her room. I don't know what's wrong with that girl. She been crying for hours."

Shay turned on her heels and rushed to Kelly's room. When she got to the door, sure enough, Kelly was whimpering with her head under the covers. She sat down on Kelly's bed next to her. The words that came out of Kelly's mouth enraged and horrified her at the same time.

"Please just leave! I'm going to tell my sister you're coming in my room."

Shay's heart felt like it exploded. Why would she say that? Was Carl sneaking into her room at night? "Kelly, who's been coming into your room?" Shay snatched the covers back to see that she had nothing on. Tears instantly flooded her eyes, and her vision went blurry. "I knew I shouldn't let you come back here! Why did I let you come back here?" Shay felt like shit because she had gone back on her word and let Kelly go back for a visit because Kelly and her mom had been begging to see each other.

"Shay, please take me with you! I don't want to be here anymore," Kelly cried into Shay's arms.

"Why are you naked?"

Kelly just kept crying.

"Kelly, why the fuck are you naked?" Shay yelled. She had a feeling but she didn't want to admit that she had fucked up. It was her fault, and she would have to live with her decision to let Kelly go back.

"He told me to get naked." Kelly looked down at the floor.

Shay shot up from the bed. "Has he raped you?" Shay could feel the food she had eaten earlier about to come rushing out of her throat. Kelly wouldn't look her in the eyes. She softened her tone, seeing that Kelly was too scared to talk. "Kelly, has he raped you?"

"No, but he comes in at night and touches me."

"Have you told Raylene?"

"No. After what she did to you, I didn't want her to leave me too."

It felt like Shay's brain went to mush. She was hearing what Kelly was saying, but it sounded like gibberish after a few seconds. Shay grabbed Kelly and held her tight. "Why didn't you call me?" Shay cried. "I would have been here in a heartbeat. You should have called me." After a few minutes, Shay wiped her eyes and let Kelly go. "You get dressed. I'll be right back." She headed out of the room in search of Carl.

But he was nowhere to be found. He had been listening at the door and wanted no part of what was to come. He figured Raylene would never believe Kelly since she didn't believe Raina. But never in a million years did he expect for Shay to come back in the picture. He had never had sex with Kelly, but he knew he had fucked up royally.

Shay searched the apartment from top to bottom, but he was ghost. "That's all right; you can't hide forever! You's a dead nigga!" she yelled.

As Shay and Kelly were getting ready to leave, Raylene came home with some grocery bags in her hands. She hadn't really been gone for hours like Carl had said. She had only run to the grocery store to get some breakfast food.

As soon as Shay saw her, she charged toward her like a raging bull, remembering the promise she had made her mother years ago. "Bitch, I told you if you let him touch her, I would fuck you up."

Raylene dropped her bags and jumped behind the kitchen table to avoid her angry daughter. She was shocked to see her at their home and what she was talking about was fucking her up. What had happened there while she took her short trip?

"What are you talking about?" Raylene was scared to death. The look in her daughter's eyes said that she was ready to kill.

"I'm talking 'bout that grimy-ass nigga putting his fucking hands on Kelly!"

Shay tried to come around the table, but Raylene moved to the other side. Finally fed up, Shay snatched the table from in between them and had Raylene by the throat up against the wall. Everything she was going through gave her superhuman strength. Shay was so mad that she couldn't stop the tears from coming down her face. "I told you years ago he was a child molester, but you stayed with him. I told you! You let the devil into our home back then and kept him there." Their faces were merely inches away. "Why!" Shay yelled.

"I don't know what you're talking about! Let me go!" Raylene shook under Raina's grip.

"Why you don't never know nothing?" She looked her mother in the eyes.

"Let her go, Ray Ray." Kelly pulled Shay off of Raylene. "She didn't know. I never told her!" Kelly cried. She was having flashbacks of the day they had left Raina, and she almost beat their mother to death, and she didn't want that to happen again.

"You shouldn't have had to! She should have known eight years ago!" Shay couldn't stop yelling.

"Kelly, Carl touched you?" Raylene was mortified. She knew she had done wrong by one daughter, but she was determined to get it right by the other one.

"Yes, Mommy." Kelly looked to the floor again, ashamed of what she had let happen to her. She really thought that it was her fault.

"I am so sorry, baby! I am truly sorry! Why didn't you say something?"

Shay just watched. She wanted to see Raylene's face when she heard the answer. Kelly didn't say anything, too afraid to hurt her mother's feelings.

"Tell her why you never said anything." Shay gave her a look to ensure her that everything would be okay.

"I didn't want you to leave me like you did Ray Ray."

That sentence sliced through Raylene's heart and soul. Was she that bad of a mother that her child would think such a thing? She slid down to the floor and began crying her heart out. Kelly went to hug her, but Shay stopped her.

"Give her time to think." Shay looked at Raylene on the floor crying. Her heart wanted to help her up, but the anger she held wouldn't let her. "You tell that muthafucka that if I ever see him again, he's dead where he stands." And with those words, they left.

"I am so sorry that happened to you!" Shay cried as they drove to her home.

"It's not your fault; don't cry. I'm just glad you came when you did. I think tonight he was going to try to go all the way," Kelly said as she stared out the window.

Shay was boiling on the inside. She wanted to shoot Carl's dick off, and she would if given the opportunity. *My mother had better do something about him before I get to him.*

When they got back to the house, Skillet was in the kitchen. When he looked up, he could tell that Shay had been crying. He thought he was the cause until he saw Kelly walk in with her bags.

"What's up?" he spoke to Kelly.

"Kelly, go to your room and let me talk to Kaylin." Shay wiped her face as she spoke.

"Why you crying?" Skillet walked up to Shay and put his arms around her. He knew he had been treating her like a stepchild and he hoped those tears weren't because of him.

"He's been touching her!" Shay cried.

"What?" Skillet pushed her back to make sure he heard her correctly.

"Carl! When I got there, she was in the bed naked and crying. When I went to find him, he was gone."

"Damn, that's fucked up! Did he rape her?" Skillet never knew he could be so fucking stressed. First the shit with Kidd, and now he had to put a fucking child molester on his list. He had grown fond of Kelly. She was a cool little chick and her being related to Shay made it even better. His anger was at an all-time high, and he felt like at any moment he would have a stroke. He knew his blood pressure had to be rising every second.

"She said no, but he was feeling on her. If I ever see that nigga, I'm gon' burn that muthafucka alive."

"Where's your moms? Is she still there at the house?"

"Yeah, I left her there. I didn't want to see her face. She let this happen," Shay fumed.

"Look, I know what happened, but that is still your moms, and you left her there with that man. What if he does something to her?"

"Then that means she deserved it." Shay was enraged that he was defending her.

"You don't mean that." Skillet shook his head. She could be so stubborn.

"Yes, I do!" she yelled.

"Yo, you can stop with all that yelling and tough shit. You know I don't do the yelling thing. I'm trying to talk to you," he said calmly. He knew she was upset, but he needed to know what she wanted him to do. He wouldn't mind putting that nigga six feet deep. Working with Kidd and Moochie had taught him a few things, so he knew how to make a body disappear.

"Okay, I'm listening," Shay huffed as she sat down in one of the kitchen chairs.

"How is she doing?"

"She all right. We haven't really talked about it yet, but she thinks it's her fault." Shay couldn't believe she was going through this with her little sister. It burned her insides to think of that man putting his hands on her.

"Well, you take care of her, and I'll handle the rest," Skillet said, not knowing she wasn't even trying to hear that. Carl was hers, and he would pay. She was going to make sure he felt her pain, all of it.

Chapter 11

One by One

"Thank you for being a friend. Traveled down the road and back again," Shay's phone sang, letting her know that Sena was calling. "What's up?" Shay asked as she answered the phone.

"You ready?"

"Ready for what?"

"Skillet ain't told you yet?" Shay looked over at Skillet. He just nodded his head, knowing what Sena was talking about by the expression on Shay's face.

"Nah, we had a li'l issue over here, but we'll talk about that later. What am I supposed to be ready for?"

"Get dressed; we going out tonight. I'll explain everything then." Sena didn't really feel like explaining everything. She was nervous and had to get her nerves together.

"I don't feel like going out. I got too much going on," Shay reasoned.

"Tell her you'll be ready."

Shay looked to Skillet and couldn't believe he was trying to make her go somewhere that she didn't want to go. "Let me call you right back."

"Let me speak to her." Skillet snatched the phone from her hands. He was getting frustrated with her, but he was trying to be patient. "She'll be ready."

"Okay." Sena hung up.

Shay sat stunned at the way he was he acting, especially after everything she had just told him.

"You going to the club tonight with Sena. She needs someone with her. You don't have to do nothing but be there," he said adamantly.

"Didn't I just say I wasn't going nowhere? I got shit to deal with!" Shay yelled.

"Didn't I just tell you about yelling at me?" Skillet said through gritted teeth as he grabbed her by the collar of her shirt, almost lifting her off the ground. "I have never asked you to do something you didn't want to do."

Shay stood frozen stiff. She had never seen him this way. Skillet noticed the tears about to fall from her eyes and he let her go. He backed away from her, looking her in the eyes, trying to read her. He could see she was scared. She wasn't a rider, which really disappointed him. "You know what, I'll get someone else to do it," he said as he tried to walk away.

"What you mean you'll get someone else? So you just got hoes on standby?" Shay asked, wanting to know who he was going to get to do it and not really caring what the situation was. Jealousy immediately took over.

"Damn, really? That's all you got to say? We trying to get shit done and you trippin' off a ho who don't even exist." Skillet looked at her as if she stank. "You know what? It would be in your best interest to get the fuck out of my face right now. I got shit to do." He left her standing in the middle of the kitchen feeling like shit.

Shay didn't know if she was mad or if her feelings were hurt. She would have done anything he asked her to do. She felt like he was telling her she had no choice in the matter. She had been bullied for more than half her life and she refused to go through it now. But she knew it had to be something serious because he had never talked to her that way or put his hands on her. He looked at her like he was disappointed in her and that hurt even worse than the tongue-lashing he had just given her. The thought of him being disappointed in her made her rethink her decision. He was on the phone when she walked into the room.

"Yeah, around eleven, she'll be there to pick you up." He chuckled a little. "Nah, my homegirl will be there; I'm not coming. And she gon' have that for you, too. Thanks for looking out."

Shay had to put her feelings in check. She wanted to bum-rush him with a fifty piece to his face. How dare he call some bitch in her home? She went to her closet to find something to wear. She'd be damned if he had to ask another bitch to do something for him. That wasn't going down at all; plus, she couldn't leave her girl hanging. He said Sena needed her, and she would be there for her. He turned around to see her looking for something to put on and he smirked.

"What you doing?"

"Looking for something to put on." She never turned to face him.

"Where you going?"

"With Sena."

"Nah, it's cool, we got somebody else. This ain't your thing." Skillet could see her flinch and her body stiffen after the words left his mouth.

"What the hell is that supposed to mean?" Shay got loud and then lowered her voice.

"It means your services are not needed." He turned his back to her and went about putting on his clothes.

Skillet had to go meet up with Moochie because, if all went well tonight, there was going be a good ol' torture party going down later. The people who tried to body Kidd didn't know who they fucked with. Their wrath would be ten times more painful than that little stunt they pulled on Kidd. He couldn't wait to squeeze the life out of somebody with his bare hands. He didn't intend to be so mean to Shay, but she had worked his last nerve, and he didn't need the added anger. He looked at her and could clearly see he had hurt her feelings by the tears that were forming in her eyes.

"Look, don't feel bad. I know this ain't for you. That's why I told you never mind. I don't want you getting hurt trying to do something you wasn't ready for." Skillet got up and walked over to her and wiped the tears off her face.

Shay knew he was right, but she wanted to be included. She wanted to help even if she didn't know what it was the she had to do. She felt like a failure. Everybody had a part to play but her. "No, I can do it." She stepped away from so he could get a good look in her eyes.

"You sure?" Skillet asked hesitantly. He never wanted to put her in any danger, but he also knew they had to keep this one close to home.

"Yes." Shay could feel the butterflies having a party in her stomach, but she would not let that deter her from her decision.

"Okay, I'll let Sena know to come and get you."

"Now you know what to do right?" Moochie asked Sena for the hundredth time. He wanted to make sure she was ready because he would surely die if something happened to her. When he had come to her with the plan, he wasn't so sure she would do it, but she jumped at it before he could finish the sentence. That's what he loved about her; her loyalty was unwavering and unquestionable.

"Yes, babe, I got it." Sena chuckled and rolled her eyes up to the ceiling playfully.

"Don't laugh at me! I want you to come back to me the way you leaving, that's all." He pulled her into his arms and placed a wet kiss on her lips.

"Damn, you act like I'm leaving for the military." Sena was cool as a fan. She knew what she was about to do was dangerous enough to get her killed, but it was a necessary evil.

"Call me before you go in." Moochie ignored her remark. He was dead serious, and here she was acting like he had asked her to go slap a bitch and not help kidnap one.

"All right. Let me go get Shay."

"Are you sure she is okay with this?" Moochie wasn't so sure about Shay being her backup. Her heart wasn't in it, in his opinion, and he wasn't so sure he trusted Shay with Sena's life. God forbid anything happened. He would be taking no prisoners.

"Yeah, she cool. We gon' be all right." Sena was sure of her friend and she never doubted her heart. Shay would be there when she needed her. Sena would never have let anyone in her circle she wasn't sure of.

After Sena left, Moochie sank into his fluffy couch and stared at the wall. He couldn't believe that, with one act, his life had turned upside down. But, then again, after all the men he had killed he knew karma would be coming for him at full force. But this was torture knowing that his brother was going to die and he would be the one to pull the plug. He figured God had to be thinking, *Since you like to kill niggas, well, voilà, li'l nigga.*

His mind traveled back to when his mother was dying. He could still see her lying in the hospital bed with tubes coming out of her mouth. Her skin was ashy and dry, and no matter how much lotion he or Kidd would put on her, it never helped much. He had never cried so much in his life. He was only seventeen when she died; and he was nine when their father left. Kidd was all he had in the world. Kidd took on the responsibility of raising him the rest of the way. Actually, Kidd had taken over when their father had left. Moochie knew Kidd had sacrificed a lot to be there for him and his mother, but he never complained.

He could remember when the doctor came into the room and told them the chemo wasn't working anymore and that it was only a matter of time before their mother passed away. It felt like he was falling with no ground in sight. His chest had caved in, and the air couldn't find its way back to his lungs. Moochie never wanted to feel that way again.

Now here he was again with the feeling of being suffocated and freefalling into a bottomless pit. He still hadn't let them pull the plug on Kidd. He wasn't ready to let go. Once the plug was pulled, it would really mean his brother was gone, and the thought of that had him scared to death.

Sena watched Shay fidget in her seat as they rode to their destination. She really hoped her friend was ready for what they were about to do. But this was the easy part. Shay didn't know that Sena would be the one to be the judge and executioner that night. As long as she had breath in her body, Moochie would never have to put his hands on a woman. That's why she was there.

"Ay, you good?" Sena asked as she cut the music down.

"Yeah, I'm good. Why everybody acting like Shay can't do shit?" She was determined to prove herself to everyone.

"Nobody's acting like that. I never once doubted you. I know you got my back no matter what, but this is a whole new ballgame, and I'm just making sure you ready for this."

"I'm good." Shay turned her head so that she was facing the window. She was very unsure of what she was about

to do, but it didn't matter. She had to do it. She wanted
so badly to prove herself. She wanted Skillet to be proud
of her like Moochie was of Sena. Everybody knew Sena
was a rider, but no one knew what Shay could do, and she
wanted to show them. She had killed a man, but no one
knew.

"We here," Sena said while pulling up to a two-family
flat. Both women took a deep breath, got out of the car,
and started up to the door. If Celeste answered the door,
they were supposed to put the gun to her head and make
her come with them. If someone else answered, they
were supposed to find a way to get in and get her out by
any means necessary.

"Safeties off," Sena said. She checked her guns then
knocked on the door. Shay felt like she was about to
throw up. "Take a deep breath," Sena coached herself
and Shay.

"Who is it?" they heard a man call from the other side
of the door.

"Damn," Shay said nervously as she looked at Sena.
This frightened the women a little. They weren't expecting a man to answer the door.

"Calm down, honey, we are all right." Sena was prepared. She didn't anticipate everything to go smoothly.
She dialed Moochie's number on her phone and put it on
speaker phone. He answered the phone and could hear
the whole conversation.

"It's Tina. Is Celeste here?"

"Nah, she went to the club." A hulk of a man answered
the door. He looked the duo up and down and was very
impressed with what he saw.

Sena stood in front of him with a strapless bandage
minidress that hugged every curve on her body, and the
blond wig just made the outfit all the better. Shay had on

some booty shorts with a tank top and some "come fuck me" pumps. Her wig was long and jet-black.

"But you can come in and wait for her," he suggested, thinking of all the things he wanted to do to these two fine women in front of him. He wondered if they were sluts like his boss's cousin Celeste, and he hoped so. Chuck hadn't had any gushy stuff in a while, and he felt he was due.

"So she ain't here? We were supposed to meet her here then go to the club." Sena looked like she was upset but she wanted him to keep running his mouth. She looked at his beard and was disgusted. It looked like he had years of food and lice all up and through it.

"Nah, she left a few minutes ago but, as I said, you can wait in here for her." He really wanted them to come in, and if they refused to give it up, he would surely take it.

"Nah, I ain't trying be around you and a bunch of men," Shay said, trying to see how many men were in the house.

"Nah, baby, it's just me and my buddy in here. It will only be us at this party." He licked his lips.

"Why would she leave us? Where she say she was going?" Sena asked, prying a little more.

"Some place called Home, some shit like that." He hunched his shoulders.

"Okay, thank you. We'll go see if we can find her there."

"You sure you don't want to come in?" He sounded like he was begging.

"Maybe after the party we'll come and have a killer party with you all." Sena put emphasis on the word "killer."

"Yeah, you do that," he said, imagining her bent over and touching her toes.

The girls hurried to their car. The big guy was giving them the creeps, and they wanted to get away before he decided to snatch one of them into the house with him.

But Sena would have let her thang rip him to shreds had he started tripping.

"Did you get that, babe?" Sena asked as she picked up her phone.

"Yeah, I'm already on my way to get Skillet. Y'all be careful, and we'll be waiting in the parking lot when y'all come out. Leave your phone in the car so I can find your car," Moochie instructed. He was referring to the GPS tracker that was on her phone. All of their phones had the GPS locator on them, but only Kidd and Moochie had the tracker under their arm. Moochie was thinking about getting one put in everybody. Things were getting hectic, and if anything went down, he wanted to get there immediately.

"Okay. I love you. Be careful," Sena said before she hung up the phone.

Moochie and Skillet sat outside of what was believed to be Celeste's home. They watched through the big window in front of the house as a group of men congregated in the living room. Moochie's blood was boiling when he had heard the man say it was only him and another man in the house, but he could clearly see about seven or eight men in the house. His mind immediately went to Sena. *What is he trying to do, get them to come in so they can do whatever they want to her?* This only angered him more. The thought of them hurting Sena did something to his psyche.

"Yo, you ready?" Skillet asked, bringing him back to reality.

They were there hoping to kill anything Celeste loved. It didn't matter if her grandparents lived there; they would surely get it too. The neighborhood looked upscale, so they knew they wouldn't be able to do a home invasion without the nosy neighbors getting involved. It was disappointing that there would be no hands-on action.

They opted for the easy route. Skillet had reached out to his man who had the hookup on explosives. They bought ten even though the dude said all they needed was one, maybe two, depending on how bad they wanted the house burned down.

Both men exited the car. Skillet went to the right, and Moochie went to the left, placing a bomb on each side of the house. Moochie ran around the back to put one there too for added measure. The men were back in their car in less than one minute and were on their way to the next part of the plan. Before they turned off the street, Skillet pulled the remotes out of his pocket. He was a little scared with the remotes on his body, but his connect assured him that they wouldn't go off until he flipped the button. He began flipping the buttons one by one. Seconds later, the left side of the house blew up, then the back, then the right. There would be no survivors in this tragedy.

It wasn't hard for the girls to find Celeste in the club. She had rented out a booth and was popping bottle after bottle like she was balling out of control. Moochie had given them the go-ahead to do with her as they pleased. He just wanted to watch. It was a must that he had to be a part of everyone's death. He wanted them to look into his eyes and see death look back at them. To let them know he was reason they were about to meet their Maker.

"Look at this bitch poppin' bottles like shit sweet out here, like she ain't just set my fucking brother up to be killed!" Sena spat. She couldn't wait to unleash on her ass. She hoped Shay was up for what was about to go down, because Miss Celeste would not be dying quick. Sena had some tricks up her sleeve. Just thinking about how much pain Moochie was in made her ready to shoot Celeste in the head right there in the middle of the club, but that would be too easy.

"I know, right? This bitch has got to get it." Shay watched her with her anger boiling over.

"Let's stand over here, blend in a little." Sena laughed once she looked at Shay shooting daggers at Celeste. She didn't want anyone to alert Celeste that they were watching her. "Girl, if looks could kill, she'd be dead ten times." They shared a laugh.

"Oh, girl, I got a lot going on. And sorry about earlier. I had just gotten back from picking up Kelly when you called."

"How she doing?" Sena hadn't really gotten a chance to spend a lot of time with Kelly, but her daughter Deonna had taken a liking to the young lady.

"She all right for now. When I got to the house, she was lying in the bed crying and naked. Broke my heart into a thousand pieces."

"What!" Sena yelled, catching the attention of a few partygoers. She smiled at them then turned her attention back to Shay. "What the fuck you mean, Shay?"

"Yes, she said Carl had been sneaking into her room at night and feeling on her."

"Damn that slimy muthafucka!" Sena gritted her teeth. "You already know the deal whenever you ready." Sena wouldn't mind adding Carl's trifling ass to the list. She was going through all this to help Moochie, but she was also getting her kicks knowing that Celeste was some kin to the people who killed her best friend Valencia. *Just throw 'em all in one big-ass blender.*

Shay thought about her sister and the situation with her mother. She didn't know what she was going to do about her mother. She still held so much anger in her heart for the way her mother had left her. Now, Raylene had let Carl touch her little sister and Shay didn't know if she would be able to forgive her mother for that. This was just too much for her right now. She felt like she was being pulled in twenty different directions.

"She leaving," Sena said, snapping Shay out of her thoughts. "Call them and let 'em know she on her way toward them."

Chapter 12

My Man's Keeper

"That was Shay. She said ol' girl on her way out," Skillet told Moochie as they sat in a throwaway car right next to Celeste's car. He had Sena double-park for him; then he moved her car over. That was the only glitch in the plan: the club was inside of the casino. But they didn't care. They would have snatched her in front of a police station if they had to.

Skillet had paid one of the men in security to have a slight glitch in the video system for about forty-five seconds in the area they were in. Skillet had sent the man a picture of Celeste before they got there so he could find were she had parked, and then he could block the spot next to her car and Sena could be right next to her. It was a lot of work to do in such a short amount of time, but the money they offered would have made him do anything they asked.

Moochie was in world of his own. His heart was heavy with grief. The days had been hard without his brother's presence and guidance. He still had the feeling that all of this was just a dream. He would wake up, and his brother would be sitting on the side of him and talking trash. Kidd had left Moochie a very wealthy man; he made sure that if anything ever happened to him, Moochie would know where everything was and that everything would trans-fer over to him upon his death. Kidd had always planned ahead for any hiccups in their plans. Moochie got it all: the cars, house, and the money. But he would trade it all in just to have his brother back. Nothing and no one would ever be able to fill that hole in his heart.

"Here she comes," Skillet said as he watched Celeste, accompanied by two men, walk out of the casino on wobbly legs.

Celeste was clearly very intoxicated. The two dudes were feeling all over her body, and she was too drunk to stand on her own two legs. One man held her up by her ass cheek, and the other was trying his best to get his hand up her skirt while she leaned on his shoulders.

"Man, look at these thirsty-ass niggas! They act like they ain't never got no pussy before." Skillet could only imagine what they wanted to do to her. Too bad they wouldn't get a chance, because he and Moochie were about to rain on their parade.

"I'm tripping off this scandalous-ass bitch! I can't believe after everything we've been through, this is the best bitch who brought my brother down." Moochie shook his head.

The horny twosome was so engrossed in Celeste that they didn't notice they had an audience. Moochie and Skillet watched as the fools literally threw her into the back seat as if she were a bag of trash.

"Watch these niggas high-five each other." Moochie chuckled at the thought.

"So what we gon' do now?" Skillet asked as he watched them pull off.

"We follow them and leave no witnesses." This slight hiccup wasn't going to stop his plans.

The duo wasted no time in getting down to business. They had Celeste bent over in the bed sucking and fucking the moment they walked through the hotel door.

"Man, this white bitch got some fire-ass pussy!" One of the dudes smacked Celeste on the ass while he ravished her from the back. Tim never in his wildest dreams thought he would be participating in a threesome with a fine-ass chick like Celeste. He was broke and butt ugly, but today was his lucky day. The drugs his friend had put in Celeste's drinks really worked.

"Nigga, I bet it is! You hoggin' it all," James said as he attempted to ram his whole penis down Celeste's throat. This was a once-in-a-lifetime type of deal for him too. He had spent his whole little paycheck on an outfit and the drinks Celeste let him buy. He wasn't ugly by any means, but he was broke in Celeste's eyes.

"Just give me a few more pumps."

"Nah, how about we cut this whole li'l scene short, period!" Moochie said as he shut the door behind him. In the men's haste, they hadn't even gotten the door all the way shut, making it easier for Moochie and Skillet to get in.

"What the fuck is going on?" Tim and James yelled in unison. Both men scrambled for a spot on the bed as Celeste lay lifeless, face down.

"No, the question is, what the fuck is that smell?" Skillet asked as he covered his nose. The smell that was emitted in that room was almost unbearable. The smell of booty, fish, and bad breath filled the atmosphere.

"I know this bitch didn't set us up!" Tim said as he looked at the men standing in front of him. They had the biggest guns he had ever seen in his life pointed at him.

"Nah, dog, it's clear y'all ain't got shit." Moochie snickered. "You just happened to be in the wrong place at the wrong time." He pulled the trigger, and the only thing that was heard sounded like a puff of wind. Tim's brains decorated the room.

"Waaaait a minute, man, you don't have to do—"

James's sentence was cut short by a bullet piercing the middle of his forehead.

Celeste was still knocked out from whatever the men had given her. She didn't know that she was about to wake up to a world of mayhem.

"Get that bitch so we can get out of here. She ain't dying that easy." Moochie threw out more demands to Skillet, taking on his role as leader finally.

"We getting 'em, big brother. We gon' get 'em all for you," Moochie said out loud.

Skillet looked at Moochie, feeling everything Moochie had just said. Kidd wasn't his brother by blood, but he was his family. He knew Moochie would never be the same. Hell, life would never be the same. He just prayed that they all made it out of this alive, so they could start picking up the pieces to their lives again.

When Shay and Sena arrived at the house, they found Celeste in the basement on an old bed. Her lips were glued shut with Gorilla Glue, and her wrists and ankles were bound to the four bedposts. She was buck-naked, with Moochie and Skillet sitting in the chair by the doorway, waiting for them to get there. Moochie had his hair pulled back into a tight ponytail. He wanted to stomp Celeste until she was flat as a pancake, but Sena insisted on him not doing anything. At first glance, Sena had to catch herself because she thought she was looking at Kidd.

Shay walked over to the bed. She admired Celeste's tattoo. It was a single black rose that sat right in the middle of her breasts with a long stem that wrapped around her body and landed at her left big toe. It had thorns with blood trickling out of them. Shay thought that was a perfect tattoo for her: beautiful, yet ugly at the same time.

She turned to look at everybody in the room then turned back to Celeste. Shay brought her arm up high in the air; then it came down hard across Celeste's face, making everyone in the room jump and turn her way.

"Wake up, bitch!"

Celeste woke up and tried to scream, but her mouth wouldn't open. She looked around frantically at the three people standing in front of her. Moochie hadn't walked up yet. He was still bracing himself. He was trying his best to gain control of his emotions. The presence of her was making him see red. He sat down in a chair across the room, breathing hard and opening and closing his fist.

They could all see that Celeste was trying to say something.

"What you say? I can't hear you." Sena leaned in so she was closer to Celeste's mouth, but all she could hear was mumbling. "Wait a minute, let me help you out." Sena grabbed her top and bottom lip at the same time and ripped them apart.

Shay thought for sure she was going to throw up. The sight of Celeste's skin from her bottom lip still being attached to the top one made her stomach hit the floor. But she knew she had better get that shit under control because Sena had only just gotten started. Celeste let out a horrendous scream, almost choking on the blood that was running down the back of her throat. But no one would hear her. They were in one of Kidd's many torture chambers. This one was soundproof, so Celeste could scream all she wanted. Their ears were deaf to her screams.

"Wha . . . what do you . . ." Her sentence stopped when she saw Moochie walk up. She turned white as a ghost as all the color drained from her face, and she pissed on herself. They could see the pee coming out like a fountain. Everyone literally watched her pee 'til the stream ended.

"What's the matter? Looks like you seen a ghost," Moochie asked as he walked up to the end of the bed.

"Look, what happened to you wasn't my fault," Celeste pleaded through bloody lips.

"Oh, you think I'm my brother?" Moochie chuckled with a sinister smirk on his face that sent chills down the spines of everybody in the room. Sena had never seen that side of Moochie. She only knew the loving, jovial side of him. Now she was seeing firsthand what his spirit could be with the right boost. But she had a side she was about to show too. "Well, Kidd is no longer with us, and it seems you are the cause."

"It wasn't me." Celeste coughed, trying to get the blood to come back up.

"Shut the fuck up! I ain't asked you no fucking questions yet!" Moochie's voice boomed and vibrated off the walls of the hollow room. He looked to Sena. "Go ahead and set up, baby."

Everybody in the room watched as Sena pulled an iron from the bag she was carrying. She plugged it into an outlet right on the side of the bed. Moochie loved it when Sena had come up with the idea. He wished he would have thought about that when he and Kidd were still doing their thing. If he had been thinking more clearly, Sena would have never known about any of what was going on. He would never want to ruin her spirit. But his rationale died when his brother was attacked. He wasn't thinking about the future; here and now was it. Never once did he think it was Kidd's karma coming back on him. No one had the right to take his brother from him. He didn't care how many brothers, fathers, and uncles they had taken away from their families.

"No, no, no, please no, no, help me, help, help!" Celeste screamed at the top her lungs, not realizing that no would hear her and that no one in the room could care less. When she saw that iron getting plugged into the wall, she thought she would shit on herself.

Skillet went to sit back in his chair by the door. He was all for killing a muthafucka, but he didn't think his stomach could take what was about to go down. He was basically there just for extra muscle and to keep Moochie as levelheaded as possible. He was grateful that Kidd and Moochie never really involved him in the torture sessions. He didn't feel sorry for Celeste in the least bit; he just couldn't watch it. He watched as Shay stood stone-faced next to Sena. He wanted to see how long she would last in the game they were about to play. If Sena was anything like Moochie, it was about to get real ugly.

"Who sent you?" Shay asked.

"Nobody sent me to do anything! I didn't do nothing!" Celeste cried as she struggled against the restraints.

"Last time. Who sent you?" Shay asked calmly.

"Nobody!"

Shay looked to Sena and Sena looked to Moochie. Moochie nodded his head and walked away. Sena picked up the iron.

"Do you know how it feels to get shot?" Sena asked as she held the iron up in the air. She put the hot iron on Celeste's chest and began to iron her skin off.

Celeste let out a loud shriek that lasted a long time. When Sena lifted up the iron, there was skin stuck to the bottom of it, and there was none left on Celeste's chest. Shay looked on in amazement, trying her best to keep from running out of the room. Sena was in the zone and ready to get the party really started. Moochie had put his headphones on and let Yo Gotti's "CM5" be the soundtrack to the movie he was watching. He had no feeling at all. His body, mind, and heart were numb to what was going on around him.

Skillet watched in horror. He had seen some shit, but damn! *What the fuck kind of person thinks to iron a person's skin off?* Skillet knew Sena was made for Moochie. They were like two peas in a pod: two fucking psychos.

"Who sent you?" Sena asked again.

"Nobody, nobody! Fuck you!" Celeste yelled. She knew they were going to kill her anyway, so why give out any info? She just hoped they would kill her quickly. She didn't know how much longer she would be able to hang on. The pain was excruciating and unbearable. She knew she was paying for her sins against Kidd and the other men she had done wrong in her life. Her whole life had been based around money. Her every thought was consumed with how to get more money. Even though her family was very wealthy, that still wasn't enough. Her greed was out of control. Now she realized she had fucked with the wrong family.

"Wrong answer." Sena set the iron in the center of Celeste's face, burning the skin off in the process.

Celeste was screaming so much that she made a mistake and stuck her tongue into the iron. Everyone could hear her skin sizzling as Sena began to pull the iron off Celeste's face, taking a good portion of skin and meat with it. Celeste's screaming had stopped because she had fainted from the shock to her system.

At that moment, Shay lost it and threw up everything in her stomach. Moochie saw Skillet get up and run to Shay and wondered what had her so upset. His mind had drifted off, so he didn't know what was happening. When he got to where Sena was standing, he looked down at Celeste and could see why Shay was so upset. Sena had really fucked ol' girl up. Her face looked like Freddy Krueger, and her lips were gone. He had done some shit, but never anything like that. He looked back up at Sena and walked away. He had nothing to say. That's what she was supposed to do. The bitch deserved everything that came to her. And to him, Sena still wasn't done yet. They would be there all day cutting her up limb by limb until she talked. He knew who made the hit, but he wanted to know exactly who was all in on it.

Celeste was in so much pain that she couldn't even scream anymore. Never in a million years would she have thought something like this would be happening to her. She was ready to talk. She knew she was going to die, but she wanted it sooner rather than later. Another second of this was out of the question. And even if they didn't kill her, she would surely kill herself. There was no way in the world she would walk around with her face burned off. Her vanity wouldn't let her.

Skillet pulled Shay out of the door so she could get some air. He knew he should have never involved her. "Yo, you all right?" Skillet was full of concern. He knew she would never see life the same after what she just saw. No sane person would.

"Yeah, I'm good. I thought we were going to shoot her, cut her up a little, pour alcohol in her wounds maybe, but not this shit. Wow, did you see that psychotic shit?" Shay knew her friend was a little off, but this was a whole new ballgame. Shit, she needed to be admitted into a mental institute.

"First off, you watch too many movies." Skillet laughed at her. "And that's why I told you never mind. I didn't want this for you. But you insisted."

"I know, and I'm still down, ain't shit changed. I just needed a breather. It was a shock to my nervous system." There was no turning back now and, truthfully, she didn't want to turn back. She looked up to Sena and wanted to be there with her. She hadn't noticed how much she admired Sena until tonight. The strength she was show-ing for her man, Shay wanted that and was determined to get it.

"You sure?" Skilled asked uncertainly.

"Yeah, I'm good." Shay walked back into the room to see Sena still standing over Celeste, but now she had a bottle of alcohol in her hand.

Celeste had fainted from the pain, but Sena was ready to wake her ass back up. She began to pour the alcohol on Celeste's chest. She woke up with a bloodcurdling scream. Shay went to stand by her friend, hoping to get some action in herself.

"You good?" Sena looked to Shay. Sena was concerned for her friend. She really wanted Shay to go home. This type of stuff wasn't for Shay. Hell, it wasn't for her either, but she was a rider and real fucked up in the head, and she knew it. She and Moochie would burn in hell together; that's how devoted she was to him. He was her world, and anything he asked of her, she would do it, no second thoughts.

"Yeah, I'm good. She still not talking?" Shay asked without looking down. The sight looked like some straight shit off a scary movie. Surely she would throw up again if she had to look at Celeste's disfigured face one more time.

Sena turned her attention back to Celeste. "Nah, but I got something for that." Sena picked up a bottle of bleach off the floor. She knew that what she was doing was horrible, but she kept in her mind that this person was trying to take away everything she loved. And Celeste had the blood of the man in her who killed her best friend. Sena leaned over Celeste's body with the bleach in her hand.

"Wait! It was Sonny! It was Sonny! Please stop!" Celeste cried.

"Who did Sonny hire?" Sena asked.

"I don't know who he hired!"

Moochie stood up and took off his headphones as she spoke.

"I knew he was looking for Kidd, so I told him I'd help set him up for some money. I'm sorry, please stop this!" Celeste cried as she tried to keep from choking on her blood.

Moochie was tired of her breathing. He didn't need to hear any more; he knew exactly who she was talking about. He had figured out everything she had just said already. She really didn't help him at all. But she would be one less person on this earth that had benefited from his brother's demise. He had no more use for her.

Moochie looked down at her and pulled out his gun. He pulled the trigger, putting a bullet right between her eyes. He felt like he had to be the one to kill her. She had stolen his heart from him. He would give his life in a heartbeat to have his brother back. After thinking about it a little longer, he emptied his whole clip into her face, turning it into unrecognizable mush.

Chapter 13

Life's a Bitch

Sonny stormed through his house like a madman. He couldn't believe one of his stash houses had been blown up, and his right-hand man had been killed during the explosion. Celeste thought she was smart by having Kidd pick her up from one of Sonny's stash houses, thinking no one would be able to find her there, and she had inadvertently brought more drama to his doorstep.

"What the fuck is going on!" Sonny exploded, looking at the so-called killers seated in front of him. No one dared answered his question. Everyone looked around, waiting for someone to break the silence.

"Somebody say something, 'cause I need to know how in the fuck one man can do this much damage!" Still he got no answers, and this only infuriated him more. But he knew the answer to his question. He knew Moochie was an undercover menace. Mr. Jackson used to tell him the horror stories of what Moochie used to do to his victims. There were three men in attendance, but he had started out with six, seven including his longtime friend who was now gone.

"We can't seem to find him. I think he may have some help," one of the would-be killers said.

Boom!

The shot resonated through the house. Sonny had decorated the room with the man's brains before he

could say another word. The remaining men sat terrified.
For one, they had no protection; they had been searched
and stripped of any ammunition at the gate. And, two,
the look in Sonny's eyes said he was ready to send them
to their Maker. His boyishly good-looking facial features
were turned into a mask of rage.

"I don't pay you muthafuckas to think; I pay you stupid
fucks to find and kill! And it doesn't seem as though you
all can do that." Sonny looked around, highly disappointed at the help he had hired.

"Moochie has a best friend that might know how to find
him," another would-be killer stated quickly.

Sonny looked at him. "Well, what the hell you sitting
looking in my fucking face for?" he yelled. The men
quickly gathered their things and got out of there.

Sonny sat back down once everyone had gone. It felt
like everything around him was crumbling down, and
the brothers were the cause of all his grief. First they had
killed his uncle and cousin; now he couldn't find Celeste.
He knew if Moochie got a hold of her, he wouldn't find
her at all. Then they went on to kill his best friend, and
they blew up a good portion of his dope and money.
He couldn't understand how two niggers could cause
so much damage to a person who was supposed to be
untouchable.

Sonny didn't know the whole story on what went
down between his uncle and the brothers, but he knew
that at the end, everything had gone wrong, terribly
wrong. He needed his uncle back for guidance; they
stole his life away for nothing. He had never liked Kidd
in the first place. He didn't like how his uncle took Kidd
under his wing and always bragged about the infamous
killer Kidd was. His uncle did all that, and Kidd turned
around and killed him over a murdering, dike bitch. If
Sonny could have found Valencia's grave, he would piss

on it, dig her up, and torch the remains. He hoped his men could find Moochie's friend, because now he was ready to get his hands dirty. He felt like he should be the one to bring his uncle's murderer to justice.

Moochie sat on the loveseat in front of his sixty-inch TV, playing Call of Duty, *when someone walked into his house. He looked up and thought he was seeing things. His heart stopped beating, and his breath got caught in his throat.*

"Nigga, why you looking at me all crazy-eyed?" Kidd asked.

"Man, I thought I'd never see you again." Moochie got up to hug his brother.

"Man, get off me, ol' sensitive-ass nigga! Let's see how sensitive yo' ass get when I'm done kickin' yo' ass in Madden."

Moochie stood in awe. He couldn't believe his brother was standing in front of him walking, talking, and laughing. His door opened, and he saw another surprise that made his heart travel to his throat.

"What's up, Moochie Mooch!" Valencia exclaimed.

Now he knew he was tripping because he had attended her funeral. She was even wearing the suit he and Kidd had picked out for her, a cream-colored Donna Karan.

"What the fuck is going on?" Moochie looked around.

"What, you ain't happy to see yo' big sis?" Valencia walked up to him and gave him a hug.

"Always happy to see you, but how are you here?" Moochie's mind was really fucking with him. He knew he had to be dreaming. If this is what his dream world was like, he never wanted to wake up. Somebody needed to give him one big-ass sleeping pill.

"Never mind the formalities. Don't try to change the subject, cat daddy. Put the game in so I can dig in that ass."

Moochie never thought he would be this happy to hear his brother talk again. Moochie watched Kidd. He was smiling from ear to ear. It had been awhile since he'd seen Kidd this happy. It was like he had found his joy again. He knew his brother wanted to be with Vee again and he was beyond happy that they had found each other. He knew his brother's spirit had long ago gone to be with Vee. He was happy his brother's spirit was free and not trapped in that hospital bed.

Vee went to sit down next to Moochie and, on the way, she slapped him in the back of the head. She used to always do that to him. It didn't matter where they were; if she got the urge, she did it. Moochie was happy to be with his loved ones again. He knew he had felt emptiness, but he didn't know how deep it was until now.

"Come on, boys, your cookies are ready," Moochie heard his mother say from behind him.

He thought for sure he was going to have a heart attack. All he could do was grab his heart because it felt like it was about to beat out of his chest. It couldn't have been his mother; she had died long ago. It had taken him a long time to get over her death and now here she was standing right in front of him. He got up and walked over to his mother and wrapped his arms around her, squeezing tight. He missed his mother with all his heart. She was his everything. The bond he shared with his mother and brother was unbreakable. Even after their death, no one would ever take their place. Tears were falling down his face. He couldn't believe he was with everyone he loved.

"Come on now, you gon' wrinkle my dress, Shawn," his mother said, calling him by his real name.

Moochie let her go so he could look at her again. His mother was still as beautiful as the day they had buried her. She grabbed his hand and led him over to where Kidd was sitting.

"Look at my two boys. Oh, how handsome you two have come to be! I want you to know that, no matter what you've done in your life, I will always love you unconditionally, and I am very proud of you both."

Moochie couldn't stop the tears from falling down as he listened to the words coming from his mother's mouth. He always wondered how she would feel about the life he and his brother had chosen. He knew deep down that any mother would be disappointed that her sons had turned out to be killers. But that's why she was the best mother; she would never tell him she was disappointed in him. He looked around and saw that everyone he loved the most was in this room, and they were all dead. And after he woke up from this dream, he would probably never see them again.

"Bye, my babies, I love you; and, Wanya, I'll see you soon," his mother said, referring to Kidd by his real name. "Valencia, don't keep me waiting too long, sweetie."

Moochie watched as his mother disappeared.

"A'ight, li'l bruh, tell my sister I love her, and you two should know I'm always here for y'all. And no weapon formed against her shall prosper as long as I'm around." Valencia blew him a kiss just before she left.

Then it was just Moochie and Kidd. Kidd looked to his little brother and tried to find the words to say what he needed to. "I know you not ready for me to go, but I need you to let go."

"I can't! How do I tell them to pull the plug? What am I supposed to do without you?" Moochie let the tears roll down his face as he looked to the floor.

"I'm no good to you like this. Look at me. I need you to man all the way up right now."

Moochie looked up. It was the first time he noticed all the bullet holes, and the blood that had begun to pour from them.

"Everyone has always been used to me leading the way, but now it's your turn. Let me go. I'll always be here with you." Kidd finally faded away.

Chapter 14

Give Me Strength

Raylene had been sitting in the dark for days. She hadn't left her apartment since Shay had taken Kelly away. She felt lower than the lowest form of life. She had failed one daughter by leaving her for dead. It didn't matter how things ended with her and Raina; it had almost killed her to leave Raina behind. Her desperation overshadowed her love for her child. But she would have never done Kelly like that. She had no intention of disappointing another child. It felt like someone had hit her in the heart with a sledgehammer when Kelly told her she hadn't said anything because she didn't want to be done like Raina. She felt numb, all over the pain she had caused her children.

Raylene hadn't seen or heard anything from Carl. He hadn't shown his face yet, but she was waiting for him. How could she not have seen him for the monster he was? Was she that desperate that she went totally blind to what was right in front her eyes? She thought about Raina and how proud she was of her. She was really happy that she had turned out all right. She really wanted to meet her granddaughter. Shay had never brought Kayla around her, but Kelly couldn't stop talking about Kayla. She would love to be a grandmother, but she understood it was going to take some time for Shay to get used to her being around again. Her thoughts were interrupted by the front door being opened.

"Kelly, is that you?" Raylene ran to the living room but stopped in her tracks when she saw Carl standing there, wobbling. She could clearly see he was drunk. He smelled real bad and looked like he had been sleeping on the streets.

"Nah, it ain't that lying li'l bitch!" he slurred.

Raylene said nothing as she tried to ease her way into the kitchen so she could get to a weapon. She was all too familiar with how he got when he was drunk, and it looked like he had been drinking for days.

"Where you going?" Carl whispered like someone else was in the house.

"Nowhere, just to get you some coffee," she said calmly.

"I don't want no damn coffee! I want to know why I'm getting the feeling you eyeballing me." His eyes were so low they looked like slits on his face.

"I don't know what you're talking about." Raylene couldn't get a read on him since she couldn't see his eyes. She prayed she made it to some sort of protection.

"Yes, you do! Those two whores of yours done got in your ear, huh?" Carl could see the anger flash through her eyes.

"No one told me anything!" She inched toward the kitchen. "When I got home, no one was here." She could see it in his body language that he didn't believe her.

"You's a liar just like them li'l bitches. I'm gon' teach you not to lie to me."

Carl charged toward her. She ran for the kitchen, but she didn't get too far. He snatched her by her hair and threw her down on the floor. He kicked her in the face and began to stomp the life out of her, all the while yelling obscenities at her.

"Bitch, you was my fuckin' downfall! I shoulda left yo' broke ass where the fuck I found you!" he yelled as pulled her face close to his.

Raylene wanted to throw up, the smell was so putrid. Carl brought his fist in the air and delivered a blow to her face so hard that they both heard the bones in her jaw crack.

"Ple . . . Slo . . . Pl . . ." She couldn't get any words out. She tried to beg him to stop, but the pain stopped her from speaking.

"Fuck you and them scheming-ass bitches!" Carl spat.

But his words made no sense to Raylene. She was too busy trying to block his blows. When his arms were tired, he let her go, stood up, and began to stomp her in the face repeatedly. She never had a chance to protect herself from his rage. All she could think about was making it out of this so she could make things right with her family.

"I wish they were here too. I would do 'em just like this; then I'd fuck the shit outta 'em!" Carl spat.

That sentence Raylene heard loud and clear, right before everything went black around her.

"I shole wish you would answer that got damned phone and tell yo' boyfriend you at home and call during your office hours." Skillet was getting tired of Shay's phone vibrating and singing across the dresser.

"Shut up! I ain't got no boyfriend." Shay hit him in the head with a pillow while getting up to get her phone. She had missed twelve calls and had twelve voicemails, but she didn't recognize the number. "Damn," she said as she sat back down, about to dial her voicemail. But before she could dial her phone, it rang again.

"Hello?" she answered, ready to give somebody the business for calling her phone that many times.

"Hello, may I speak to Rianah?" the voice on the other end asked, pronouncing her name wrong and shocking her at the same time because they knew her real name.

"Who's calling?" Shay wasn't ready to give up any information.

"This is a social worker from Barnes Jewish Hospital, and we found your number in the pocket of one of our patients. When she was brought in, she had no identification on her."

Shay jumped out of bed to go check on her sister. But when she got to the bedroom, Kelly was sound asleep. She got back on the phone. "This is Raina. Who do you have there?" By now, Skillet was standing behind her, wanting to know what made her jump out of bed.

"As I said before, the only thing she had on her was your phone number."

"Well, what the hell does she look like?" Raina knew in the pit of her stomach they were talking about her mother. She was only other person who would call her Raina.

"She's looks to be about forty-five years old, a hundred and thirty pounds, with long black hair—"

"Stop!" Raina tried not to feel anything for her mother, but her heart wouldn't let her. "That's my mother," she stated. "Is she all right?"

"I really can't discuss it over the phone. If you can come up to help fill out some paperwork, we can go from there."

"Okay, I'm on my way." Shay looked at the clock and saw that it was three-thirty in the morning. "I don't need this shit right now. When it rains it pours," she huffed.

"What's wrong and where you going?" Skillet asked.

"To Barnes. Something happened to Raylene."

"You want me to come with you?"

"No, I need to be alone. I need time to think. It's too much going on around me." Shay felt like she was going to have an anxiety attack. The walls were closing in on her slowly.

"It's going to be okay. If you need me to come up there, let me know. Are you going to wake Kelly up?"

"Nah, I have to find out what's going on first. She's been through enough as it is," Shay said with an exaggerated sigh

"Okay, well, keep me posted." Skillet really wanted to go with her, but he knew how it felt to want to be alone with your own thoughts. She gave him his space when he needed it, and he would do the same for her.

When Shay got to the hospital, she didn't know what to expect. She had all kinds of questions going through her head. Why had they called her? Why hadn't Raylene called to tell her what was wrong? She actually hoped that it wasn't anything really that bad. She wouldn't wish harm on anyone. She may have said a lot of mean things about her mother but, no matter what they went through, she was still her mother. When Raylene had first left her, she was hurt beyond belief and didn't know what to do with that hurt anger, so she reacted horribly. She now understood that, and it still didn't make what her mother had done to her right.

Shay walked up to the nurse's station and approached a nurse who looked like she had seen better days and was ready to get off work. "Excuse me, I'm looking for a patient named Raylene Dillard."

After she got the info, she headed to the nurses' station. "Hello, I'm looking for the social worker for Raylene Dillard."

"Okay, let me page her for you. Could you have a seat in the waiting area?"

"Raina Dillard?"

Shay looked up to a short, fat lady standing in front of her. "Yes, ma'am." Shay stood up to go with the lady.

"Follow me."

"Can I see my mother?" Shay was anxious to see what was wrong with her mother.

The lady turned around to look at her. "I would like to explain what happened."

"Well, I would like to see her while you explain." Shay was getting tired of all this talking. "Look, can you just take me to her?"

"Yes, ma'am." She could see that, no matter what she said, the young lady wanted to see her mother. She just hoped that Shay could handle it.

Shay felt like she was walking the green mile. She had no idea about what she was about to see. She really didn't know how much more she could take. Her life was slowly spiraling out of control. She just wanted to get a grip on things. When she walked in the room and saw her mother, everything around her started spinning and then the struggle to breathe kicked in, and she lost the battle with staying conscious.

When Shay woke up, she was in a bed on the side of her mother. She stared at Raylene in the bed. Raylene was bandaged from head to toe. There was a big bandage wrapped around her head. There was a wire holding her jaw together, and she had a cast on her right arm. From what she could see, she also had two black eyes. She looked away and saw the social worker sitting on the other side of her bed.

"You had me scared for a minute. Are you all right?" She looked at Shay through saddened eyes.

"Yeah, I'm all right, but what happened to her?" Shay turned her back so she was looking at an unconscious Raylene again.

"Apparently, she was badly beaten. A neighbor found her on the floor of her apartment. He was awakened by her screaming. When he came to his door to see what was going on, he saw her boyfriend running from the apartment and covered in blood. He immediately called the police. He said she had a young daughter, but we couldn't locate her."

"Because she's at my house," Shay said in a daze. She couldn't believe Carl had the nerve to come back to the house. He had struck again. "I told her to get rid of him," Shay said more to herself than to the social worker.

"Will the child be able to stay with you until she gets better?"

"Yeah. Do you mind giving me a few minutes alone with her?"

"No, not at all. Let me know if you need anything."

Once the social worker left, Shay pulled a chair up to the side of Raylene's bed and just stared at her. She couldn't seem to find any words. She had an "I told you so" feeling. Out of all the times she had wished harm on her mother, never did she imagine this. She just sat there. She could not think of anything to say to Raylene, so she just sat with her for a few hours.

Chapter 15

No Bond Stronger

Sena thought she was dreaming when she felt Moochie's hands roaming over her body. She shivered under his touch. He hadn't touched in her weeks. She knew he was stressed, so she didn't press him, but she had missed this feeling.

Moochie had missed the feel of his woman. He knew he had been neglecting Sena. He also knew she was kind of a nympho, so he had to jump out of his funk for a second to tend to her needs. It felt like her skin melted under his touch, and he could feel the goose bumps forming on her body. He slowly pulled himself on top of her.

"I missed you," Moochie confessed as he placed long, wet kisses along her collarbone.

Sena pulled his face up to hers and kissed him long and hard. She could hardly contain her excitement. He finally pulled his face away from her and slowly kissed down her body until he got to the treasure he had been neglecting. He spread her legs out as far as they would go and admired the juices flowing from her box and down the crack of her ass. He bent down to lap it up before it fell on to the bed. He didn't want to miss a drop of her essence. Her body shivered feverishly.

"Aahhh, ssss!" she hissed.

Sena could hear the ocean waves crashing and the good morning birds chirping in the background as Moochie brought on an orgasm that felt like it was coming from way deep within. He sucked on her clit, softly pulling on it. As he spread her pussy lips apart, he wished he could climb inside of her. His dick was so hard that it felt like it was about break off. He watched her shiver as her moans got louder, then subsided as her orgasm high came down. He wanted her to enjoy every second of it. If he could, he would make it last forever. He wasn't done tasting her yet, but she wanted to feel him inside of her.

"Come on, baby, I want you inside of me," Sena moaned.

Moochie climbed back up to the top of the bed so they were face to face. He loved the way she looked right at that moment, like she was bracing herself for what was to come. She opened her legs, inviting him in, and he gladly entered.

"Ahhhh," they sighed in unison.

Moochie just lay there, loving the feeling of just being inside her. Her pussy sucked him all the way in. It felt like his dick was sitting in hot pudding. She didn't want him to move either. She wrapped her legs and arms around him so he could stay just like that.

"I love you," Sena whispered in his ear.

"Say it again." Moochie could never get enough of hearing that. To know that he wasn't left alone in the world made life worth living. At times he felt alone, but Sena tried her best to let him know he wasn't alone.

"I love you, I love you, I love you."

He started to move. "I love you too," he grunted.

The feeling that was building in his nuts was indescribable. His strokes got harder and went deeper, making her gasp with each stroke.

"Ohh, shhh." Sena could feel her body tingling all over. Her body stiffened, so he knew she was on the verge of an orgasm.

Moochie sped up his pace, pumping hard into her, bringing on an orgasm that she didn't think her body would be able to handle. Her eyes rolled to the back of her head and her body locked. Her hot box had a death grip on his love stick, making him nut before he wanted to. He fell on top of her drenched in sweat, breathing hard and instantly snoring.

Sena watched him sleep as she softly pushed him off of her. He was smiling a little. She knew that just for a slight moment in time, all his worries were gone and she was happy she could be the one to make that happen. He was her world, and she would give anything to make his pain go away.

When Sena finally woke up, she was in the bed alone. Moochie had left her a note that he was going to see Kidd. She took in a deep breath.

"I just wish this were all a bad dream," she said aloud. She thought about her friend Shay. They hadn't talked in a few days, so she decided to give her a call. The phone rang about seven times before Shay answered.

"What's up, chick?" Sena asked as Shay answered the phone.

"A whole bunch of mess, girl. What's going on with you?"

"Nothing. You want to take the kids to zoo so they can play? I need some kind of recreation."

"Yeah, I need to talk to you anyway. We can meet at the zoo in an hour."

"Okay."

"Girl, I don't know if I'm coming or going nowadays. Every day it's something new. If anything else goes wrong, I think I'm gon' have a nervous breakdown," Shay vented to Sena while they watched the kids run around in the play area. "How can this much shit happen in such a short amount of time?"

"So, what are you gon' do about Kelly? Have you told her about your mother yet?"

"No, I haven't. I don't know how." Shay looked defeated.

"How are you taking it?" Sena knew how Shay felt about her mother, but there had to be some love in there.

"I don't know. You know, I wanted to say 'I told you so' so bad, but it wouldn't come out. She looked so broken."

"So, my next question is, how are we gon' handle this?" Sena asked, looking Shay right in the eyes. "You know I got you, no matter what. We pullin' kick-dos, drive-bys, whatever, I got my nine and my stun gun. You know we can wreck shit!" Sena mocked one of her favorite movies, *A Low Down Dirty Shame*. They shared a much-needed laugh.

"I know, crazy! But I don't know where to even look for Carl."

"What? Girl, do you not know who our men are? Shit, they could find a piece of rat shit in a pile of burnt rice. Girl, you better get yo' mind right." Sena looked at Shay like she had lost her mind.

"I don't want to involve Kaylin and Moochie. They got so much going on with Kidd and everything, and I don't want to add to their stress."

"I have to disagree. When my participation begins, I must inform my man. For one, his ass got me on lockdown. He on some paranoid shit times ten. If I need to pull him in, I need him to be fully aware of the situation."

"I guess you right. I'll get back with you on that. Anyway, how is Moochie doing with Kidd?"

"Horrible." Sena exhaled loudly. "I just wish this were all a bad dream and we could go back to the way things used to be. I would give up everything if I could have the last two years back." Sena looked to up to the sky and could see the sun was shining bright and the sky was as blue as the ocean. She stared at the clouds. They were in a shape of a smiling face. She prayed that was a good sign.

"How does it feel?" Shay asked.

"How does what feel?" Sena had a confused look on her face.

"When you lost Vee." Shay could see the sadness that quickly consumed Sena's eyes.

Sena looked at her, not able to really find the words to describe the pain. It broke Sena's heart every time she heard Vee's name. It never failed; the pain was still as fresh as if it happened yesterday. But she could tell Shay sincerely wanted to know.

"Like someone hit you in the heart with a sledgehammer over and over again. You feel like you want to go with them, like the air in your lungs has been sucked out. I could go on forever, but you can't sum it up in a couple of words." Sena wiped the tears away that had started to form in her eyes.

Both women sat there in their own world, watching everything around them but not really seeing anything.

"Girl, that little Deonna looks just like Moochie. All you did was spit her out," Shay said as she admired how beautiful Deonna was, trying to brighten the mood.

"I know, right? But I wouldn't have it any other way." Sena loved the fact that Deonna looked like Moochie. She had his eyes, lips, honey brown skin tone and, of course, the long sandy brown hair that hung down her back.

They sat there for another two hours, just catching up and laughing at the kids. For that short moment in time, there were no worries in either of the lady's minds. All was right with the world: no murders, Kidd wasn't dying, Moochie and Skillet were out having drinks. It felt like old times, and if either one of them had the power of God, this moment would never end.

***

Skillet had been riding around for about an hour with no destination in sight. He just needed the fresh air. It was starting to feel like the walls were closing in on him. The last two years of his life had been like being on a roller coaster. He could remember him, Moochie, and Kidd chilling and living life to the fullest. His life had always been pretty easy. Kidd made sure of that. He didn't want Skillet to get into their world, but Skillet wouldn't let it go. He had to be in the mix with Moochie. Kidd didn't want Moochie in it either, but there was no telling him no. Whatever his big brother did, Moochie did. And that's how Skillet felt: whatever his brothers did, he wanted to do. Kidd and Moochie were his only family for a long time. His mother was around. She did the best she could do, and he loved her to death, but it was Kidd who kept him under control. If he knew Kidd wouldn't approve of it, it wouldn't get done. The thought of losing him hurt him to his core. He could only imagine what Moochie was feeling. He knew deep down that Moochie would never be the same.

Skillet was snapped out of his thoughts when he heard a screeching sound. He had to quickly step on his brakes to keep from smashing into the car in front of him. All of a sudden, he was surrounded by four black cars. Before he could react, his window was being shattered, and two big hands were snatching him through the window. Now Skillet wasn't a small dude, so this meant the person grabbing him had to be something huge! The last thing he remembered was the sun shining in his eyes before there was nothing but silence and darkness.

When Skillet woke up, he was in a basement tied to a chair. His phone vibrating snapped him out of his slumber. His mind was racing a mile a minute, trying to figure out what was going on. All he could think about was his baby girl and Shay. Would he ever see them again? And Moochie; what would happen if he lost another brother? The gash on the back of his head was bleeding badly. He could see the blood running down his shirt. Other than that, they really hadn't done too much to him, at least not in his opinion. But if someone was looking at him, they would have thought he was knocking on death's door. Skillet hoped they weren't trying to get any info out of him because, if so, then let the torture begin.

Skillet could feel his phone vibrating in his coat pocket. He hoped it was Shay's or Moochie's tenth time trying to reach him because, if that was the case, they would surely be on their way to get him. He was happy as hell they hadn't taken his phone. If he went too long without contact with anybody, he knew the hounds would be out looking for him. Moochie was on some paranoid "everybody's after me" type of shit lately. He had recently fussed at Moochie about it and he hoped this wasn't the one thing Moochie decided to take his advice on and that they got there before his life ended. If he died that day, he wouldn't change a thing in his life. He had lived and loved life at its best.

"Hand me my phone." Moochie could see it vibrating. "I hope that's that nigga Skillet. I done called him about five times today." Sena handed him the phone. "Aww shit!" He shook his head and braced himself for the worst when he saw Shay's number come across the screen. His stomach dropped to his feet. She never called his phone.

"What's up, Shay?" He almost didn't even want to hear her answer.

"Where in the fuck is Kaylin? If that bastard is with you, I'm fucking him up!" Shay yelled into the phone. She had been calling Skillet for hours, and he had yet to answer his phone. Her mind immediately went to thinking he was with some other chick and, if that was the case, there was going to be hell to pay. He wouldn't play her twice.

"He ain't with me. I been calling him all day." Moochie didn't think anything of it at first. He knew his partner in crime used to be a big ho. He too had ventured on the ho-ish side, but Sena shut all that shit down. She was practically a porn star in the bed, so he had no need to step out. Sena took very good care of him. Now, he didn't know the depths of Shay and Skillet's relationship, but he hoped Skillet wasn't out on some bullshit. There was too much going on right now.

"The last time I talked to him, he was supposed to be with you," Shay said suspiciously.

"He got his phone with him?" Moochie knew if he had his phone, they would be able to find him.

"Yeah. I talked to him earlier when me and Sena were at the zoo." Shay was in full panic mode now. Her anger had quickly turned into worry. It wasn't like Skillet not to contact anybody. He and Moochie were practically attached at the hip, so she knew something was wrong if Moochie had no clue where he was.

"Okay, hold on a minute. Babe, call Shay's phone," he told Sena as he hung up to turn on the family locator on his phone. He was thinking the same thing that Shay was thinking. It wasn't like Skillet not to call just to say what's up. The last two times he looked at his phone to locate someone, his world got flipped upside down.

"I can't take no more hits. I just can't, babe. Shit gon' get real ugly in minute." Moochie could see Skillet's phone was still on and there was an address of the location on the screen of his phone. Not recognizing the address, he picked up his house phone to call Skillet one more time. He didn't answer, making Moochie imagine the worst.

"Ask her if she knows this address." Moochie handed her his phone, and Sena read it off. He got the response he didn't want to hear. He was highly protective and he made it his business to know the whereabouts of his people at all times. Everyone knew if you were going someplace new to call and let someone know, especially now with everything that was going on. There were to be no disappearances.

"Tell her to meet us at that address."

Moochie really wished he had his brother there with him. Kidd would know what to do and how to go about it. But he had to get used to doing things without his mentor. He only had one friend, and they were about to go save him. From what, he didn't know. But he knew he needed the girls with him. Not knowing what the situation was, he needed someone to bounce ideas off of. He stared out the window, hoping that he got to his friend before anything happened to him. The world seemed darker these days. The sun didn't shine in his eyes, and it felt like a terrible storm was coming. They had no plan whatsoever, but it didn't matter. If they had to pull a kick-door in broad daylight to get his friend back, they would.

"You know I'm down for whatever you need me to do," Sena stated as they drove to the unknown destination. She said nothing else after that. She didn't need to say anything else.

Moochie already knew she would do anything for him. He looked over at her and admired her beauty. He knew deep down he had tainted her soul, but she would never let him know that. She was his heart, his rock, his everything. He decided right then and there that once all this was over, he was going to propose to her. He wanted to spend the rest of his life with her. He didn't know how long that would be, but he wanted it to be spent with her being Mrs. Deshawn Brown.

"Do you know how much I love you?" he asked her out of nowhere. He could tell she was shocked by his sudden question.

"Yeah." Sena looked over at him and smiled. It seemed like he wanted to say something but couldn't find the words.

"No, I mean really, do I show you? If not, is there something I can do to show you?" Moochie was in his feelings about some things. He had a feeling like his time would come to an end, and he didn't want to leave without her knowing how much he really loved her.

"If I left the earth today, right at this moment, I would die a happy woman knowing I had real love in my life. You may not think you show me, but I wake up every morning knowing I'm loved. And that's why there is nothing in this world I wouldn't do for you." She loved this man on the side of her with every ounce of her being, and she would kick down the gates of hell to get him.

"I think that is it," Moochie said, looking at a two-story brick home.

They sat adjacent to the house. The neighborhood looked quiet, and nothing seemed out of order. *Maybe we overreacted,* Moochie thought. He hoped he hadn't just made a mistake and brought Shay to the house of one of Skillet's chicks.

Shay got out of her car and went to sit in the car with Moochie and Sena. "I hope this ain't the house of one of his bitches 'cause, if so, it's about to get real ugly around this mutha." Shay was thinking the same thing Moochie was thinking. This didn't seem like the kind of neighborhood where shootings happened.

"Where his car?" Sena asked as she looked around at the quaint little neighborhood they had just invaded.

"Let's wait a few minutes to see if anyone goes in or out," Moochie suggested.

Chapter 16

Ghost of Vengeance

Sonny rode in the back of his Town Car while his driver raced to get the destination his minions had given him. He couldn't believe it had taken this long for him to get a solid lead on finding Moochie. He felt as though he was ready to jump out of the car and run full speed to get to Skillet. He wasn't dressed in his usual getup. Today was sweatpants and a T-shirt, not the Hugo Boss suits that normally he wouldn't be caught dead not wearing. But he had business to tend to, and he planned on getting his hands dirty. By the end of the day, he wanted Moochie's head on a platter.

Sonny still couldn't believe his uncle had chosen Kidd over him. He would have never betrayed his uncle for anything in the world. He couldn't help but think of the irony of it all. His uncle had chosen Kidd over him and Kidd had chosen a bitch over his uncle. Sonny didn't know the whole story and that it wasn't Kidd who killed Mr. Jackson. Moochie had done it because Mr. Jackson had turned against Kidd.

His uncle, Mr. Jackson, had tried to make Kidd kill the love of his life, but he couldn't do it. Mr. Jackson wanted Kidd to suffer for falling in love with the woman he thought had killed his daughter. In the end, everybody's family was being killed over a person who really didn't even exist. Mr. Jackson would never have found Valencia had it not been for his daughter, the twin of the girl who was killed. She had stumbled upon Valencia in the mall one day shopping and placed a call to her father. But in the end, she ended up getting herself killed too. Moochie was taking no prisoners that night. He came in blasting, taking down everything in his path like a weed-whacker. Ever since the day Sonny found his uncle's and cousin's remains in the basement of one of their stash houses, he had been dead set on finding and killing the deadly brothers.

Sonny arrived at the house, not noticing that he had an audience. He jumped out of the car while it was still moving. He felt like if he didn't act fast enough, Skillet would disappear.

When Moochie saw Sonny jump out of the car, he knew something was terribly wrong. He had never really encountered ol' boy but knew him from riding with Kidd. He never got a good vibe from Sonny, but Kidd told him not to sweat him. He watched Sonny practically leap from the car and run up the six steps to the house in two strides. He felt his muscles twitching, and the temperature seemed to have gone up a hundred degrees.

Moochie turned to Sena. "Yo, you stay here."

"What the fuck you mean stay here? Who was that guy?" Shay inquired, getting an attitude with Moochie. She could tell something wasn't right by the way Moochie reacted to seeing the man. She saw the way his jaws clenched shut.

"Right? The hell you bring us for if you just gon' leave us in the car?" Sena questioned.

Moochie knew she had a valid point. He didn't know why they were there. But, hell, they were his only backup now. He knew how the Jacksons got down and he didn't want to put them in that kind of danger. But he also needed some eyes and ears on the outside.

"What the fuck I just say? Stay the fuck in the car. When I come out, have the car ready to pull off." He looked at Sena and could see she wasn't even trying to hear that shit.

She rolled her eyes as if to say, "Nigga, please!"

Moochie frowned. "You bring yo' bald-headed ass in that house, and I'm gon' fuck you up!" he warned. But he knew it went in one ear and out the other. He took a deep breath and looked in the back seat at Shay. "Keep her in the car, please?"

Shay rolled her eyes at him also.

Moochie checked both his 9 mms to make sure the clips were full and then he got out of the car and started toward the house. He looked around cautiously to make sure no one was watching as he placed silencers on the ends of both guns. As soon as he ducked around the corner, Sena sprang into to action.

"What the fuck are you doing?" Shay asked while watching Sena check the clip of her brand new .380 to make sure it was full.

Sena pushed the lighter in, and out popped her secret compartment with her silencer inside. She made sure it was securely on the end of her gun. She ignored Shay until she felt she had everything she needed.

"The fuck you mean, what am I doing?" Sena couldn't believe the questions her friend asked sometimes. Didn't Shay get it that Sena would do anything for Moochie, even die? There was no way in the world Sena was letting Moochie go into some shit like this by himself. She would go up against an army with him and for him.

"He said to stay here." Shay knew Sena was going in. She wished she were as brave. She was all for going toe to toe, but they had no idea what was going on in that house. But she knew if Sena went in, there was no doubt about whether she was going with her.

"Girl, fuck what you and that nigga talking 'bout! Are you coming or not?" Sena left without giving her a chance to answer.

Sena could feel her stomach in her throat, but there was no turning back. Either they were going to leave together, or die together. She knew she was thinking selfishly because she would be leaving her daughter behind. But if Moochie died, she wouldn't be any good for her daughter in the first place. After losing Valencia, she didn't think she could take another death. The thought of Moochie leaving her was unbearable. She had waited her whole life to be loved the way Moochie loved her. That kind of love came once in a lifetime, and nothing was going to take that away from her. She would burn down the whole block just to make sure the both of them left together alive.

Sena looked around at the quiet neighborhood as she approached the back of the house where Moochie had gone. She checked to make sure the safety was off. Moochie always yelled at her about keeping the safety on. He would say, "How the hell you gon' be ready to blast on somebody if you got to get to the safety first?"

Moochie felt like he couldn't get inside fast enough. He could feel his heartbeat in every inch of his body. He bent down to look through the basement window in the back of the house, and he could see Skillet tied to a chair. It looked like he was bleeding from everywhere. They had put a beating on him something terrible. Moochie had a feeling of déjà vu. He had walked in on Kidd sitting in the same position. He didn't like it then, and he sure as hell didn't appreciate it now. His blood was boiling, and he couldn't wait to put that steel to someone's head. There was no one in the room with him who he could see, but he could tell there was someone in there with Skillet because he was laughing at something.

Moochie had seen all he needed to see. His friend was still alive. Now it was time to get the show started. He got up off the ground, went to the back door, and looked in the window. He could see a kitchen and a door that looked like it led to the basement.

"Fuck you, white boy!" Skillet laughed. He didn't give a fuck what they did to him; there was no way in the world he was giving Moochie up. He would never betray Moochie like that. He was willing to die that day knowing his family would be well taken care of.

Moochie was his brother, and their bond was as strong as if they had come from the same womb. He thought about Shay and his baby girl and he wanted to cry at the thought of never seeing them again. But he knew this was the way it had to be. "You's a pussy!" He sucked the blood from his mouth and tried to spit it all on Sonny. His body was in so much pain, but he would never show them that. He had been trained by the best, and he knew how to hold his ground.

"You're a real tough guy, huh?" Sonny asked. He couldn't understand why Skillet hadn't cracked yet. They had beaten him to a bloody pulp and still no information. Sonny figured either this guy was really loyal to the brothers or he was really scared. "Why won't you just tell me where I can find this cockroach? Are you scared he'll come for you?" Sonny thought that maybe he could offer protection for some information.

"Scared? Fuck I got to be scared for? Never that! But you should be! I can't wait to watch you take your last breath, bitch!" Skillet couldn't help but to laugh at this wannabe gangsta.

It fucked Sonny up that he was still laughing at him.

"This ain't even yo' type of game, homeboy. You swimming with sharks now, guppy."

If Sonny didn't feel like Skillet was his last chance at finding Moochie, he would have put a bullet in his head.

"Real fuckin' funny, huh? No worries though; I don't need you to talk. I'll find him and your family on my own." Sonny hoped to scare Skillet by threatening his family.

"Is that supposed to scare me?" Skillet smirked, popping Sonny's bubble. "Nigga, my bitch would pop you the moment she saw you coming, pussy!" He could see he was getting under Sonny's skin, so he dug deeper. "Moochie is going to make sure you die a torturous death, and I'll be there to watch." He laughed again, pissing Sonny off even more. Skillet knew Sonny was a pussy. There was no way in the world Sonny would still be alive had the shoe been on the other foot. They would have killed him hours ago and disposed of his body already.

Sonny stormed out of the basement. He claimed to be gangsta, but he really wasn't. All his life he had been living off the family name. His iron fist was more like wood. He had been dreaming of what he would do once he was close to finding Moochie. He had one brother down, and now it was time for the other to fall victim to his wrath. He really wished his uncle was there to see him in action but, in reality, he really hadn't done anything of any importance. The only reason his henchmen stayed around was because they were paid very well and his connections were strong. None of them respected him or really cared for the Zac Efron lookalike.

Moochie snuck into the house unnoticed. He slowly opened the door to what he hoped was the basement. Seeing no one was on the steps, he walked down slowly, watching his surroundings like a hawk. No one had hopped out on him yet, but he wasn't foolish enough to believe Sonny was there alone. Even the lousiest of bosses had a flunky or two.

As he got to the basement, there was a mirror straight ahead, and he could see a big man standing guard outside of the door, but he couldn't tell if there was anyone else in the room with the big man. The only thing he could hear was muffled sound coming from the other side of the door. He watched the man's every move, waiting for him to turn his head or make a move in the wrong direction so he could spring into action.

The man turned his head, trying to hear what was going on in the room he was standing in front of, and that's all Moochie needed. He took aim and put two bullets in the back of the man's head. Moochie ran to catch the man before he could hit the floor, not wanting to alert anyone of his presence; then he dragged him to another door and pulled the man inside. He hated that he was alone. Going into random rooms without knowing what was on the other side wasn't something he would normally do. But he had to keep it moving and get it how he could.

As Moochie was walking out, he was stopped short by a big-ass .38 Special pointed at his head. He looked his killer right in the eyes, waiting for his demise. He raised his hands in the air and closed his eyes, ready to die. He was sorry he had put everyone in the position they were in, and he wished he could have told them how much he loved everyone. He heard two poofs and then felt the big man fall on him.

When he opened his eyes, Sena was standing in front him with a smoking gun on some Charli Baltimore–type shit. Once again, he was thankful for her being there for him, but he would get in her ass later about not doing what he had told her to do. He'd told her to stay in the car, but she never did as he told her, so why should today be any different?

"There are three of them in that room," she whispered. "One is standing right behind the door. The white dude is on the other side of the basement sitting at a desk, and the other is standing by Skillet." She had looked in the same window Moochie had before she came in behind him. They must have come back into the room while Moochie was trying to hide the body.

Moochie just looked at her. He couldn't believe she was his. He couldn't have built her with his bare hands to be the woman she was.

"Text Shay and tell her to ring the doorbell and let her know what's up. And you go back to that window. Start blasting if you see anybody coming in after me." Moochie kissed her on the lips and sent her on her way. He figured if he could get at least one of them out of the room, the odds would be better.

Sena pulled out her cell phone as she tiptoed back up the steps. Before she could get out the door, Shay answered and agreed to do as Sena asked. Sena was glad she hadn't listened to Moochie. If she had, he would have been dead. She had almost lost Moochie before so she knew she had to be on her toes. One wrong step and everybody could be dead. She went back to the window to watch what was going on.

Shay got out of the car to go and ring the doorbell. She made sure her gun was securely on her hip. Sena had left her the gun she usually kept locked away in her glove compartment. Shay hadn't shot a gun since Tory's death. She figured it should be just like riding a bike. She had no idea what she was going to do after she rang the doorbell. She didn't know if she should start blasting on sight or try to get invited inside. All she knew was that she was leaving with her man. She prayed they made it in time.

Shay thought about the time Skillet got shot up in front of her house. She thought she had lost him. He was everything in her life that was right. With everything that was going on in her life, this was the last thing she needed.

She wished she could press rewind and everything would go back to the way it was.

Once Shay got to the door, she made her decision on what to do. She just hoped everyone was in sync. She stood at the door, texting Sena before she rang the doorbell to let her know what was up. Sena got the message and forwarded it to Moochie. All this happened within ten minutes of them arriving.

Shay rang the doorbell again, getting in her sexy stance. She figured she looked pretty good in her black liquid leggings, white collared shirt with a red stomach belt, and red knee-high flat cowgirl boots. Had she known what the situation was, she probably would have changed her clothes. All Moochie said was to meet him at this house. He didn't say they were going on a rescue mission. But, nevertheless, here she was all dolled up, ready to fill someone up with hot lead. She knew Sena would have gone into a war zone to get Moochie, and that's the mentality she was trying her best to get herself into. She didn't know when her obsession of becoming like Sena kicked in, but it was in full effect.

Sena couldn't see where the man had gone, but she knew he was going to answer the door. She watched for her signal.

Moochie watched from his hiding place as one of the killers ascended the steps. He listened for his signal before he went in blasting.

Shay felt like she wanted to throw up when she heard someone yell, "Who is it?"

"Hi, my name is Kim, and I hit your car when I was parking. I wanted to exchange information with you," Shay said through the door. She could feel the man looking at her through the peephole. She knew her looks alone would get him to open the door.

The man swung the door open, trying to get a better look at the beauty on the other side of the door. He licked his lip and straightened his hair before he got the door all the way open. Once he finally got it open, he was met with two bullets to the head.

Moochie heard the body fall to the floor. That was his cue. With one kick, the door came off the hinges. Sena saw the door go flying and let off four shots into the window, hitting the back of the head of the man who was standing next to Skillet. Moochie locked his gaze on Sonny. He was squeezing the gun so hard his hand had started to hurt.

Sonny looked like he was about to shit on himself. He raised his hands in surrender. He had no weapons on him whatsoever. He had his head so far in the clouds that he didn't think he needed any. He figured that's why he had his many bodyguards.

Moochie could see Sena and Shay come into the room and they started untying Skillet. Shay felt like her legs were going to give out on her when she saw Skillet all bloody.

"Now what was so important that you had to talk to me about that you had to go get my peoples?" Moochie nodded toward Skillet.

"Look, you don't have to kill me." Sonny's pleas fell on deaf ears. He knew he had violated in a major way.

"You ordered a hit on me and my brother." At the thought of Kidd, Moochie felt his rage boiling over. His teeth were clenched so tight it felt like they were going to crack at any moment. This man who destroyed his life was breathing, talking, walking, and living. Moochie could not allow that to go on any longer.

"Look, you and that lesbo-loving brother of yours—"

Sonny didn't get to finish his sentence. All the rage Moochie had built up in him came out of the end of his gun. Moochie couldn't believe he had the nerve to mention his brother and Valencia in such a disrespectful tone. He didn't need to hear any more words come out of that snake's mouth. He had no conversation for the man, so he let his guns do the talking. Moochie emptied both his guns into Sonny's torso, landing all twenty-eight shots. As he got closer, he kept pulling the trigger as if more bullets would magically appear. He turned as he saw the girls holding Skillet up and waiting for him at the door.

"Go get the car," Moochie told Sena as he took Skillet's arm from around her neck and placed it around his.

As they were walking, Skillet stopped and looked at his friend. "I knew you was coming, and I told him I was going to watch him die." Skillet laughed.

Chapter 17

Turn Back Time

Shay watched Skillet sleep peacefully in their California king bed. She studied all his bumps and bruises. After they got all the blood cleared away, it wasn't as bad as everybody thought. There was a big gash over and under his right eye; it was swollen shut. He had a few broken ribs but, other than that, he was all right.

Shay thought about how close she had come to losing him again and she couldn't control the tears that started to fall. It had been a week since they got him back and she had been crying nonstop the whole time, thinking about what he looked like when they found him. She thought about how she would be able to explain to her baby that her daddy was never coming home. How would his mother take it?

Shay had gone to get the kids two days ago. She missed their laughter and needed some sort of joy in her life. Even though she had gotten Skillet back, she felt something was wrong deep down in her heart. She had a nagging feeling that she couldn't shake because she still hadn't told Kelly about their mother. She decided that she was going to take Kelly to see their mother that day. There was still so much she had to deal with. She felt like her young heart and mind were going to explode with her mother being beaten and dealing with Kelly being molested.

As soon as everyone was in a better place, she was going to pull Skillet's and Moochie's coats about finding Carl. The very thought of him made her skin crawl and her anger boil to an all-time high. He had ruined her life, and now he was trying to ruin Kelly's. But he wouldn't succeed in this lifetime if she had anything to say about it. She kissed Skillet on the lips and went to make breakfast.

As everyone was finishing up with breakfast, Skillet walked into the kitchen. "What's up, bubble butt?" He addressed Shay. "What's the dealio, Kelly?" He looked to Kelly as he picked up baby Kayla.

Shay got up to get his plate out of the oven. Kelly nodded. She couldn't really talk with a mouth full of food.

They hadn't really talked about what happened yet. He wasn't feeling good, and Shay didn't want to upset him. She knew there wasn't much to be told. He had gotten kidnapped, and they got him back, but she wanted to know how he was feeling, what was going through his mind. She wanted to make sure he was all right. She still didn't know how she felt about what happened. Her emotions were all over the place but, in her heart, she felt she had done the right thing. She'd killed another man in hopes of saving her own man. Playing God was something she never wanted to do again, but she had to play the hand that life dealt her.

"Hey, Daddy's baby," Skillet cooed at his daughter.

"Dadda," she said back, smiling big.

Skillet looked over at Shay. She frowned and rolled her eyes. "Why he get such a joyful greeting? That's a bunch of bullshit," she said, clearly jealous.

"'Cause they know daddies do the most, that's why." He and Kelly shared a laugh. Shay gave him the middle finger.

"Don't you do the most," she said sarcastically. "Well, I hope y'all continue to bond today because me and Kelly are going for a ride."

"Where y'all going?" Skillet looked at her. She avoided the questioning look Kelly was giving her.

"Kelly, go get ready and put some clothes on Kayla for me."

"Are we going shopping?" Kelly asked excitedly.

"Already you got her transformed into a li'l mini you! Damn shame." Skillet shook his head.

"Well, what else is she supposed to be other than just like me?" Shay winked at him. "Yeah, we can go shopping later on. And, boy, stop. You know we stay fly, ya dig? Just wait 'til Daddy's little girl gets a hold of the wallet. It's a wrap! That's why I'm getting mine now." She patted his front pocket on her way to put the plates in the sink. Kelly scooped up Kayla and did as she was told with a big smile on her face.

"So I'm a trick, huh? You just pimping me?" Skillet turned toward her and stared at her. She was looking good in her pink pajama shorts and tank top to match. He walked up behind her, put his arms around her waist, and started tongue kissing her neck.

"Now don't start nothing you can't finish!" Shay rubbed her ass against his hard dick. She hadn't felt it in a while, and her body was screaming for it.

"Who said I can't finish it?" Skillet reached around and slid his hands down the front of her shorts and started rubbing her pussy. He could feel her juices running all over his fingers instantly.

Shay laid her head back on his chest and let out a soft moan. Her hot box was aching. He took his fingers out of her and put them in his mouth, relishing the taste of her. He turned her around.

"Get up on the counter," he instructed her.

"Boy, no, the kids will hear or walk in." Shay looked around like they would pop out at any moment.

"They're upstairs running around. I bet they ain't even getting ready yet. Now get up there. I just want to taste my pussy. You gon' deny me that?" Skillet stuck his hand back down the front of her pants. He ran his fingers up and down her swollen clit. Slowly he started pulling on it, squeezing it between his thumb and index finger, making her feel like her legs would give out at any moment.

Shay thought about it for only a second. It had been way too long since she had any good loving. "Well, who am I to deny you such a treat?" She smiled and slid up on the counter. "You get three minutes."

"Yeah, a'ight."

Skillet slowly went down to his knees. He wasn't really able to do much with his broken ribs, but he needed this more than she did. He had missed the taste of her for far too long. He slid her shorts to the side and stared at her pretty pussy sitting in his face. He wished like fuck he could slide his throbbing dick inside of her. He sucked her clit into his mouth with ease. She grabbed the back of his head and let her head fall back, forgetting all about her little sister and baby running around upstairs. His head game was lethal, and he was taking her to another planet. Within seconds, she was coming.

"Can you fuck me?" she asked in between moans. That wasn't enough; she needed more. She wanted to feel him fill her up.

Skillet stood up, not giving it a second thought. His adrenaline took over and erased any pain he may have been feeling. She looked so sexy sitting on the counter with her legs spread, exposing her dripping-wet hot box. He slid inside of her and just stood there. They let out a sigh in unison, relishing in the feeling. The feeling of her walls wrapped around his dick was indescribable.

"Damn, I missed you," he whispered in her ear as he bit down on her shoulder to keep from screaming out. Her nails in his back let him know he was hitting her spot as he went in slowly and tenderly. He didn't want to move his ribs too much or make her scream too loud.

"I missed you too baby. Umm," she moaned. She could feel his pace start to quicken, but he really couldn't move, so she started throwing her pussy back at him to help him out.

"Ahh. Thank you," he said as he felt his nuts release a heavy load.

Shay couldn't respond; she was breathing too hard. Everything around her was spinning. She felt like she was floating in air. Skillet backed up from her and pulled his pants back up. She grabbed a paper towel to wipe the cum that was sure to run down her legs when she stood up.

"You gon' have to take Kayla with you. I'm 'bout to go back to sleep." He smiled.

"Whatever! Ain't nobody tell you to do that." Shay threw him a paper towel too.

"Yeah, whatever. Nah, you ain't ask; you was begging for it," he joked.

"Really? I got to beg now?" she joked.

"Nah, you ain't gotta beg; this is all yours whenever and wherever you want it." He grabbed his crotch.

"What you thank me for?"

"For being there for me and coming to get me," Skillet said sincerely. He was truly thankful for the part she played in his escape. Moochie had told him what she had done, and he couldn't have been prouder of her. She came through for him in a major way. There was nothing in the world he wouldn't do for her.

"I'ma keep it funky with you, I thought I was coming to fuck some bitch up." Shay laughed.

"Yeah, I bet! You and that crazy-ass sidekick of yours was coming to wreck shop, huh?" They laughed at his little joke about Sena, even though he wasn't really joking. He really thought something was wrong her, but his homie loved her dirty drawers. He knew they were made for each other because she and Moochie both had a few screws loose.

"And you know this, man!" Shay pushed him in the forehead and walked out of the kitchen. She had to get herself together. Whatever Kelly couldn't get done with Kayla, Skillet would have to finish.

"Where we going, Ray Ray?' Kelly asked Shay as they rode down the highway toward the hospital.

"To see Momma," she answered, looking straight ahead. She didn't really know how to tell her about their mother.

"Really? I've missed her." Kelly was excited.

Shay took in a deep breath. "She's in the hospital, Kelly."

"What? For what? How long has she been there?" Kelly asked, panicking.

"A week," Shay said, unable to look at her little sister.

"A week? So you've known all this time and didn't tell me? What happened to her?" Kelly asked, feeling some kind of way about Shay not telling her.

"I didn't know how to tell you. We had been dealing with everything that happened to you. I didn't want to worry you. I'm gon' be straight with you. Carl attacked her," Shay blurted out. That's the only way she knew how to say it.

Kelly couldn't hold back the tears that started to flow. It hurt her to her heart to hear her mother was beaten. "It's all my fault. I should have never said anything!" she cried.

"No, it's not your fault. It's that pervert's fault. He is a sick man. Don't blame yourself for what someone else has done. You have no control over the next person's actions. You remember that."

"She's been in the hospital by herself all this time?" Kelly asked

"No, I've been to see her. She hasn't woken up yet. I didn't want you see her like that, but I didn't want to keep you away from her either." Shay watched Kelly stare out the window. She did not need this right now. Lately, it'd just been one thing after another. She longed for the days when she used to just sit around and laugh all day.

"Mommy! Mommy!" Little Deonna came bursting into the bedroom, waking Sena from her sleep.

"Hey, my baby." Sena smiled and looked at her daughter with her hair everywhere. She looked over to where Moochie was supposed to be.

"My daddy say we jummmmm him?" Deonna put her hands on her little hips.

"He said will I do what?" Sena laughed at her grown little baby. She almost thought she was trying to say, "Will you marry me?" but she figured that couldn't be it.

"Huhhhhhh?" she huffed as she ran to the door. "Her said she don't know." Sena could hear Moochie laughing from the hallway. Then she heard him whisper something to her.

"Tell her I said come here, baby."

Deonna just looked at him not fully comprehending what was going on.

"Try it again for Daddy," Sena heard him say while he was laughing.

"K." Deonna turned on her heels and ran back into the room.

"You ready now?" Sena asked, smiling big because she now knew that what she thought was happening was really happening. She was so excited, but she wanted to let her daughter finish her part before she burst from the excitement alone.

"Mmm-hmm. Him said come." Little Deonna waved her hand so Sena could follow her. "Daddy?" she yelled into the hall.

"Yes, baby." Moochie couldn't help but laugh some more. He thought it was a good idea to include their baby, but she couldn't get it right so he had to go to plan B.

"What in the world y'all got going on?" Sena asked as she got of the bed and went into the hallway.

What she found almost made her faint. She stood frozen stiff. Moochie was down on one knee with a ring in his hand. He was looking so handsome. His dreads were freshly done, but all he had on was a tank top and some pajama pants. She kept looking from him to the ring.

"What she was trying to say is will you marry me?" Moochie grabbed her hand. "I never thought I would ever feel this way about a woman. I tried my best to avoid feeling like this, but you stole my heart and won't give it back. I love you more than life itself." He looked to his daughter standing next to Sena and nodded for her to come to him. He pulled her into his arms. "We want to know; will you marry me?"

Sena's mind had gone blank. "Yes," was trying to leave her mouth, but nothing would come out. After a few more seconds, she found her voice. "Yes, yes, yes, yes, yes!"

Deonna just watched. She didn't know what was going on, but seeing her mommy so happy made her happy. "Yaayyy, Mommy!" She jumped up and down while Moochie grabbed Sena up and kissed her long and hard.

Moochie couldn't believe he finally did it. But his joy was short-lived. He had no family to share the joy with. Sena could feel his body language change.

"They're here, baby. They right here with us, enjoying this moment with us."

Moochie couldn't hold it in any longer. The dam had broken. He let all of his frustrations out as he cried like a baby in Sena's arms. He cried for his mother, for Kidd, and for Valencia. He missed them with all his heart. Sena let him get it all out. He needed this; hell, she needed this.

Moochie lay down for a nap, but he was awakened by Beyoncé blasting through every speaker in the house. He almost jumped out of his skin. The music was loud as hell. His heart was beating so fast and hard he thought he was about to have a heart attack. He lay there for a little longer so he could get everything in his body to working at a normal rate again. He knew Sena was in one of her moods, and that was his cue to get the hell out of Dodge. He didn't feel like trying to convince her to turn that shit down, and you better not even think about telling the girl she couldn't sing. She went in extra hard when it came to Beyoncé.

Moochie got dressed and went downstairs to find his daughter trying to do everything Sena was doing. Both had microphones, and their hair was big and wild. You couldn't tell Sena she wasn't another Beyoncé in another life. He laughed watching them dance around the room to "Love on Top." He cracked up at his baby because she didn't know how to say the words like her mother, but she was trying her best. Sena, on the other hand, knew every word, ad-lib, breakdown, and note. She had once told him that she was going to get a petition going so she could get a Beyoncé game like *Michael Jackson: The Experience.*

"I'm out of here!" Moochie yelled over the music.

Sena still hadn't paid him any attention. She just went into overdrive, swinging her hair all over the place. He watched her teaching their daughter how to do the hair throwing thing. This was exactly why he was leaving. He walked over to the stereo and turned it off, ready to get yelled at.

"What the hell?" Sena turned around to see Moochie standing there, looking good enough to eat. He wore all black, but it still looked good on him. She had gotten used to his dark mood, but she hoped his bright, colorful spirit would come back soon.

"You lucky you looking good right now, 'cause you was about to get the business, cutting off my Beyoncé." She rolled her eyes.

"Yeah, yeah, yeah. I'm 'bout to go to the hospital. I'll see you later."

"Okay. I'm going to drop Deonna off at Momma Rogers's house." Sena walked over and gave him a kiss before he left.

Chapter 18

Letting Go

After celebrating with Sena and Deonna, Moochie sat next to Kidd in his hospital bed, watching him sleep. He couldn't believe it was almost time to let him go. The self-ish part of him wanted to keep him around just to have him in his presence, but he knew his brother wouldn't want to be hanging in limbo. Moochie was waiting on Skillet and Sena to come so they could do it together. Sena had to drop Deonna off at Skillet's mom's house.

His heart was wrapped in joy and hurt. He was happy to be getting married, but his family wouldn't be there with him when he said, "I do." He looked around at all the machines keeping his brother alive and felt an overwhelming sadness take over him. He felt like he shouldn't be happy with his brother laid up in a hospital bed about to die. His brother was the one who made his life so easy and worth living. Kidd helped him through so much in his life, and now he was about to pull the plug on him. If he could switch places with his brother, he would in a heartbeat. Even with all that was going on with Sena, he would still trade places with Kidd. He couldn't wrap his head around the fact that he was about to bury his brother. His thoughts were interrupted by the doctor walking into the room.

"Hello, Mr. Brown, are you about ready?" The doctor looked at him sympathetically.

"Not yet, sir. I'm waiting on the rest of my family."
Moochie couldn't even look up. His heart was hurting
so bad, he didn't think he would ever be able to mend
his broken heart. He would have been able to take it a
little better had he just found out Kidd was killed, but the
thought of him being the one to have to give the go-ahead
cut him deep down to his soul.

"Okay, I'll come back in a little while." The doctor
walked back out of the room to leave him.

Moochie looked back over to his brother and stared
at Kidd's facial features. Even though they were practically a replica of his own, he knew he would never see
them again after today. He knew he was prolonging the
situation, but he just wasn't ready to let go. Moochie had
tried his best to keep Kidd looking presentable by hiring
a private duty nurse. She was supposed to make sure
his hair stayed cut, he always smelled good, and his skin
didn't get ashy. She was supposed to be there when he
wasn't there.

"Hello, Mr. Brown," the nurse, Tia, said nervously. "I
just stepped out to take a lunch break," she explained
quickly. She was a homely looking young lady, not the
prettiest girl, but she did her job well. To Tia, Moochie
was fine as hell, but there was something behind his eyes
that made her skin crawl. It looked like he was possessed
by the devil. When he had first hired her, she was a bit
apprehensive about doing that kind of work. She felt like
she didn't go through all those years of nursing school to
do nurse's assistant work. But Moochie could be quite
encouraging, so she did as she was told. The money he
offered her was something she couldn't turn down. He
didn't want her to do anything but take care of Kidd.

"It's cool. Here." He handed her an envelope that con-
tained her final paycheck. He didn't even look up at her.
He couldn't. It felt like his shoulders weighed a thousand
pounds. He also didn't want her to see his silent tears fall.

"Thank you. Is it my last day?" she questioned. Even though Moochie scared her shitless and his crazy girlfriend didn't make her feel any better, she liked taking care of Kidd. She knew it was wrong to be looking at Kidd in a sexual manner, but she couldn't help it. He was the finest man she had ever seen in her life, and the fact that he was well-endowed didn't hurt either. All she could think was that it was a waste of a perfectly good specimen of a man. She would have worshipped the ground he walked on.

"Yeah, thank you for all your help. I put a li'l bonus in there for you, and sorry for asking you to step out of your comfort zone. I know this was not something you would normally do. I appreciate you taking such good care of my brother." Moochie looked straight ahead and never even looked her way.

Tia was used to this treatment. He never acknowledged her presence really; he just looked straight ahead all the time. They never even held a conversation. As a matter of fact, this was the most conversation she had gotten out of him since she began working for him. She didn't know if it was because he thought she was so ugly that he didn't want to look at her or if he was too stressed. Maybe his girlfriend was as crazy as she seemed. She'd bet on the latter.

"You're welcome. And anytime you need another nurse, give me a call." She went to gather her belongings. She didn't know if she meant that.

"Check to see if your pay is okay." She had taken very good care of his brother. Of course, she had no choice, or he would have not hesitated to shoot her in the head over his brother. That's why he had hired extra help. He didn't want to be in the position to have to hurt someone. He had heard horror stories about the infamous Barnes hospital, and he would have hated to have to burn the building down.

"Okay." She began to open the envelope. Even if it wasn't enough, she wasn't going to say anything. She would be too scared to say anything. Once she pulled the check out, she felt a dizzy feeling take over at the sight of all those zeroes. Instead of the ten grand they had agreed to, it was $100,000. He heard her gasp for air. Before she could thank him, he stopped her.

"Don't worry about a thank-you. You took good care of my brother, and I just thanked you. You can go now." Right at that moment, Moochie didn't want to see anyone smiling or laughing.

Tia quickly left the room, feeling like taking a month or two off work to get all her affairs in order. She silently thanked him and God for the wonderful blessing. She definitely would take another job if he offered it to her. She would just have to put her fears in check.

When she left, Moochie thought back to when Kidd had taken over the family and took care of him and his mother.

"So you're just going to leave us?" Teresa asked her husband Ken as she watched him loading his suitcases.

"Don't make it such a big deal. This marriage has been over for years," he said nonchalantly, as if it were no big deal that he was leaving her to raise two boys on her own.

"How can you say such a thing? We have been together for twenty years, and you're just going to up and leave? I have been fighting for my marriage, and you just want to throw it all away." She prayed he wouldn't leave. They had been together since high school; she had never worked a day in her life. She didn't know what she would do after he left. How would she take care of her sons? That was her only concern. She could live out of a cardboard box, but she would never let her children go without.

"You look desperate, so go clean yourself up and get over it," he said cruelly. He laughed at her. She looked so pathetic to him. He had been over their marriage for years, but he stayed to help her out. Now he had a whole other family who needed him.

"Momma, why you begging this nigga? He ain't never done nothing for none of us anyway," Kidd came in and asked. He had heard enough of his mother crying and begging only for that man to talk down to her as if she was nothing. He hated him and was glad he was leaving. Whenever their father came around, his mother would get sad and depressed, and she wouldn't be her normal happy, singing self. He loved to see his mother happy because she did everything in her power to make them happy.

"Wanya, go back to your room," she pleaded with him. She didn't want him to see this.

"Yeah, little boy, go before you step into grown man shoes."

"I been in my grown man shoes and I'm standing in them." Kidd stood his ground. His heart was beating rapidly, and he didn't know what he was going to do, but he did know he was not getting ready to stand and watch this man disgrace his mother like that. He loved his mother to no end and, if he had to, he would definitely fight for her honor.

"Oh, you getting your grown man on, huh?" Ken walked up to Kidd, and they stared each other down.

"Don't do this. Let me handle this," Teresa pleaded with them. She could tell they were about to lock horns.

"Handle what, Ma? If the nigga wants to leave, let him go."

At the end of his sentence, Kidd felt his father's fist connect with his chest, knocking him backward and knocking the wind out of him. He fell back into the wall, desperately gasping for air to come back to his lungs.

"Why would you do that?" his mother screamed as she jumped on his back and started hitting him in the head. She may have loved Ken, but she loved her kids way more and would die to defend them against anybody.

He threw her off of him, and she flew against the wall. The sight of his mother being thrown set Kidd's soul on fire. He jumped up and charged for his father, but he was caught in midair by the throat. His father tried to squeeze the life out of him with his bare hands. Kidd swung widely, trying to get him to let go, but his grip was like a vice grip, and his punches slowed down due to not being able to move at all. Everything started to get blurry, and he started to see dots. He heard a crack and then felt the ground. He looked up to see his little brother Moochie standing there with a bat in his hands. Moochie looked around at what had happened and flipped out. He swung that bat in every direction, trying to break every bone in the body of the man he called Pops.

"Wait! Stop, Shawn! Stop it, stop it!"

Moochie heard his mother yelling, but his anger wouldn't let him stop. His father had violated them in a major way. Kidd jumped up and grabbed him before he killed the man. He could still hear his mother crying.

"Oh, my God, what have you done?" Teresa looked at her husband on the ground and then looked to her sons standing there huffing and puffing. She couldn't help but to think this was all her fault. Moochie was still holding the bat. She took it out of his hands.

"Go get cleaned up." She had to think of something to keep her son from going to jail. When they left the room, she looked down at her husband one more time before she hit herself with the bat in her hands. She figured her best bet would be to plead self-defense. He wasn't dead; he just looked like he was knocked out. She wished she had the strength to wish him dead. He

had tried to leave her and hurt her sons in the process. But no matter what, she still loved him.

"Momma, I'm sorry!" She was startled out of her thoughts by Moochie.

"It's okay, baby." She waved him over and put her arms around him.

A few years later, Moochie sat at his mother's bed side. She had been admitted with stage four brain cancer. She had been fighting it for a few years, and it was her time to let go and let God have His way. She looked so sick. Her skin was ashy, her head was completely bald, and she had red spots all over her body from radiation and chemo treatment. Moochie and Kidd tried everything to keep her looking beautiful. They combed her hair before it all fell out and kept lotion and grease on her at all times. She had beautiful scarfs all over her room.

"Boy, why are you still here?" his mother had asked him.

"Where else am I supposed to be? I'm with my favorite girl in the whole wide world." He smiled at her lovingly. It hurt him to watch her dying slowly, but he couldn't imagine being anywhere else. She would not die alone if it was up to him. She was still beautiful to him. She was his heart. Moochie thought she didn't deserve what she had been through. She unconditionally loved a man who didn't love her, and then she ended up getting brain cancer and suffering every day of her life. He and Kidd did their best to make her last days happy.

"Where is your brother?" They were always there. She didn't want her sons' lives to revolve around her anymore. When her husband had left, she knew Kidd had taken to the streets like a madman. He was gone day and night. He had taken over the role of man of the house to heart. He took very good care of her; she *wanted for nothing. Even now, he paid her hospital bills. She wasn't proud of the way Kidd got his money, but she was proud of the fact that she knew he was doing it for his family.*

"He'll be up here later. It's just me and you for now, kid." He shrugged his shoulders.

"I'm fine with that." She studied her son. "Boy, what is you doing with those worms sticking out your head?" She rubbed her hands through his wild hair. He had only been growing it out for a couple of years. It was in that awkward stage where it wasn't short, but it wasn't long.

"It's gon' be down my back in a little while, watch and see," he boasted.

"You know you and your brother gon' have to get used to me not being around." She looked at him.

"Momma, don't start! You ain't going nowhere." Moochie could feel his tears starting to form in his eyes. He did not want to hear anything about her dying. He wasn't ready to face the truth even though it was staring him right in the eyes.

"Listen to me—"

"No! I don't want to hear it." He stood up, getting mad all over again at what was happening.

"Boy, sit down and listen to me," she pleaded. She didn't have the strength to yell at him. He was so stubborn! She didn't know who was worse: him or his older brother.

"Ma, I don't wanna hear 'bout no death and all that mess! Please, not now!" He couldn't imagine not ever having his mother around. She was always there for him no matter what. Whatever he wanted, it didn't matter how big or small, she made it happen. They were true momma's boys and they catered to her, making her feel like a queen. After their father left, she was devastated, but they helped her through it.

"Okay, we'll talk about something else. I know you young and not thinking about a girlfriend, but when you do find that special one, please be good to her."

"Ma, I ain't trying to find no woman." Moochie waved her off.

"I know, ain't that what I just said? Now shut up and listen!" They both laughed. "I just want you to be good to her and treat her how you would want me to be treated, that's all. And give me lots of grandbabies I can look after when I get to heaven."

"See, here you go." He rolled his eyes. "I'll be back when Kidd comes back. You depressing me." He stood up, kissed her on the cheek, and started to leave. She was making him mad, and he didn't want to be mad at her.

"Okay, baby, I'll see you later." She didn't press the issue. She could clearly see he wasn't ready.

Moochie went to go find his brother. He jumped into his 2000 Grand Prix that Kidd had bought him. It was a bribe to keep him in school, and it had worked for a little while, but Moochie was hell bent on getting into business with his brother. He knew he wouldn't have to look hard. Kidd was always in the same spot. It was one of the trap houses his boss, Mr. Jackson, owned. Kidd had been working for Mr. Jackson since he was thirteen years old. He started out as a lookout then graduated to selling weed. Now he ran his own trap house.

Moochie walked into the apartment and looked around. There was no one in the empty living room, but he could clearly hear someone talking in the back. He knew Kidd worked alone and there was usually no one there with him. Only he and Skillet hung out there. He couldn't wait for Kidd to put him down with what he was doing, but Kidd was on some "you going to college" bullshit that Moochie was not trying to hear. He wanted to do whatever his big brother was doing. He just didn't know Kidd would have given anything to be able to go to college. It had been his dream to be a lawyer, but when they said his mother's illness was terminal, that put a twist in his plans.

The conversation Moochie was hearing didn't sound like both parties were happy. He stopped outside the door and could see someone holding a gun in the air, aiming it toward Kidd. Moochie knew where everything was in the apartment, so he tiptoed back and went to get one of the guns he knew was hidden in the couch in the living room. It was the only piece of furniture in the room. He had never shot a gun before, but he figured if he put it right to the back of ol' boy's head, he couldn't miss, could he? He was scared shitless. What if he couldn't save his brother? What if he missed? What would he tell his mother? The death of her firstborn would surely kill her. When he got back to the room, he could see Kidd putting stacks and stacks of money into a bag.

Kidd was steaming mad when he found out he was about to get robbed. He could have kicked himself for not being more careful. When dude came to knock on the door, he was on the phone with the doctors, and he was distracted. The doctor had just informed him that his mother's breathing had slowed all the way down and she wouldn't make it through the night. He hoped he would be able to make it through to be able to tell his mother good-bye. He didn't want his death to be the one thing that pushed her over the edge. He would never be able to forgive himself if she died without him being there. He thought that he should have just gone to the hospital with Moochie.

Moochie took a deep breath and tiptoed full speed toward the would-be robber. Before he could react,

Moochie pulled the trigger, blowing his brains all over the place. It actually looked like a scene out of the cartoon Tom and Jerry when Tom the cat would be trying to sneak up on Jerry and eat him.

Kidd jumped because he had his back to the whole scene. He was packing money up. He felt around his body as he turned around. He thought the dude had gotten trigger happy and shot him. But when he looked up, Moochie was standing there with the gun in his hand and a smirk on his face.

"I told you that you was gon' need me." Moochie showed all thirty-two of his teeth as he smiled because he knew Kidd was getting too big to be working alone. Kidd would have to let him in or else he would force his way in. Either way it went, he would be there to protect his brother.

Kidd took in a deep breath. He couldn't believe his little brother had just killed someone, but he was glad he had come through for him. He just didn't know this would be the first of many men to fall victim to Moochie's wrath. Moochie thought he would feel some kind of way about taking a life, but he didn't. It was going to either be the guy or his brother, and he would choose his brother any day.

"Let's clean this mess up. We got to get to the hospital." Kidd wasn't ready to talk about what had just happened. He just wanted to get to his mother before she took her last breath.

"I just left. What happened?"

"The doctor told me he said he tried to catch you, but you were already gone." Kidd didn't want to tell Moochie what the doctor had said; he just wanted to get to the hospital.

When they walked into the hospital room, tears instantly hit them both. Kidd felt like he had been hit by

a Mack truck. His mother looked like she was already
dead. Her face had sunken in, and her eyes were just
open, looking up at the ceiling. Moochie looked at her,
and his brain felt like it had exploded. He had just left
her not even two hours ago. How had she gone downhill
so fast?

Both boys rushed to opposite sides of the bed and
grabbed one of her hands. She could no longer talk, but
they knew she was only hanging on until they got there.
Kidd picked up a towel and wiped the sweat off her
face. He bent down and kissed her on the forehead and
whispered in her ear, "You can go now, Momma. Suffer
no more." He cried as he spoke the words. He couldn't
believe his mother was about to die. Their family was so
close. It would never be the same without her smile and
laughter around.

Moochie couldn't find any words to say. He was
lost. What would he do without his mother? Even
though she was sick all the time, she was still there
for them. Moochie said a small prayer for her then
kissed her on the cheek. His body collapsed on top of
her. He slid his arms around her and held on to her
for dear life. His heart was breaking, and his world
was turning upside down.

Kidd watched as his brother held on to their mother
with a tight grip. He was crying so hard that his body
was making the whole bed shake. He held her 'til he
couldn't feel her chest moving up and down anymore.
He kissed her once more then he told her to go be with
God. With those last words, they watched her take her
last breath. From that day forward, the brothers had
been inseparable.

When Skillet finally got to the hospital, he found
Moochie sitting in a chair, still staring at Kidd. It didn't

seem as though he was looking at him, but through him. Moochie looked so broken. He wasn't his normal jovial self, making everyone laugh. You could tell his spirit had been darkened. He was sitting there in all black, and if anyone was normally colorful, it was Moochie. You could catch him on a normal day in lime green, yellow, or turquoise. In other words, he was very vibrant in his choice of clothes.

Skillet looked around the room at all the machines and plain white walls. There were a few pictures of Kidd posing with everyone scattered around the room. The only sounds that could be heard were the breathing machine that was keeping Kidd alive. Skillet walked over to the other side of the bed and sat next to Kidd. Not too long after, the girls finally arrived. For about two hours, everyone sat around talking and remembering the good times.

The doctor walked back in, and silence fell upon the room. "Are you and your family ready, Mr. Brown?" the doctor asked somberly.

Moochie grabbed his brother's hand and said a silent prayer for him. Then he got up and walked over to a corner of the room. He took a deep breath and nodded his head, saying yes. Everyone watched as the doctor walked over to the machines. Suddenly the beeps turned into one long beep. Moochie finally let his brother go.

Chapter 19

Don't Take This the Hard Way

Moochie watched Sena sleeping peacefully. He had been up all night trying to figure out how to tell her he was leaving and that he needed to be alone. After the funeral, he felt like his life had taken a complete halt. Through the whole thing, he kept seeing himself in the coffin instead of Kidd and he wished like hell they could trade places. He knew Sena was going to hit the roof and possibly try to cause him bodily harm and he knew he would deserve it because even he felt like he was deserting her. He had just proposed to her, and now he was saying he needed to get away. But his emotions were all over the place, and he didn't know what to do with himself, so it would be better if he was alone at the moment.

Constant thoughts of his family not being there with him haunted him day in and day out. He had chosen this life. Even if he could rewind the hands of time, he still didn't know if he would change a thing. But he did know he would have never brought Sena into this life. She was his heartbeat, and he wanted nothing more than for her to be happy for the rest of her life, but he thought he was bringing nothing but pain to her life.

"What's up?" Sena asked with her eyes still closed. She could feel Moochie watching her. Even though he wasn't moving, she could still feel his gaze burning a hole through her. She could always feel when something was bothering him.

She opened her eyes and could see that something was wrong by the way he was looking at her. She knew him like she knew herself and it looked almost like he was about to cry. She knew he was going through a lot, so she wanted to help him through whatever was bothering him. They were as one, so she knew something was wrong but she wouldn't push him to talk about it until he was ready.

"Nothing, just thinking." Moochie didn't have the heart to tell her right then. He needed to get his bearings. He was trying to prepare himself for the altercation that was going to happen. They'd only had one argument ever, and he said he would never do anything to make her mad again.

"Okay. You want to talk about it?" Sena looked at the clock and saw that it read 3:30 in the morning.

"Nah, I'm good. You finish sleeping. I'll get with you in the morning." He kissed her on the forehead and went to get some fresh air.

When Sena woke up the next morning, Moochie was sitting in the living room with some of his clothes packed. He had a blank stare in his eyes.

"What's all this?" Sena felt her heartbeat speed up instantly.

"I have to go away for a while." He looked down at the floor. He could feel the sweat building in his hands and his pulse quickening.

"Excuse me? Run that by me again." Sena got closer to make sure she had heard him correctly from across the room.

"I have to go away for a while." Moochie looked up at her.

Sena paused for a minute and stared at him. "I thought that's what the fuck you said. So where you going?" She folded her arms across her chest, trying to control her anger. She felt like she had been karate chopped in the throat.

"I don't know. I just have to get away." He could barely hold eye contact with her. He felt so guilty.

"Get away from who, and what? It's always something with your ass. Selfish son of a bitch! You act like you the only one going through shit. I stuck with you through everything. I was there for you, no questions asked. Now you want to leave? Fuck that! You got to come up with something better than that bullshit to tell me!" Sena was hurt and enraged, and it showed with every word that she said. She wanted to hit him in the head with a bat.

"I don't know how to explain it." Moochie didn't know what to tell her because he didn't know what he was doing, so what was he supposed to say?

"Well, you need to figure it the fuck out 'cause I ain't getting it! What you need to get away from, me?" With every passing second, the climate in the room shifted from hot to cold back to hot, then cold again. But at that moment, it felt like all the air in the room had evaporated.

"No, I don't need to get away from you." Moochie could tell this was about to get ugly. With every question asked, her voice got louder. The veins in her neck were bulging so big he could see her pulse. He was relieved to see there was nothing close by she could use as a weapon but, knowing her, she could use a cotton ball as a weapon.

"You proposed to me, asked me to spend the rest of my life with you! Now you want to leave me? What are you going through that we can't get through together? Aren't those your famous words?" she yelled.

"I got a lot of shit on my mind right now, and I just need some space!" Moochie matched her tone. He hadn't meant to yell, but she was yelling at him, and he didn't know how to react any other way.

"You need some space?" Sena looked at him like he had a real bad odor about himself. She couldn't believe the shit he was saying. "Nigga, fuck you and your whole atmosphere!" She paused for a minute. "Space? I been giving you space for a long time now. If you want to go, then get the fuck out. I told you before I ain't into keeping a muthafucka who don't want to be kept. Space?" She squinted at him, really trying to figure where he was going with this conversation. "Muthafucka, please! Take all the space you want. Just don't expect me to be ready and willing when you ready to share your space again."

Moochie jumped out of his seat and charged toward her. Sena got in a fighting stance, never backing down.

"Nigga, I wish you would!" Sena gritted her teeth. "Please do it. Give me a reason to act an ass in the muthafucka!" She was not scared.

"You gon' make me fuck you up!" Moochie grabbed her by the collar of her shirt. "The fuck you mean, fuck me?" Those words stabbed him a thousand times because it sounded like she meant it.

"You heard me! Fuck you and the white horse you rode in on." There was a fire burning in the pit of her stomach that was radiating throughout her entire body.

"All I said was I needed a little space. Damn! Now you talking 'bout fuck me? What the fuck you mean you not gon' be here when I come back?" Moochie knew he deserved it, but he wasn't ready to accept it.

"What you want me to do, sit around and wait while you go out and do you? No, fuck that! Bye, nigga, get gone!" Sena yanked her collar out of his hands.

"Why the fuck you gotta be so damn extra?" Moochie didn't know why he asked that question. That's what he loved about her: her rowdiness and willingness to go to war with anybody in a heartbeat, no questions asked. He was hoping it didn't get that far with them. He would never really hit her, no matter what she did. He could never see himself putting his hands on her. He figured grabbing her up wasn't hitting.

"Extra?" Sena couldn't believe what he was saying. All her anger turned into hurt as she looked into his eyes. The man staring back at her was not the love of her life, her soul mate. No, he was something else she couldn't name at the moment. "You leaving me for no reason and I'm being extra?" The tears started falling down her face. "You are a real piece of shit. I could spit in your face right now. Get away from me!"

She didn't hit him because she knew once everything turned physical, there was no going back. She knew if she hit him, all the love she had for him would be gone and she wasn't ready to accept that yet. "Know this: I won't wait around for you. Take all the time you need." She looked him up and down with disgust written all over her face and she walked into their bedroom, yelling, "Fuck you!" before she slammed the door.

When Sena heard the front door slam, it felt like it had slammed shut on her heart. She couldn't believe he had left her. This had to be a bad dream but, if so, why hadn't she woken up yet? She wanted to beg him to stay, plead with him to make him understand why they needed to be together, but her pride wouldn't let her do it. If he had changed his mind in that same second, she would have forgotten all about what had just happened. She wanted him back the moment he said he was leaving. She felt numb all over, and she just wanted this whole thing to go away. She wished she could rewind the whole day and she would never wake up, just sleep the day away so she could avoid this.

"Thank you for being a friend. Traveled down the road and back again," Shay's phone sang, letting her know Sena was calling.

"What's up, *chica?*" Shay sounded like she was in a cheerful mood.

"He left me!" Sena cried into the phone. All her toughness melted away when Moochie had walked out of their home. She felt like her soul had flown away, and every morning she woke up alone, it felt like her lungs were being deflated over and over again.

"What you mean he left?" Shay asked, trying to get a better understanding.

"I mean the muthafucka left, talking about needing some space and some more bullshit." Sena rolled her eyes to the ceiling, trying to get the tears to stop from falling.

"Get the fuck out of here! That bastard!" Shay yelled, highly upset for her friend. "Where are you?" Shay was walking around gathering up her things so she could go comfort her friend.

"At home," Sena cried into the phone.

"I'm on the way."

"I can't believe that punk son of bitch," Shay said to herself.

"You can't believe who?" Skillet asked, watching her pacing back and forth looking for something.

"Have you seen my keys?" Shay stopped and looked at him, full of frustration.

"Yeah, they in your hand," Skillet pointed out.

"Oh shit, okay." She stopped walking and looked at Skillet. "Have you talked to your friend?" She put her hands on her hips. "Did you know what he was going to do?" She looked at him with questioning eyes.

"Who, Moochie? What he do?" Moochie hadn't told Skillet what he planned on doing.

"Yeah, that asshole," she said as she laced up her tennis shoes.

"Nah, why?"

"That jerk left Sena!"

"What? And went where?" That was totally out of character for Moochie but, lately, anything was liable to happen with Moochie's mind being all over the place.

"I don't know. I'll call you with the details after I get them all myself," Shay huffed and walked out.

When Shay got to Sena's house, she was sitting on the couch watching Deonna play. It had been three days since Moochie had left and Sena was a total wreck. She had on some stretch pants and a tank top with her hair pinned up wildly. She hadn't called Shay immediately because she needed some time to think and recuperate. She had been crying nonstop though. She wanted to drop Deonna off over at Momma Rogers's house, but she also didn't want to be alone. If she didn't have a distraction, she probably would have gone crazy.

"Hey, honey, how you doing?" Shay asked when she walked in.

"I'm doing better, just kind of still stunned about the whole thing." Sena looked up.

"Has he called?"

"No, not even to check on the baby." Sena laughed humorlessly.

"Wait, how long he been gone?"

"Three days."

"What? And you just now calling me?" Shay sat stunned.

"I had to be sure he was really gone. I guess I'm sure now." Sena shrugged her shoulders.

"Don't worry, we'll get through this."

For the next three weeks, Shay stayed by Sena's side, helping her deal with the depression she was feeling. Shay's company was good for the day, but when she would leave, Sena would cry her heart out. Moochie hadn't called the whole time he was away. She hadn't called him either.

Every time she looked at Deonna, she couldn't help but to think of him. Deonna looked just like him. Sena could tell their daughter was starting to wonder where her father had gone because she kept saying, "Daddy," a lot and looking around the house. Sena watched the clock day in and day out, waiting for Moochie to call. She had told him she wouldn't wait for him, but she knew she needed him like she needed her next breath. If he knocked on the door and asked if he could come back, she wouldn't hesitate to say yes.

At night, she could still feel his presence with her in the bed. Sometimes she thought she felt him touching her. She called out his name in her sleep. She could feel his breath on the nape of her neck, his hands roaming all over body. The pillow that she slept with at night was drenched in his cologne and her tears.

Moochie sat in the back of the strip club watching a woman on stage climb up and down on a pole, each time in a different position and direction. He could remember a time when this would have been considered fun and entertainment, but now he was just passing time. Feeling like the lowest form of life, he sat in that corner drinking his life away. His body was so numb that he almost didn't feel the light tap on his shoulder. Startled, he turned and looked up, ready for war with his hand resting on the pistol in his lap.

"Now is that any way to greet an old friend?" one of his many stripper friends asked with a big smile spread across her face. She wore nothing but a lime green thong, and finishing the outfit were some seven-inch "come fuck me" heels. She could see he was reaching for his gun under the table.

"Aw, what up, Carmel. Long time no see," he drunkenly slurred as recognition set in. He was sobering up quickly because, once again, he had been caught slipping.

"Can I get a quick dance for old time's sake?" She twirled one of his dreads around her fingers.

"Nah, I ain't really on it like that tonight, but here you go anyway." He handed her a couple hundred-dollar bills. He wasn't in the mood and just wanted to drink 'til he couldn't see straight.

"Thanks, good looking out, but I got to rap with you for a minute about something I overheard." She and Moochie went way back. He was always fair with her and treated her cool.

"What's up? Talk to me."

She had his full attention now. She slid down onto his lap and started to grind slowly on his pole, which was slowly coming to life beneath her. "You see Frick and Frack over there in the red Cardinals hats?" She nodded toward two dudes sitting in the corner getting lap dances from three girls.

"Yeah." Moochie looked the duo up and down, trying to see if he knew them from somewhere. "What about 'em?" he said as he tore his eyes away from them.

"Well, I was giving someone a dance and overheard them talking 'bout getting at you." She paused for a minute because the look he was giving her made her skin crawl. "Ummmm," she stuttered a little. "And they said that they couldn't wait to give your head to somebody named Sonny. I couldn't hear everything over the music, but I thought it was still worth saying something."

"Oh, yeah?" Moochie smiled inside and out. He was going to have some fun that night. He started sweating and got an instant adrenaline rush at the thought of what was to come. "Okay, do me another solid. Go over and stand by them and say something to get them to follow me into the bathroom." The wheels were turning in his head. That little killing he did at Sonny's place did nothing to feed his appetite.

"All right." Carmel stared at him for a second. She knew Moochie well enough to know shit was about to get ugly.

"Oh, and take this with you to make sure you get their attention." He handed her a big stack of hundred dollar bills.

Carmel almost fainted at the sight of all that money. She broke her loving gaze from all the money and looked at him with questioning eyes.

"Yeah, you can keep it," he said, reading her mind. If he could have, he would have paid her ten times that amount for looking out for him like that. "Thanks for getting me hip to the fuckery." He winked at her.

"Anytime, baby. You know I got love for you, and I wish I could have looked out in a different way. But I know you all wifed up now." They shared a laugh. She smiled and winked back at him as she walked away.

Moochie watched her ass cheeks jiggle like they had a life of their own and that poor thong didn't have a prayer in the world for its survival. He shook his head at the thought of all the freaky shit they used to do back in the day. That seemed like many lifetimes ago. His smile faded when he felt his phone vibrating. It was Sena calling. He felt his heart cry. He wanted to answer, but he didn't want her to think he was out living life while he left her alone. He put the phone back in his pocket as he watched Carmel run her mouth to some more strippers. Whatever she was saying, it was working. He could feel the heat from the stares he was getting.

Moochie staggered as if he were too drunk to stand on his own two feet. Walking on wobbly legs, after a few feet he leaned on a table for support and looked out the corner of his eyes to see what the two men were doing. Right before he walked into the bathroom, he saw them getting up and heading in his direction. He was waiting behind the bathroom door, ready to attack anything that walked through it. He was squeezing the pocketknife that he often carried around so hard that his knuckles turned white.

The door swung open and, in a fast fury, Moochie grabbed the first dude who came through it. He stabbed the first one in the throat then in the eye in two swift movements, and blood splattered everywhere. At first, he didn't know what he was going to do, but thinking quickly on his feet had been his MO lately, since there hadn't been too much time to think during current events.

Before the other man could react, Moochie had his gun pointed at his head and his finger on the trigger. The would-be killer put his hands up in surrender. Apparently, they hadn't thought this whole thing through.

"Lock the door," Moochie said, looking like a crazed maniac. His dreads were flying all over the place with every word he spoke. Blood had splattered all over his face and arms.

"Man, what's all this about?" the dude asked, trying to play it off as he watched his fallen comrade twitch one last time before he took his last breath. The duo's botched plan at getting the ransom money from Sonny had gotten them into a sticky situation. When they found out about the ransom on Moochie's head they jumped at the opportunity not fully thinking the situation through.

"The fuck you mean, nigga? You and fuck boy was trying to get at me!" Moochie yelled, his voice matching the bass coming out of the speakers in the club. "But you didn't know who the fuck I was, did you?"

Moochie brought up the makeshift shank and stabbed ol' boy under his armpit, causing him to scream out.

Luckily no one heard over the music. Realizing time wasn't on his side, Moochie stabbed him again as he fell to the floor. He brought the knife down into the guy's guts, opening his stomach all the way up like a he was about to perform surgery. Once he got the guy all the way open, he stuck the gun into his stomach and emptied his clip.

Once Moochie came down off his high, he realized the mess he was standing in, literally. He washed himself as best he could and walked out the back door, avoiding anyone who would recognize him. He wanted to go back and have a talk with Carmel. In due time, he would find her again.

"You ready to go?" Shay asked Raylene when she walked into her hospital room. It was finally time for her to leave the hospital. Shay had offered her one of their spare rooms. She knew her mother couldn't go home, so she did the right thing and offered her a place to stay 'til she found somewhere else to live. Shay had mixed emotions about everything that was happening, but she had to get over it, if not for her, then for her little sister; also she wanted Kayla to get to know her grandmother.

"Yeah, I'm ready." Raylene was bursting with joy that Shay had offered her a place to live. This was her opportunity to show Shay that she had changed and she couldn't wait to spend some time with her granddaughter she had never met. She was happy for the opportunity.

When they finally got to Shay's home, Raylene's joy was overflowing. She could barely contain herself when Kelly and Kayla came running into the living room, sounding like a herd of elephants.

"I'm so glad y'all got all this damn energy, 'cause y'all sure gon' need it to clean this mess up! Really, who plays with this many toys at one time?" Shay looked around at the mess they had caused. "Where is Kaylin? I cannot believe he let y'all do this."

"Hi, Mommy!" Kelly yelled as she ran into her mother's arms. Kelly had really missed her.

Once Raylene let go of Kelly, she looked down at her granddaughter. She got down on her knees so she could get a good look at Kayla. "I'll clean it up, don't worry," Raylene said as she picked Kayla up with tears flowing freely down her face. She couldn't describe how she was feeling, but it felt good.

"Don cwy? Momma, her sad?" Kayla looked to Shay innocently.

"She is so smart and beautiful, Raina." Raylene looked up as Skillet walked into the room.

"Raylene, this is Kaylin. Kaylin, this is my mother Raylene," Shay said dryly. She was really fighting within herself to hide the feelings she was feeling at that moment.

"Nice to meet you, young man." Raylene beamed.

"Same here." Shay had already informed him of her decision to let her mother move in. Skillet didn't object because he felt they should have some kind of relationship and this would only make them closer.

"Let me show you to your room." Shay led the way to the basement.

Raylene put Kayla down and followed Shay. She admired the home. It was well decorated, and the basement was bigger than her whole apartment. It had its own bathroom, bar, a mini kitchen, and a bedroom with a queen-sized bed that looked like you could fall into it and never find your way out.

"Make yourself at home." Shay began to leave the basement.

"I'm real proud of you, Raina!" Raylene called out.

Shay stopped walking and turned around. She never knew how much those words coming from her mother's mouth would affect her. Instead of reacting, she turned back around and continued on her way.

"You done real good for yourself. I'm gon' make you proud of me, I promise."

Shay shut the door and kept walking. She really did hope her mother meant the words she was speaking.

When Shay woke up, she found her mother and the kids in the living room, living it up. Kayla was showing Raylene the little dance kelly had been trying to teach her. Shay didn't think she would ever see this scene happening in her house. She was kind of happy her daughter was getting to meet her other grandma.

"Well, what's going on in here? Y'all having a party without me?"

"Nah, we just showing Momma how to dance," Kelly said.

"Is that right? I remember when Momma used to dance around the house all day long." Everything got quiet for a second until Kayla broke it up.

"Look at me, Momma!" She put her hands on her knees and started shaking her butt.

"Whoa, whoa! Not my daughter! Who done taught you that?" Skillet came in highly disturbed by what he just saw. "Y'all done tainted the baby. Daddy don't want to ever see that again. You hear me?" He picked her up and smiled. He didn't really want to show her how pissed he really was.

Shay knew how mad he was, but she didn't care. This was too funny to her. His precious baby almost gave him a heart attack.

"Boy, please! If she is anything like her mother, she gon' be a lot more than that! Raina used get down, honey, singing and dancing all over the house."

Everyone was laughing and having a good time. These were the times that Shay prayed for. She missed just sitting around and laughing. For some reason, her mother being around made it a lot better. She just prayed her joy would last forever.

Chapter 20

When I Needed You

Sena thought her day would never end. She and Deonna went to the mall, and she let her run around the playground that they had there. She hadn't done that in a while with everything that had been going on. She felt like she hadn't been putting in enough time with her daughter. Deonna seemed to be growing an inch a day, she was getting so big. She put Deonna in the bed and went to take a long, hot bath.

Sena felt like she was getting stronger every day. The pain in her heart was getting a little better. She had been feeling a little sick for about two weeks. She put it off as just her not having an appetite and that her body wasn't taking it too well. Moochie had left her broken, and now she was slowly putting the pieces back together. Even though she missed him like crazy, she felt a tinge of hate for him. How dare he just up and leave when she had stayed through everything and sold her soul to the devil to make sure he was all right?

Now she lay at night by herself, facing her demons alone. She couldn't understand why he hadn't called, not one time. She knew in her heart he hadn't left to be with another woman, but that didn't change the fact that he had left her with a shattered heart. She wished he would walk through the door, throw his keys on the table, and ask her to get him something cold to drink. She missed everything about him, and she just wanted him home.

Sena walked into the bathroom to start her bath. She turned on the stereo and let Ledisi's CD sing to her. At that moment, she was singing about having to get back to her man. Sena loved that CD. Ledisi had officially made it to the list of her favorite artists.

She sat and thought about her life and how she had made such a drastic change. She now had Moochie and Deonna, she basically had everything she ever wanted, but there was no Vee in the picture. Never in her life did she ever imagine life without Valencia would be this hard. Actually, she had never imagined life with Vee not in it. They were supposed to be having birthday parties and family gatherings together, gossiping and lying poolside with each other. But she was all alone. She had Shay, but she would never even come close to being what Valencia was to her.

After soaking in the tub for about an hour and checking on Deonna again, Sena lay down and stared at the ceiling in deep thought. Once again, her thoughts drifted to Moochie, but they were interrupted by the sound of someone coming through her front door. Her stomach filled with butterflies at the thought of Moochie coming home, but when she got up to see him, she was met by four men in her home.

She immediately ran back into her room to get her phone. She could hear their footsteps speeding toward her. She locked herself in the bathroom to buy a little time. She called Moochie, but he didn't answer. She called him again, and after three times trying to reach him, she left a message, saying, "Please help me."

Sena thought about how much she had loved the fact that they didn't have any regular neighbors. There were only two other couples living in the building, but they were travelers. Now she wished she had one of those creepy old ladies living next door who never missed a thing. Right as she was about to call the police, the door came crashing in. She jumped in the tub. One of the men marched toward her with a scowl on his face. The first thing she noticed was that they weren't wearing any masks, so she knew she was going to die tonight. She had never been so scared in her life.

"Ahhhh!" she screamed as she was yanked out of the tub by her hair.

Sena swung wildly, trying to get away from the man. She swung at his head, connecting a couple of times before he punched her in the face, knocking her out cold. He dragged her by her hair back down the hall to the living room.

"What you knock her out for? We ain't got that much time, dumb ass!" Tyrell exclaimed as he yelled at his partner in crime. He couldn't wait to tell Mr. Jackson he had found where Moochie lay his head. He could see all that money and he saw himself spending it all in the mall.

Tyrell was a short, stubby, goofy-looking, young dummy trying to make a name for himself. He was also unaware that Mr. Jackson was dead and he had no idea what he was getting himself into. He had never heard of Moochie or Kidd, with good reason. The only way anyone knew about the brothers was if a person was high up in whatever organization they worked in. He was a mere street cat trying to make his name ring some bells. He didn't know that if Sonny was still alive, he would have never killed Moochie's woman while Moochie was still alive. Everyone who knew anything about Moochie knew that you had to kill him before you fucked with his family because he was sure to come back ten times as hard and kill your whole family tree and even your dog.

"She kept punching me in the fucking head, so I hit her back." He shrugged his shoulders, then bent down and started rubbing on her breasts. He had a big-ass smile on his face until he felt Sena squeezing his balls so hard it felt like they were going to pop.

"What do y'all want?" Sena gritted her teeth as she applied more pressure to his balls.

Tyrell immediately let her go, clenching his teeth in pain. She looked around the room with blurry vision. Her head was pounding hard. He had punched her so hard in her head that she couldn't hear out of her right ear. She looked at the four men in all black and tried to remember as much as she could about the men.

"Where the fuck is that pussy nigga?" the leader yelled while he kicked her in the face so she could let his peoples go.

As soon as Sena let him go, he instantly went to grab his crotch. He wanted to shoot her in the head right then and there, fuck the rest of the plan.

"What, nigga?" Sena was trying to play dumb as she spat blood out of her mouth. She hoped she would come out of this with her teeth intact. She began to prepare herself for what was about to happen. No matter what Moochie did to her, she would never give up any information. But she couldn't help but wonder where he was and why he wasn't busting down the door right then to save her. He had promised to always be there for her, but now he was nowhere in sight.

"Bitch, you trying to be funny?" Tyrell brought his foot down hard across the center of her stomach, bringing up the food she had just eaten. As Sena curled over in pain, she noticed blood starting to stain her panties. The pain that was radiating through her body was unheard of. She had never felt like that in her life.

"Where in the fuck is he?" he snarled while snatching her by her hair.

Sena spat blood in his face. He came with a hard right to the nose, blacking both her eyes instantly. The pain was almost unbearable, but she refused to let the pain get the best of her.

"Fuck you!" Sena swung on him, connecting with the left side of his jaw, making him let her go.

But he wasn't done with her yet. He stood up and lifted his foot high in the air then brought it down hard across her stomach and chest repeatedly, knocking the wind out of her. She screamed out in agony. After he was done stomping her, he turned to his partners.

"This bitch ain't talking. Let's just shoot her in the head to let the nigga know we on him," one of the gunmen said.

Sena noticed they were deep into their conversation and she took that as an opportunity to make a quick dash for her gun. If she was going to die today, she sure as hell was going to take somebody with her. She raced for her room, feeling pain with every stride she took. As she ran to her room, she passed Deonna's room, remembering her baby was in the house. Now she was really mad at Moochie. She asked herself again, *why isn't he here?*

As soon as Sena got to her gun, she felt a hard impact hit her in the back of her left shoulder. She turned on her heels to pull the trigger. A bullet ripped through her arm, causing her to pause for only a second. Her adrenaline wouldn't let her feel the pain. She pulled the trigger, hitting two of the armed men. After that, a barrage of bullets came at her, hitting her everywhere as she fell to the floor.

"Fuck! Let's get the fuck out of here!" Tyrell yelled, mad at the botched attempt at finding Moochie. The men ran out of the apartment, leaving Sena for dead.

Sena lay on her bedroom floor, crying while she listened to her baby cry for her. She couldn't move; her body was burning all over. She wanted to pray to God, but she felt she didn't deserve His mercy. She had sinned big time in her life, and she felt like she deserved everything that came to her. If she was paying for Moochie's sins, she wouldn't change a thing. Even with him not being there for her, she still could not deny the fact that she would die for him. Her eyes had swollen shut. She hoped someone would find her before she died on that cold floor alone. Before she blacked out, she sent a small prayer for her daughter.

Moochie sat in Kidd's basement, looking at all the pictures they had taken. He missed his brother so much that he didn't know what to do with himself. He felt like the lowest form of life. Three people in his life had died, and he couldn't do anything to help them. He had packed up his things and was ready to go home. He didn't want to be alone anymore. He watched as Sena's name flashed on his screen. He wanted to answer, but he needed just a little longer before he was able to face her. She had called like four times then left a message. He wanted to hear her voice, so he dialed his voicemail.

"Please help me!" Moochie could hear someone ramming the door in the background.

His heart nearly stopped, and he had to listen to the message again to make sure he had heard her correctly. When it said the same thing, he jumped up and ran up the stairs taking three at a time. His heart was racing as he ran out the house. He dialed Skillet's number. It felt like his brain was going to explode. The words from her message kept replaying: *"Please help me!"* He had never heard Sena sound so scared.

"Hello?" Skillet sounded asleep.

"Meet me at my house. Something is going down. Sena just called me. Hurry up!" Moochie sounded panic-stricken. He hoped his family was all right. If not, it would be time to release the beast. The streets of St. Louis wouldn't know what hit them. He would find anybody who had anything to do with this happening and he would spread their body parts all over the city.

When Moochie finally arrived, he bypassed the elevator and ran up the eight flights of steps like a professional sprinter, taking three and four steps at a time. When he saw the door open, he could feel it in the bottom of his soul that something was terribly wrong. His whole body felt numb, and he felt like he had to shit. He had never in his whole life been so nervous at the thought of what was to come. His not knowing what was around the corner was driving him crazy.

"Sena!" he yelled while he looked at all the blood on the living room carpet. He could hear Deonna crying. He pushed the door open and saw she was safe in her crib. He closed the door and went to look for Sena. When he turned the corner, he saw two men lying dead at the entrance to their bedroom. Sena had landed one shot in one of their heads, and the other got hit in the chest. He didn't see Sena anywhere when he looked around.

"Sena!" Moochie yelled again, about to lose his mind. He needed to know what the hell had transpired in there. This was all too much for him, and he didn't even know what had happened yet. He had a quick flashback of when he had found his brother's deceased girlfriend in a pool of blood, and he prayed that wouldn't be the case here. His blood ran cold at the thought of Valencia beaten and bruised.

"Mooch," he heard Sena say faintly.

He followed her voice, and when he found her, he thought he died. He dropped to his knees, crawled over to her, and felt his heart shatter into a million micro pieces. She looked so bad. There was blood coming from everywhere. He turned her over and saw she had been shot so many times. He let out a roar that could be heard from miles away. He pulled her to his chest and hugged her tightly. Instantly tears flooded down his face. The pain he was feeling was indescribable. "I'm so sorry, baby, I'm so sorry! Please don't leave me. You can't die on me too, please!" he cried as he kissed her face all over.

After a few seconds, survival mode kicked in. He called the police and told them to get there immediately. He got to his feet and slowly and gently lifted Sena into his arms. He wanted to run, but he didn't want to move her too much.

When Skillet and Shay got there, Shay flipped.

"Oh, my God! What happened to her?" Shay cried. She watched as Moochie carried her to the elevator.

Moochie wanted to meet the ambulance at the door. As he walked, it looked like a scene out of a movie when the action hero is walking in slow motion with the damsel in distress in his arms. She was bleeding, and he had to get her to some help.

"Go get Deonna," Moochie said to no one in particular. He ignored Shay. He didn't even look at Skillet. His mind was on getting Sena some help.

Shay went in to get the baby. Skillet looked at Moochie one more time before the elevator doors closed. He went into the home to see what had happened. When he walked through, he ran into Shay and the baby.

"What the fuck happened in here?" Shay asked in tears. "It's two dead muthafuckas laid out in the bedroom, and Sena is covered in blood!" She was hysterical.

"I don't know, babe." Skillet was in total shock at all the blood everywhere. He looked at baby Deonna and was happy to see she was all right. "Damn, this shit is fucked up and the last thing we needed right now." He knew his friend was about to lose his mind. They had gotten the people responsible for what they had done. Now if Sena was killed too, there would most definitely be a lot of bloodshed. He knew there would be a mission coming on soon.

"Let's go."

They ran out. When they got downstairs, they found Moochie pacing back and forth with Sena still in his arms. He was praying for her to stay alive. He could tell she was slipping away.

"Come on, baby, don't die on me." Moochie kept kissing her all over her face. He moved the hair that was stuck to her face. He looked at her, and everything went blurry because a rainstorm of tears started falling all over again. He pulled her closer to him. He couldn't believe this was happening to him. God must have really been angry with him to take everyone he ever loved away from him. He now felt Kidd's pain. Kidd had to sit and watch his girlfriend's brains get blown out right in front of him.

"Where the fuck is the ambulance?" he yelled. "Come on, baby, stay with me," he coached her. "Skillet, go double the surveillance tape and keep it. Then show the police the room so they can see whatever happened."

Moochie knew Sena would be okay with any charges they tried to bring about with the dead bodies in her house. She was legal and licensed to protect herself. He needed a copy of the tape so he could identify the culprits. His heart was burning with rage.

"Where were you?" Sena managed to get out.

Moochie looked down at her. The tears hadn't stopped since he had found her. It had only been about four minutes, but it felt like forever before he finally heard the ambulance coming.

"Come on, baby, they here, stay with me. I'm right here and I ain't going nowhere ever again, I promise. I'm sorry. Just don't leave me, please," he pleaded. "Please, baby, stay with us! Deonna needs you. I need you. Just please don't leave us."

"God, please don't take her away from me!" Shay cried. She would die if Sena was taken from her. Sena was her only friend in the world. She would be totally fucked up if Sena was killed. She finally got a glimpse of what Sena was feeling when Valencia was killed because it sure as hell felt like someone had hit her in the chest with a sledgehammer. She had never in her life seen so much blood and felt so much pain.

When Moochie saw the ambulance pull up, he ran outside to get Sena to them as quickly as possible. He jumped into the ambulance after they had her strapped in and watched in horror as they worked on her on the way to hospital. He saw about fifty police cars pull up as they were pulling away.

Shay and Skillet stayed behind to talk to the police. Moochie knew they would be barging in with a million questions and he didn't have the patience at that time to answer them. He himself couldn't wait to see what those tapes showed. He hoped he could identify the would-be killers; he had so many torturous plans for them. Sena had gotten two of them. He only hoped she left someone for him to release his fury on. The walls were caving in on him, and he didn't know if he had the strength to push back.

Moochie looked back down at Sena as they worked on her and he prayed she made it through. He felt like he had no right to be praying, but what else was he supposed to do? He needed God right now in the worst way. He only hoped God hadn't given up on him yet. He had already changed his life, but situation after situation kept pulling him back in. But Moochie promised that, if God made Sena better, he would never take another life as long as he lived. He wanted revenge, but if God granted him this prayer, he would have no choice but to let it go, because if he reneged, there was no telling who He would take away next time.

"So, ma'am, can you describe what happened here?" a police officer asked Shay.

"No, sir. Me and my boyfriend got a call from Sena's fiancé, and he told us to meet him here, that she had called him and that something was wrong. When we got here, he was carrying her from the back of the apartment." Shay started crying at the visions that were going through her head.

"Sir, did he say anything to you?" the officer asked Skillet.

"Yeah, he wanted me to make sure you all saw the surveillance tape."

Skillet signaled for the officers to follow him. They walked into Moochie's computer room and waited for Skillet to pull up the surveillance footage. They watched Sena's interactions with the men and sat in awe as she fought back. They couldn't see what happened in the bedroom, but they could see each man she hit flying backward in the hall. After everyone was finished watching the tape, they sat in shock. No one knew what to say. Sena had gone toe to toe with a group of men and had taken two of them down with her.

"We will be taking this down to the station," the officer said as he ejected the DVD from the machine.

When they finally got to the hospital, Moochie was sitting in the waiting room with his head down. He knew he needed to stay strong for his daughter, but his life would surely end if Sena was removed from his equation. There was no him without her.

"Did they say anything yet?" Shay asked as they walked up to him.

"Nah, not yet."

Moochie finally looked up, and they could see that life had taken its toll on him. His eyes were swollen, and he looked like he did the day they brought Kidd to the hospital, only worse this time. He was covered in blood, and his hair was all over the place. He looked at his daughter in Shay's arms and almost had a complete meltdown. How would he explain to his daughter that Mommy wasn't coming back if she didn't make it? Everything got quiet until Shay broke the silence.

"Where were you?"

"Huh?" Moochie and Skillet looked at her.

"Where were you when my friend was having a fucking shootout with them niggas?" Shay looked at Moochie with pure disgust written all over her face.

"This ain't the time for that right now, babe," Skillet whispered.

"No, fuck that! She laid up in the operating room with God only knows how many bullets in her, and this ain't the time?" Shay looked at him like he couldn't be serious. "No, nigga, where were you?"

Moochie just stared at her. He felt the muscles in his face start to twitch, but she was right. He wasn't where he should have been.

"Stop it, Shay!" Skillet yelled. He could see she was upsetting Moochie and he didn't want to have to choose between them tonight. He did not want them butting heads. This was not the time. He knew how much Sena meant to both of them.

"If she dies, you deserve it, you selfish muthafucka! How in fuck you gon' leave her after everything she did for you? She would have gone to the moon for you, but you couldn't be there for her." Shay could see Skillet getting upset, so she stopped her beatdown on Moochie, but she now officially hated him.

"Just give me my daughter." Moochie reached out for his baby. He sounded defeated.

After Shay handed the baby to him, Skillet grabbed her and pulled her to the other side of the room.

Moochie had no defense for her; she was totally right. He held his daughter in his arms tightly, kissing her all over the face. He was barely holding on to his sanity, and she made him feel loved. If Sena was to be taken from him, Deonna would be all he had left in the world.

"Mommy, mommy?" Deonna called innocently, not knowing what was going on.

He couldn't ask God why this was happening to him, because he knew he deserved everything that was happening to him. He had ruined a lot of lives while he was working. Now karma was coming back with a vengeance and taking everything away from him.

"The doctors are helping her. She got hurt." Moochie got choked up and felt the tears about to fall down his face, but he stopped them, not wanting to cry in front of his baby. He didn't want to worry her.

Sena had been in the operating room for about two hours before someone came out and said something to them. He watched and held his breath as the doctor walked up to him. He handed his baby back to Shay. He'd almost dropped her, his body felt so numb.

"Mr. Brown?"

"Yes, sir. How is she?" The anticipation had his stomach doing a million flip-flops.

"Everything went well. We removed four bullets from her arms and chest, and one from her hip. We also closed up the holes where the bullets went in and out. She must have an angel with her, because each bullet was only fractions of an inch away from her vital organs. We couldn't see any nerve damage, but she may walk with a bit of a limp. However, we couldn't save the fetus. There was too much damage."

Moochie looked at him for a second to let what he had just said sink in. "The fuck you mean 'fetus'?" Moochie stepped closer. He thought he needed to hear him better. He had to be mistaken. This couldn't possibly be happening, not now, not ever. A tingly feeling fell over his body like it went to sleep.

"Yes, sir, she was about eight weeks along."

At that moment, the doctor wished he hadn't been the one to deliver that message. It looked like he was standing in front of a firing squad the way everyone was looking at him. Moochie's whole face turned into a mask of fury.

Skillet quickly walked over so he was standing in between the doctor and Moochie. He didn't make a scene; he stood there just in case. It looked like he was about to flip all the way out.

"So when you say fetus, you mean baby, right?" Moochie seemed a bit confused, because the doctor was saying she lost a baby like she had just stepped on a bug or something, like it was nothing. He just knew he couldn't be saying what he thought he was saying.

"How many times was she shot?" Shay asked, because it looked like Moochie was about to lose it. She wanted to switch the conversation. She felt bad for her friend, and she didn't want Moochie getting locked up for murdering a doctor to add to her stress.

"Seven," the doctor stuttered. "She will be in the ICU for the next twenty-four to seventy-two hours for monitoring." He kept a close eye on Moochie in case he saw any movement. He would surely be running for his life.

Everyone was listening to the doctor talk until they heard Moochie's roar boom through the hospital halls. He couldn't believe they had killed his seed. His unborn child would never take his/her first breaths, and Sena would never get to see her son or daughter grow up. His breaths became shallow. It felt like he was losing all the air in his lungs. He began throwing furniture all over the room. He needed to release his anger on something, and the furniture was the closest thing to him.

He could hear the doctor saying something and Deonna crying and yelling, but it all sounded like jumbled words at that point. He'd heard something about a limp, but he didn't give a fuck a about a limp as long she was still with him. He would love her blind, crippled, and crazy. She was his heartbeat, and if she died, he would go with her.

Skillet ran over to Moochie to keep him from hurting himself or anyone else. When Moochie felt Skillet's hand on him, he collapsed to the floor. He didn't know what he would classify this feeling as, whether it was a nervous breakdown, anxiety attack, or psychotic break.

"They killed my seed, man!" he cried on his knees. This was the worst thing he could have ever heard. How was he going tell Sena this? He didn't even know the words to say.

"Come on, man, you gotta be strong for Deonna. She watching you," Skillet whispered.

"They killed my baby. How am I gon' tell her this? She ain't never gon' forgive me for this." He just knew Sena was going to leave him for this. Why wasn't he there for her like he promised he would always be? *I should have never left,* he kept thinking. He thought he was doing the right thing by leaving. He didn't want to burden her anymore with his problems. But now he could see he only made everything worse. He really needed his brother there with him to help him through this. He was lost in his own misery and couldn't seem to find his way out.

"Come on, look." Skillet pointed to a crying Deonna. Moochie tried to pull it together, but you could clearly see the turmoil written all over his face.

"Can I see her?" Moochie asked the doctor. He needed to be with her, to see her to help him keep from going crazy.

"As soon as she is awake in the recovery room, someone will come to get you." The doctor wanted to get the hell away while he could.

"Okay, thank you, sir, for everything." As the doctor walked away, Moochie turned to Skillet. "Can you take Deonna over to your mom's house for me? I don't want her here around all this mess."

"I'm staying here," Shay stated defiantly.

"Nah, come back with him. I want to be alone with her for a while."

"I ain't going no-gotdamn-where! Ain't that a bitch? You wanting to be alone is what got us in this situation in the first place."

"Yo, you pressing yo' muthafuckin' luck with me." He didn't raise his voice, but everyone could clearly see the devil coming out of him. "You got me mistaken for someone who gives a fuck right about now. You need to get the fuck away from me before you cause some problems between me and my mans."

He hadn't moved out of his chair, but Skillet knew Moochie moved fast as lightning, so he stood in between them. He saw this collision about to happen. He was never really worried about Moochie putting his hands on Shay; that wasn't in his character. But this was a whole new situation, so he took precautions. They needed to stick together. This was not the time to fall apart.

"Yo, man, calm down, she leaving." He was trying to not get upset with Moochie. He knew how much Moochie was hurting and Shay wasn't making it any better.

"I ain't better do shit! You gon' let him talk to me like that?" Shay looked to Skillet.

"Don't start no dumb shit. Really, you on that shit when you started it with him? I told you this wasn't the fucking time start that shit." Now she had pissed him off by testing his manhood. If it were any other nigga, his brains would have been on the floor. He knew there were only so many people in the world Moochie wouldn't put his hands on, and she was one of them only on the strength of him.

She had failed to recognize the magnitude of the situation. Moochie would rip anyone apart at this moment in life. He would have bet if Moochie had been alone when the doctor came in telling the bad news, he probably would have tried to choke the life out of him with his bare hands. He could tell Moochie was ready to pull his gat out and start shooting anything breathing.

"You know what? Fuck you two lousy muthafuckas!" Shay rolled her eyes and walked away. She was pissed that Skillet didn't defend her. *Fuck Moochie! He should have been there for Sena!* She didn't give a fuck about his feelings. She let her anger override her better judgment. She knew Moochie was a very dangerous man, but at that point, she didn't care.

"I'm sorry, man." Moochie apologized for what he had said to Shay. "She was hitting my pressure points. Everything she was saying was the truth. I wasn't there for Sena. I wouldn't have been any good if she was taken away from me too." He could feel himself on the verge of tears again. He hadn't cried so much in his whole life.

"Don't do that yourself. It wasn't your fault that this happened." Skillet tried to console Moochie, but it wasn't working. He honestly didn't have a clue what to say to Moochie.

"Whose fault was it then? They were coming for my head, and she got it instead of me. Man, I was too late. I had all my shit packed, ready to come back home. Huh." He exhaled hard and put his head back down. "I don't even remember why I left." He looked up at Skillet. He and Skillet had been close as brothers since they were kids, so he didn't have a problem expressing himself in front of him.

"I got that tape for you."

Moochie stood up. "Yeah? What it look like?" He was anxious.

"Man, yo' woman is a straight-up beast! She went in on 'em. It was four of them. The dude who looked like he was calling all the shots got away, and the dude who did the most damage did also. The camera got good angles, so we were able to see all of their faces." Skillet rubbed his hands together in anticipation of what they were about to get into. Now they were going into his type of thing. When they talked about feelings and shit, he tried to be there, but when they got into some gangsta shit, he was the first one there.

"Do you recognize any of them?" Moochie was hoping he did because he couldn't wait to punish them. He promised he wouldn't kill anyone else, but he never said anything about punishing the culprits who had done Sena so wrong and killed his seed. They could live, but the question was, would they want to live after he was through with them?

"Nah, but I'll get Lil Tony on it," Skillet said, referring to their go-to guy for any information they needed.

"Okay, I'm about to go in here with Sena. Let me know the deal as soon as y'all find out anything." Moochie began to walk away. "Ay, and tell Shay I'm sorry." He really felt bad about the way he had talked to her. He knew she was only taking up for her friend.

"A'ight, I'm out." They gave each other dap and a half hug and parted ways.

Chapter 21

Promise Me You'll Stay

Moochie went in to see Sena, and he felt like his next breath would be his last. She looked so broken. He could feel the tears in the back of his throat trying to choke him to death. He took notice of all the machines that were hooked up to her body, and it felt like déjà vu times four. He had been through this too many times in his life. First he had to watch his mom suffer in the hospital for years until she died, then Skillet got shot, next Valencia got beat to a bloody pulp, then she was killed, then after all that, he lost his brother and had to be the one to pull the plug. Now Sena was lying there looking like she was about to join everybody he loved.

Moochie pulled up a chair next to her bed, picked up her hand, and rubbed it up against his face. He admired her engagement ring. She had never taken it off, even after he left. His heart wouldn't allow him to feel anger at that moment. All he wanted around her was love. Even though his heart was boiling over with rage, he wanted her to feel the love he had for her.

"I'm so sorry, baby. I could never tell you how sorry I am." Tears fled from his eyes. It seemed lately all he did was cry. "I never left you; I was there. I'm sorry I wasn't there when you needed me most. You have to believe I would never leave you. You are the best part of me and the reason my heart still beats. Please know I love you with all of me. I promise we gon' get them back, you and me, Bonnie and Clyde style." He continued to study her body. She looked like she was in so much pain, and if he could, he would gladly take all her pain in for her and even switch places with her.

Two days later, Sena was stable enough to leave the ICU.

"Sir, we are ready to move her to a private room." A nurse came in, breaking his train of thought.

"Okay. Will there be a bed or something for me in there?" He was not leaving her side until she woke up and told him she forgave him. He wanted to be the first person she saw when she opened her eyes.

"Yes, sir, the room has something like a let-out couch in it."

"Okay, I'll be there in a hot second." Moochie needed to call Skillet. He was dying to see the tape. He dialed Skillet's phone when he got outside so they could get everything together. He knew it would take a while to move Sena with all the machines and things that needed to be moved.

"Ay," Moochie spoke into the phone.

"What's up, something wrong?" Skillet tried not to panic, but it seemed like nowadays anything was possible. Every day it was something new.

"Nah, I just want you to bring that tape down so I can watch it. It's killing me not knowing what happened. I can't wait any longer." Moochie felt like his head would explode from all the guessing games he was playing in his head.

"A'ight, I'm on my way."

"Cool." They hung up, and Moochie went back in to be with Sena.

"*Now you know you can't stay here with me, right?*" Valencia looked at Sena with caring eyes.

"*But I don't want to go back. This is the only time I get to see you!*" Sena cried as she looked into the eyes of her deceased best friend. "*I miss you like crazy! Nothing's the same. Everything is falling apart,*" Sena cried. Sena loved to be asleep because that was the only place she could see Valencia. Her friend would come and talk to her in her dreams, and she looked forward to escaping into her little dream world where she and Valencia were back together laughing and talking like the good old days.

"*Nothing is falling apart, honey. God has a plan. He knew me and Kidd could never be together in life, but now we are here together.*" Vee smiled.

"*But what about me?*" Sena cried. "*You left me.*"

"*Moochie and my niece need you. You know he is taking it hard. Everyone around him is dying, and he's trying to learn how to deal with it. Don't give up on him yet, baby. He loves you more than you know.*"

"*And you know I love him with every piece of me, but he wasn't there for me when I needed him most, and I would have never left him hanging. I would have cut off my right arm before I did something like that.*"

"*I understand that, sweetie, but forgive him. His heart and mind are all over the place, and he's trying to figure things out the best way he can. He never had to do anything alone. He's lost, but you will help him. He's here now; that's all that matters. He came as soon as he thought something was wrong with you. Do you think he would have left you if he knew something was going to happen to you?*"

"*No.*" Sena looked down and began to cry even harder. "*Why is it about him? I'm the one hurting.*"

"It's not about him; it's about the both of you. He won't make it without you, and you won't make it without him. I'm trying to get you to think before you make any decisions since you are such a 'react now and think later' type of person. You two need each other more than ever now."

"Can't you come back?"

"I'm always here for you whenever you feel like talking. I may not always respond, but just know they will never succeed at getting rid of you." Vee laughed a little. *"No matter how bad you get on their nerves, they are stuck with you."*

"Shut up, skank!" Sena found herself laughing too.

"I love you, Sena, and you be strong for your family. They need you."

"I love you too."

Moochie sat next to Sena's bed with his head lying next to her and her hand resting on his face. He had started to drift off until he felt her hand rubbing his face. His head snapped up and saw she was looking at him. They stared at each other for a few minutes. His heart felt happy, but his eyes were hurting from seeing her this way. He was just happy she had woken up.

"Hey, baby," he said in a whisper.

"Hi." Sena's voice squeaked and sounded really hoarse. It hurt like hell for her to talk.

"Don't talk, babe, just rest." Moochie didn't know what to do. He sat there staring at her like he had never seen her before.

Sena also stared back at him, wondering what he was thinking. She loved to look at him. No matter how mad she was at him, his presence was always needed and welcomed.

"What you thinking about?" Sena couldn't help it; she needed to know what was going on in his mind. It felt good to be around him, to feel him.

"How sorry I am that this happened to you and that I would have lost my mind if you were taken away from me."

She let the tears roll down her face.

"And how much I love you and I will never leave you again. I promise with all my heart I will never leave you again, never. If you going to the bathroom, I'm going with you. I'm gon' be sitting right on the tub watching you." They both shared a laugh. He wanted to tell her about the baby, but not right then. He wanted her to get better before he told her the bad news.

"So when are we going to find out who did it?" Sena appreciated his honesty and feelings, but she was ready for some get-back. She wasn't ready to deal with him not being there just yet. Even though she couldn't move an inch of her body on her own, she was ready for some revenge.

"You don't have to worry about that yet. You just get better, then we will get on the mission. But Skillet is on his way up here to show me the tape of what happened." Moochie just shook his head. He knew there was no way in the world he would be able to leave her out of the loop.

"Don't you try to leave me out." Sena couldn't wait to get her hands on the men who tried to take her out. They would pay severely.

Skillet and Shay walked in with teddy bears and GET WELL balloons. Shay speed-walked and gently jumped in bed with Sena, trying to avoid any IV lines or tubes and not wanting to hurt her but wanting to be near her.

"Hi, honey. You scared the hell out me." Shay looked at Sena with such admiration. She couldn't believe her friend was still hanging on with everything she had been through.

"You know it will take a lot more than some funky bullets to get rid of me," Sena joked, but the room fell silent. No one found the joke to be funny at all.

"Glad to see you awake," Skillet said, breaking the silence as he put the stuff down on the bedside table.

"I am so sorry about the baby," Shay said without even thinking whether Moochie had told her.

"What baby?" Sena looked around.

The silence spoke volumes, and Moochie just put his head down. He couldn't believe Shay had said something about the baby. He could have kicked himself for not warning them not to say anything yet.

"What baby, Mooch? Where is Deonna?" She tried to raise her voice, but the burning feeling from where tubes had scratched her throat halted that. At the thought of something happening to her daughter, she wanted to die. She could feel the air in her lungs leaving. She needed to hear him say the words out loud to let her know this was really happening.

Moochie took a deep breath before speaking. "Deonna is fine. You were eight weeks pregnant, and the baby didn't survive," he said sadly. He tried to grab her hand, but she pulled it away.

"Don't touch me," she cried.

Moochie was taken aback because he wasn't expecting that reaction. "Sena—"

"Shut up!" Sena cut Moochie off. She needed to breathe, but she couldn't seem to bring any air into her lungs. She felt like her whole body had gone numb. She needed to think for a minute.

The room was quiet. No one said anything, too afraid to make her even more upset. She stared off into space as the tears rolled down her face. She unconsciously rubbed her stomach, thinking of the baby she didn't even know she wanted until it was taken away. After a few minutes of silence, she took in a deep breath. It hurt like hell, but she knew there was nothing she could do at that point.

"Where is the tape?" Sena asked, not looking at anyone in particular. A feeling of emptiness swept over her.

Skillet looked at Moochie to make sure it was okay. Moochie shrugged his shoulder as if to say, "Go ahead." They all sat in silence as they watched what happened. Moochie could feel his muscles burning. He was so mad as he watched the man rain those blows down on Sena. He felt gut-wrenching pain shoot through his body when he saw the man stomp her in the stomach.

Sena felt like she was reliving the whole thing again, as if she could feel each blow every time she saw it happen. The gunman had stomped her in her stomach so many times that she felt like she had to throw up from watching the blood flow from her body. They watched her get up and run, and the next thing they saw was the shootout happening. They watched as the men tried to invade the room but were stopped short by an onslaught of bullets.

Moochie couldn't watch anymore. He was seeing red. He felt that beast in him raging to get loose. This would surely bring a lot of death. The streets of St. Louis had better hope they found the culprits fast because Moochie had no problem going through their whole family tree to get to him. They were dead men walking and didn't even know it.

They sat and talked for a little while. Skillet and Shay had left and gone to do as Moochie asked of them. Moochie wanted them to show Lil Tony the tape to see if he could identify any of the culprits. Knowing Lil Tony, he would be able to lead them in the right direction.

Moochie watched as Sena slept. He could see her chest rise and fall. She had cried herself to sleep. He watched as she inhaled and exhaled, realizing that these small opportunities were almost taken away from him.

His young life had taken a turn for the worse. He was watching everyone around him being taken away. He decided at that moment that he wouldn't bury anymore of his loved ones; they would bury him. If it took his last breaths to get the people responsible for hurting Sena, then so be it.

Chapter 22

Where Do Broken Hearts Go?

Sena was in the hospital for three weeks before she was able to be released. She thought for sure she would go crazy if they didn't let her out soon. It was getting too crowded in her hospital room. With the doctors, nurses, the personal nurse that Moochie had hired for her, Shay, Moochie, Skillet, and Skillet's mom coming to bring the kids, she felt like the walls were about to close in on her. She appreciated the love, but she needed to be alone to deal with what had happened to her. She still didn't know how she felt about it all. She knew she felt a little anger toward Moochie for not being there. She wouldn't feel right until she got it off her chest, but she knew now was not the right time. She needed to heal.

Once she made it home, she went right to her room to lie in her own bed. She just wanted to fall into a comatose slumber until all her pain went away. She had told everyone she wanted to be alone, but her nurse wouldn't leave.

Sena looked up to see the nurse sitting quietly and reading a book from her Kindle Fire.

"Why are you still here?" Sena asked with her head halfway under the covers.

"I was told not to leave your side, ma'am," the nurse stated nervously, looking up at the lump in the bed that was Sena. She was praying that Sena didn't start any shit again. When she had first gotten hired, Sena threw a whole fit, but Moochie wasn't paying her any attention. He had basically told her to shut the hell up and deal with it because Tia wasn't going anywhere.

"Well, you can go now." Sena didn't realize the situation she was putting Tia in. Moochie clearly told her that if she left Sena's side and something were to go wrong, he would cause her great bodily harm. So, Tia didn't give a fuck what Sena said. If she needed to blow her nose, Tia would gladly hold the tissue for her. She was scared shitless of Moochie, but she couldn't pass up the money. He had compensated her very well on her last job, and she was really looking forward to seeing what she would get this time around.

"No, ma'am, I cannot. Look, please don't make this harder on me. I'm only doing my job; plus, I am way more scared of Mr. Brown than you." She added a little chuckle to lighten the mood. Even Sena had to laugh at that one.

"Huh!" Sena pulled the covers back over her head. She didn't care to finish the conversation because she knew there was no winning. Moochie had spoken, so there it was. She was stuck with this woman until she got better. She began to wonder where he was and why he wasn't there with her. She didn't want to turn into one of those women who worried every time their man was out of sight.

"Where is Moochie?" Sena asked from under the covers.

"He took little Deonna to the park for a little while. She kept trying to come in here and wake you up. He thought you needed your rest. He said for me call him when you woke up. Do you want me to call him?"

"No, don't call him. Can you run me a hot bath and help me get into the tub?" She still couldn't get around as well as she would have liked. She figured if the girl was going to sit there and stare at her, she may as well put her to some use. While she was in the hospital, she did a little physical therapy and was told she would finish at home but, for now, she had to walk with a walker.

"Yes, ma'am." Tia was thanking God that Sena was coming around. Sena had been home for a week, and this was the first time she had actually asked her to do something for her. All Sena did was sleep with all the pain pills she was on. Basically, all Tia did was sit and watch Sena and help her with her meds. Sena's wounds had closed and begun to heal, so there were no wound dressings that needed to be changed. So, she just played in the background and collected her money.

Once Sena was in the tub, she picked up her remote and turned on the radio. She found her mix playlist and Beyoncé's "I'd Rather Die Young" flowed through the speakers. Sena felt like Beyoncé had written this song for her personally. She really related to the song because that's what she had been proving for some time now, that she would rather die young than to live her life without Moochie. The song really hit close to home, and she couldn't help the tears that started to run down her face. She was so into the song that she didn't notice Moochie had come into the room and was watching her sing.

Moochie smiled because he hadn't heard her sing in way too long. Now she couldn't sing to save her life, but he still loved to hear it all the same. The house was too quiet without her around. For weeks it was just him and Deonna. He wanted to stand there and watch her for a while. He could see she was getting into her feelings because the tears started to roll down her face. Beyoncé always got Sena emotional.

He listened to the words: *And what I'm gonna do is be a woman and you can be a man. And I wanna say nobody understands what we've been through.* Moochie had heard Sena play this song a thousand times over, but he'd never really paid attention to the words until now. They struck his heart like lightning.

"You need some help?"

Sena almost jumped out of her skin. Moochie put his head down because she was afraid in her own home. It hurt him to see her react that way. She used to be so strong. He just hoped this didn't break her. He knew she was hurting and he just wanted to be there to help her through it.

"Yeah, thanks." Sena handed him the towel and sat up slowly so he could get her back.

They were quiet for a while. All you could hear was the water splashing and the music playing. Neither knew what to say to the other. He looked at the scars left from all the bullet wounds and the surgery she had. With her being so light-skinned, there was no hiding the scars. He felt so bad because these were supposed to be his scars and his heartbreak, not hers. He just didn't know that, even with losing the baby, she would still have rather it be her than him. To watch him in pain would be way worse than what she was going through.

"I am so sorry," Moochie said just above a whisper.

"The only thing I would change about what I went through is the fact that I couldn't find you. Other than that, I would do it all over again. I would have never given you up." Her loyalty may have seemed crazy to someone else, but she couldn't give a fuck about what the next person thought. Moochie was her everything. In her opinion, it wasn't for someone else to understand. She wanted to be mad at him, but she knew deep down inside that he would have never left her if he knew something was going to happen to her.

"I know, and that's why I'm so sorry. I should have never left. You were right. And I will never forgive myself. Just promise me you won't leave me." He couldn't help it. He was scared that she would leave him for a more peaceful life. He kept seeing her face the day he left. She had so much anger in her eyes and hurt, and that would forever be sketched in his memory.

"I told you before I would never leave you." Sena finally turned to look at him.

"Why not? Is it the money?" Moochie could feel the tears burning the back of his throat. He was hurting so badly, and he didn't understand anything that was going on around him. All he knew was the life that his brother had provided for him. There had never been a problem that Kidd couldn't help him through. Now he didn't know what to do. It would literally kill him if Sena really left him. "You don't have to do that. I would take care of you wherever you went. I don't want anything else to happen to you. I have been bringing nothing but bad shit to your life." He was really on a pity wagon and didn't know how to get off.

Sena would have taken that as insult had it not been for the tears in his eyes. She could tell he honestly didn't know why she was still with him, even after everything they been through together. He just didn't know that was the reason she wanted to stay with him. Everything they had gone through together made their bond stronger. She wouldn't trade a day of her life with Moochie for anything in the world. The good far outweighed the bad.

"I don't know how to explain to you that you are my life, and I love you with every piece of me. With you is where my heart is and where it will remain." She wanted to be mad at him, kick and scream, but her heart wouldn't allow it. No matter what she was going through, she would gladly put it on the back burner to help him.

Moochie just stared at her. He didn't really know what to say. He just knew he was grateful for her.

"Daddyyyyyy," they heard Deonna sing from the other side of the door. Both of them laughed. She was such a funny little girl.

"Let me go get her together. I'll send Tia in."

"Nooooo!" Sena pleaded. "Please not her!" she whined as she slid her whole body under the water, head and all.

"Stop it! The sooner you get up and about, the sooner she will leave. And I know you can still hear me." Moochie laughed as he walked out the door. He knew Tia was driving her crazy, but he didn't care. She was not to be left alone. Tia was only there during the day, then Moochie or Shay took over. Moochie had the nights.

Tia came in and helped Sena finish washing up, then helped her get back into bed. Moochie fed Deonna and put her down for a nap.

"Ma'am, Shay has been calling all day. If you could please call her before you fall back asleep, that would be a great help to me. She has threatened me more times than I care to count. She has threatened to shoot me, torture me, and make me disappear. Please call her. She thinks there's some funny business going on."

Sena couldn't help but to laugh, but Shay would have to wait. Her pain pills were kicking in.

When Sena woke up, Moochie lay behind her with his arms wrapped tightly around her. She melted into his body; it felt so good to be in his arms again. She just didn't know Moochie held her day in and out. She was just always sleeping. She lay there for a few minutes not moving, just relishing the moment of tranquility. Everything was silent. Moochie slept peacefully, and it was so quiet that all she could hear was the ticking of the grandfather clock in the far corner of their bedroom. Both were startled out of their sleep when they heard Shay yelling at poor Tia.

"Girl, if you don't move the fuck out of my way! Who the fuck are you anyway? You are nobody, with yo' cockeyed ass!" Shay yelled as she stormed into the house. She was pissed that neither Moochie nor Sena were answering their phones, and she was going to get to the bottom of that shit.

"Your friend is going to drive that poor girl insane! I'm starting to think you done wore off on her. She a little bit loopy now herself." Moochie laughed.

"No, she's not. She worried about me, that's all." Neither Moochie nor Shay had told Sena about their little spat at the hospital. She didn't need the added stress. They both wanted her to get better.

"Umm hmm, if you say so."

Shay knocked then walked right in as Moochie was getting up.

Skillet stayed in the living room, not wanting to be in there with all the commotion. He knew Shay was beyond pissed about being told to call back so many times. She had literally dragged him out of bed and made him come with her.

"What the hell is going on around here that I can't get in contact with anyone of importance?" Shay yelled, taking a shot at Tia. She didn't give a shit about her feelings. She figured she had better learn her position before she was put in it very roughly. Shay was not fond of this new woman hanging around Sena at all, even though she was working and not necessarily hanging around Sena. Shay thought she didn't need to be there. She felt like she could take care of her friend.

"We are trying to rest, that's all, Shay," Moochie calmly told her as he stood up.

"Yeah, what the fuck ever! Y'all resting and I'm worried sick. Stressing the fuck out." Shay looked him up and down as he attempted to go out the door. "Nigga, where you going? Put a damn shirt on. Don't be giving that retarded-looking heffa no thoughts that will get her fucked up!"

Sena burst into laughter after that one. Moochie just shook his head, turned around to find his shirt, and then kindly removed himself from the equation. Most definitely Sena had worn off on her.

When he made it into the living room, Tia looked like she was about to break out into tears. He felt sorry for her. He knew Sena was a handful on her own, but somewhere along the line, Shay had joined in the ranks.

"You can go now. You will get a big bonus for having to deal with nutty and nuttier. And I don't know which one is which just yet." Moochie laughed, trying to make Tia feel a little better.

"Okay, sir. Do you need me tomorrow?"

"Yeah, she starts physical therapy. They will be coming here."

"Okay." Tia gathered her things, almost too happy to get away. If she didn't need the money so badly, she would have been gone. She had paid off all her school bills and bought a car with the money from the last job, and she was hoping for another big bonus again. This job was a little easier though because she had help with Sena. But it was a total strain on her mental status. Those two women were going to drive her crazy. With Kidd, it was just her and him and an occasional nurse or doctor to step in and update her on things.

"Lil Tony got at me about ol' boy and 'em," Skillet stated as soon as Tia was out of earshot.

"What's up?" Moochie asked anxiously.

"It was some ol' nothing-ass nigga named Tyrell trying to get that money Sonny had put on your head. He just didn't know that Sonny was dead." Skillet picked up the bag of Red Hot Riplets sitting on the table.

"Who was the other dude?

"His li'l flunky Dion. They say if you see one, the other is not far away."

"Just how I like 'em! That makes it easier. I want them to watch what happens when you fuck with me and mines, pussy niggas!" Moochie rubbed his hands together with anticipation. He wanted to squeeze the life out one of them with his bare hands. He had to keep his feelings in check because of the promise he made to God. He hoped God would be busy helping someone else on the day they found the culprits.

"Hiiiii!" Deonna yelled as she ran and jumped into Skillet's lap. "Where Kay?" she asked, looking around the room for Kayla.

"What's up li'l pimpn, you got it." He couldn't help but think she should have been a boy. Skillet thought Sena was going to ruin her.

"I'm good." She smiled big.

Both men broke into laughter. She was too much.

"Yo, man, you need to put a boy in that woman before she ruin your precious baby girl."

Moochie laughed some more. Deonna was too beautiful with her long pigtails that hung past her shoulders and her little Elmo pajamas. She was Sena all the way: girlie as all get-out, but she talked like a nigga.

"I know, right?"

"Where Kay Kay?" Deonna had a habit of giving everybody a nickname when she didn't feel like trying to pronounce their whole name.

"She at home with her grandma and Kelly."

"Ooooweee, Daddy!" The kids seemed to have taken a liking to Raylene.

"You just gon' leave me?" Moochie faked like his feelings were hurt.

"Daddy, I wanna!" She jumped down off Skillet's lap about to have a melt down.

"You can't leave me. How long you gon' be gone?"
She pulled his fingers.

"But I want to hang with you." He pouted some more. But he knew there was no telling her no.

"You know she's always welcome." Skillet threw that in.

"Daddddyyyyyy!" she sang.

After everybody left, Moochie looked in on Sena and saw that she was resting again. He knew she slept like a log when her medicine kicked in, so he went into the living room to think. He turned on the radio and Tyrese's cut "Stay" started talking to him. He could really feel that song. He never understood why Kidd used to listen to slow music all the time, but now he could see that it had tamed him. It helped him to relax, and if need be, to express how he was feeling. And right then, Moochie was feeling this song so much he put it on repeat. He let his head fall back on the couch and he began to relax for the first time in a long time. He knew his relaxation would not be long-lived because he had a lot of ruckus to cause. The would-be killers thought they had gotten away with something, but he was only letting Sena get back right before he struck. He had gotten all the info he needed from Skillet. He would call Skillet in if his services were needed. He planned on him and Sena doing the deed together like he had promised.

It was like everyone was suffering for someone who never even really existed. Raven was the cause of all this turmoil everyone was going through. He never blamed Valencia because she was just as much a victim as anyone else. But he couldn't help feeling like if they had never met Valencia, everything would still be the same. No one would be dead, everyone would be happy, and he and his brother would be somewhere laughing and joking. But if he hadn't ever met Valencia then he wouldn't have Sena or his daughter in his life, and they meant everything to him. They were the best part of him. He most definitely wished his mother could have met them. He knew she would have spoiled Deonna rotten and loved Sena as if she were her own daughter.

Sena limped into the living room using her cane. She refused to use the walker because she thought it was for old people. She watched as Moochie bobbed his head to the music and every now and then he would sing a note or two. She could tell the song was really touching something in him. She walked over to him and slowly slid down on his lap, facing him. He looked up and stared into her eyes. She laid her head down on his shoulders and wrapped her arms around his neck.

"Can you hold me?" she whispered in his ear.

Moochie pulled her in to his body tight and held on to her for dear life. He loved the feeling of her being in his arms. She sat that way for about five minutes before she started to feel him growing under her. She could feel him getting harder and harder, but he never stopped holding her. She sat up and pressed her lips against his softly. As they kissed, his holding turned into rubbing. It had been way too long for both of them. Her pussy was aching for this. Her heartbeat had traveled all the way to her screaming clit.

Moochie pulled Sena's tank top over her head. He looked at her chest and began to kiss every scar to let her know he didn't care about all that. She lifted herself up so he could pull her shorts off along with his. She pulled his shirt over his head as she slid down onto his throbbing pole. Even though she was on top, Moochie would still have to do most of the work. He knew this, so he raised her up by her ass, meeting her every time she slid back down. He started to feel that tingle in the bottom of his nuts, so he pushed her up and slid down 'til she was sitting on his face. He sucked her pussy into his mouth gently, wanting her to enjoy every minute of what was happening.

"Ummm, shhhh!" Sena's back arched as her eyes rolled all around in her head. A few minutes later her body started to spasm out of control when electrical shock waves shot all up in through her body. She hadn't felt that feeling in so long that it was a shock to her. When her body loosened up, he slid from under her and lay her down on the couch to reenter her. He held her legs up as he ground all in her walls, driving both of them insane.

"I love you," Moochie said with each stroke.

Sena couldn't respond immediately because he was digging all in her spot. He watched as her teeth clenched and her jaw muscles got real tight. He knew she was about to cum again.

"You gon' stay with me?" Moochie dug deeper.

"Huh?" Sena's body still hadn't started to cooperate.

He pulled her body up off the couch and asked again. This time he got the answer he was looking for.

"You gon' stay with me?" Moochie looked into her eyes.

"Forever!"

Chapter 23

Together 'Til Never

Ay, ay!" Moochie came in the room yelling the next morning, waking Sena out of her deep sleep.

"Boy, what the hell is wrong with you? Why you yelling?"

"I got something for you. Come with me. I got a wonderful morning planned for you before you start therapy."

Sena went to grab for her walker, but Moochie signaled that she wouldn't need it. He held out his arm for to hold on to. "Close your eyes," he said to her when they got to their guest room.

Sena did as she was told. When he opened the door, in front her was a whole spa room he had made just for her. There was a massage table and an area for her to get her feet done and nails done. There was a place where she could pick out her own oils she wanted to use. The smells that were emitting throughout the room were a mixture a vanilla and lavender. A few minutes later, she was greeted by a host of people carrying trays of fruit and food for her to eat. She was so overwhelmed that she couldn't do anything but stand there in awe.

"I can't believe you did all this for me!" She was so touched.

"I would give you the world if I could. Enjoy yourself. I'll be back in a little while when it's my turn with you." Moochie winked, then left her to get pampered and treated like the queen she was.

After Sena had gotten her mani/pedi and facial, she stuffed herself with so much fruit that she didn't think she would be able to handle anymore. She was instructed to get undressed and lie on the massage table. After everyone had left, Moochie walked in wearing nothing but his boxers, caring a tray that was covered.

He turned down the lights and commenced massaging her all over. Sena felt like she was in heaven, it felt so good. She never knew getting your hands rubbed could feel so good. The way he was rubbing all over her thighs and ass cheeks had her hot box leaking juices all over the table. After he was done, he hit her with the bombshell.

"How you feeling?"

"Um, I'm feeling too good," she moaned, not wanting it to end.

"Turn over on your back," Moochie instructed.

Sena gladly turned over, thinking she was about to get dicked down again. But she was sorely mistaken. She turned over to see him standing there with a waxing kit in his hand.

"We need to get this hair business under control," Moochie stated in a matter-of-fact tone. When he was finished sucking on her the day before, he had made up his mind that the hair had to go. He was used to her being groomed, and if she couldn't do it herself, he sure as hell was going to step in to help. He was not into choking on hairballs.

"Nigga, is you retarded? You think I'm gon' to let you put that hot-ass wax on my shit and yank out some hair?" Sena couldn't believe this shit. She had never in her life waxed anything but her eyebrows, and if that shit brought tears to her eyes, she knew this would most definitely bring on a storm of tears. No, she was not feeling this at all. Why couldn't they just finish the morning off with a quickie and keep it moving like normal people?

"You don't have a choice." Moochie said it like he was simply suggesting she change her hair color or something.

"You say what happened?" She raised one eyebrow.

"I said you don't have a choice. I'm not gon' to shave you or put that Nair shit on you. It stinks like perm, so this is the next best thing." He shrugged his shoulders like it was nothing.

"You done fucked up my whole moment." Sena was totally thrown off by the suggestion. She looked down and could see a small curly 'fro starting to develop. She was all for keeping herself groomed, but there had to be a better way. Clearly, this couldn't be the only option.

"Just chill and let me do this, 'cause please believe that fur ball is not going back in my mouth until the hair is gone. Damn near choked to death off all that damn hair."

On that note, Sena really didn't have a choice anymore, because she couldn't bend over to do it herself and she was most definitely not passing up some head! Moochie could see the recognition of what he had just said run across her face.

"I thought so." He went to setting up his little waxing station.

Sena nervously watched him prepare. "You look like you having a little bit too much fun for my taste," Sena said as she watched him turn on the wax warmer and lay out the strips of tape.

"Just chill out, I got you." He winked at her and smiled. "I watched the video and everything. I even waxed a part of my arm to make sure I knew how hot I wanted it to be. That shit hurt like a son of bitch! I don't see how you women do this shit on a regular. But you always say beauty is pain, right?"

"Yeah, whatever!" Sena huffed.

"Okay, open your legs," Moochie instructed.

Sena did as she was told. It felt like her heart was about to beat out of her chest. Moochie began to rub the wax on the lips of her pussy; then he spread the waxing tape on. Before he could rip it off, she jumped.

"Wait a minute!" Sena yelled. "Uhhhh, OMG!"

Moochie was laughing so hard at her that he had tears coming out of his eyes. "Man, lie back down!" He pushed her in the forehead.

"Man, fuck you! Wait a minute. This is not funny! Shit, urrrr!" Sena growled, trying to psych herself up. She knew there was no turning back now that the wax was already on. She took in deep breaths, but it wasn't working.

Moochie continued to laugh. The look on her face was priceless. "You need a distraction?" he asked as he dropped his boxers to the floor.

"Umm," Sena moaned as she ogled his pole hanging down his leg. She wanted to slide it right down her throat.

Moochie could see that it had helped a little. "Okay, you ready?" He laughed some more.

"Yeah, man, go ahead!" Sena yelled as he yanked the tape off. "Whoo, shit, muthafucka, gotdamn!" Her pussy lips felt like they were on fire. That little diversion didn't help one bit. He didn't even give her a chance to brace herself.

Moochie couldn't help laughing. He wished he could have recorded it. "I'm almost done. Believe me, it's gon' be well worth it." He licked his lips.

"Whatever, man, just finish it. You done fucked up my whole day. You can put that little shit up." She was referring to his dick that was still dangling in the air. "Don't nobody want to see that bullshit. I don't want to see yo' ass the rest of the day. Where the hell is Tia?"

Chapter 24

The Take Down

"I can't believe you still watch this movie like that," Raylene said as she plopped down on the couch next to Shay.

"Yeah, you know this my movie. It takes me to a happier time in my life." Shay looked to her mother and could see the shame flash across her face.

"I'm sorry," Raylene said just above a whisper. She felt horrible for everything her daughters had been through. She knew there was no excuse for what she had done to Shay, but she would try to make it up to her for the rest of her life.

"I know." Shay looked back to the scene that was unfolding on the screen. Eddie King and Baby Doll were singing a song about going on. This was one of her favorite parts of movie. The two sat there for hours watching movies.

Raylene got up to start dinner.

"Ma?"

Raylene stopped in her tracks, because Shay hadn't called her "Ma" or "Momma" in so long. She didn't think she heard her correctly. "Did you say something to me?' she questioned, wanting to make sure she really did call her "Ma."

"Yeah." She figured she might as well start letting go of what her mother had done to her. Her mother had forgiven her for what she had done; she was ready to let bygones be bygones.

"What is it?" Raylene would do anything she wanted her to do.

"I need to know where I can find Carl."

Raylene swallowed the lump that had formed in her throat. She knew that Shay was going to try to have something done to Carl. She didn't know if she wanted Shay to participate in something like that. He could die a thousand horrible deaths, but she never wanted that kind of karma on her daughter's aura.

"What are you gonna do, Raina?"

"Ma, I just need to know where he hangs out at. I'm not going to do anything, but he can't get away with what he did."

"Okay." She paused for a minute. "He hangs out at a bar in the city on Taylor. That's all I know. He never let me go anywhere with him." She didn't want to start an argument with her daughter right when they were starting a new relationship, but she hoped that Shay wouldn't get herself into any trouble messing with that lunatic Carl.

"Thanks, Ma, I'll take care of it from here."

"Raina, don't go getting into any trouble."

"Are you still cooking?" Shay tried to change the subject.

"Yes, ma'am. Is everyone still coming? 'Cause I did it big. Ain't that what y'all say?" She laughed.

"Yeah, that's what we used to say." Shay laughed at her mom's attempt at being hip.

"Yeah, well, whatever! I got a new dress and everything, and the food gon' be finger-licking, mmm-mmm good." Raylene was so excited. It was her time to shine. She knew everyone had been under a lot of stress, so she wanted to cook a big dinner to get everyone together and to have a good time.

Skillet had given Raylene a ton of money to go buy whatever she needed and to get herself something to wear for the occasion. She had gone all out with decorations. She had flowers all over the living room and the dining room. She had gotten the kids their own little table that would sit by the grown-ups' table. She had six new place settings that looked like they were made out of black marble. She also got silverware that was twenty-four-karat gold. She couldn't wait to start decorating and cooking.

Raylene watched as Shay got up and went into the basement. She assumed that's where Skillet was. She went to get everything together as she turned on her music. Kelly had taught her how to download music on the iPad. She had gotten it and was going with it. She cut on her playlist, and Anita Baker led her the rest of the way. Four hours later, she was greeting people at the door as they arrived.

"Hey, honey, you're looking beautiful!" Sena squealed as she took in Raylene's beauty. Indeed, Shay's mother was beautiful. She looked gorgeous in her all-white summer dress.

"You ain't half-steppin' yourself, suga!" She noticed Sena was looking nice in her multicolored maxi dress. Sena was feeling good. She had finally gotten rid of Tia and got her house to herself again, not to mention she and Moochie were fucking all over the place.

"Can we get in the house? Y'all can trade fashion stories later." Moochie interrupted their little moment.

The last to arrive was Momma Rogers, and then the party began. Everyone was having a good ol' time. Laughter filled the air. It had been so long since they had heard this much laughter going on. At that moment in time, no one had any cares in the world.

"Momma, you put yo' foot in this food!" Shay exclaimed. She was proud of her mother. She had really outdone herself with everything.

"She ain't lying, Ms. Raylene! This food is the bomb," Moochie stated with a mouth full of food.

"I'm just glad I got somebody else to cook for the holidays now," Momma Rogers stated as she put more food into her mouth. "I been cooking all the meals for years. Now I can visit once in a while and get a good home-cooked meal, 'cause between Shay and Sena, they think steak and potatoes is a good meal." Everyone laughed because they knew she was serious.

After everyone let their food digest, the kids pulled out the Wii console, and *Michael Jackson: The Experience* was next on the menu. While the kids were playing the game, the grown-ups were out on the balcony talking and laughing.

"I'm ready to tell you all about how I came to St. Louis and why I changed my name." Shay paused. "And also why I had so much anger for my mother."

Everyone got quiet, giving her their full attention.

"Wait a minute; let me go top my glass off." Sena went to get a refill of peach Cîroc. "Okay, let me hear it."

"Okay, well, my real name is Raina, as you have heard. My mother left me when I was fifteen and went to stay with her boyfriend, Carl. And . . ." Shay took a deep breath and went into detail on her life story.

They stayed out there for about an hour, just listening to Shay talk about her life and how she felt about everything that had happened in her life.

"Soooo, you just a stone-cold killa in the cut playing good girl, huh?" Sena broke the silence that had fallen upon everyone once Shay had finished. Sena chuckled a little. "I knew there was a reason you was my bitch! I know how to pick 'em."

"You know how to pick 'em, huh? I thought I knew her first," Skillet said, claiming his woman. For some reason, hearing her story made him more endeared to her.

"I got one more person on my list," Shay said as she looked around at everyone in attendance.

"I told you whenever you ready, I can get him."

"No, I want to do it; I have to be the one to do it. He has done so much to the people I love, and I want to watch him suffer for a long time."

"Say no more. Me and my mans will get right on it."

Everybody looked over to Sena to see if she was ready.

"Y'all ain't got to look at me! I been ready. I been waiting on y'all slow asses," she stated matter-of-factly as she gulped down the last of her drink.

It had been two weeks, and everyone was ready for some get-back. Moochie had gotten the phone call he had been waiting for. He'd put a bug in Carmel's ear and told her the next time Tyrell and his peoples came through to hit him up. Lil Tony had given them the info on where to find them. He didn't want to go to their houses because he didn't want to have to kill any unnecessary people, just the fools responsible for hurting Sena. He told Carmel that he was looking for them and that she would be given a $100,000 each if she was able to get them both to come along. He also informed her that it would be detrimental to her if she mentioned their conversation with anyone else. He hated that he had to involve an outsider, but he couldn't seem to find the slimy worms for nothing.

Moochie usually never had this much trouble getting to someone, but these days were different, so he had to roll with the punches. It was time for him to get his grown man on. This was the first real lead he had. Every time someone said they had seen them, they would be gone by the time he got there. But this time, he made sure someone was leaving with them. He sat tapping his foot in his mortuary on wheels, watching the club doors, waiting on them to exit. He hated waiting because he still had to wait for Carmel's signal that they were ready for him to come in and get them. She was supposed to drug them, wait 'til they were out, and call him in. He actually wanted to blow their heads off on sight, but he knew this was going to be a long process. Sena wanted to teach them a few lessons on how to treat a lady. She was hell bent on getting her get-back in the worst way. He wanted her to move on with her life, so he would basically serve them on a silver platter to her.

Meanwhile, Carmel rode in the back of Tyrell's Tahoe, giving him the meanest head he had ever gotten in his life.

"Man, this bitch got this head game shit on lock, hands down, my nigga! You got to see what this shit be like!" Tyrell slurred to his partner in crime Dion. The drugs had started to kick in already. His lips had already started to droop to one side.

Carmel hoped the driver wasn't feeling the same way just yet. She needed to make it home in one piece.

"Man, my dick harder than a muthafucka listening to them slurping sounds." Dion grabbed his crotch, looking through the rearview mirror. Carmel met his eyes and smiled at him with a mouth full of dick. He was too drunk to see the daggers her eyes were shooting at him. If looks could kill, he would have dropped dead right at that moment.

"Um, daddy, this dick big!" Carmel exclaimed as she licked up and down his shaft. She wasn't lying either. Tyrell was working with a major piece. She just couldn't get over how such a beautiful piece of meat was wasted on such a slimeball. All she could think about was how these two ignorant-ass bastards were about to get theirs in spades.

Carmel hated both of them with a passion. They always came in the club treating the girls like trash, as if they were nothing, calling all of them bitches and hoes and none of them by their names. They would slap them on the ass and stick things in them when they were dancing. The owners let them get away with it because they spent a lot of money there. She was all too happy when Moochie had reached out to her. She would have done it for free if he had asked her to. But that $100,000 bounty on each of their heads was just the icing on the cake. With that money and the money she had saved, she would be on the first thing smoking out of St. Louis, for good.

"I know it is, bitch, now keep sucking until I tell yo' funky ass to stop." Tyrell laughed as he pushed her head down farther.

Carmel gagged but held it together. She was almost tempted to bite it off, but that $200,000 and Moochie's warning for her not to fuck it up kept her grounded.

Carmel felt the truck come to a stop. She looked around and could see they were at a seedy-looking motel. That was fine with her. It would be easier for her to get away. She knew them trifling sons of bitches were going to try to fuck her six ways to Sunday in that raggedy-ass motel, but she had something for them. The fact that they were about to die made her extra happy about the part she was going to play.

As they were getting out, Carmel had to literally hold Tyrell up because he was so out of it. They were so dumb they couldn't tell that they had been drugged. Tyrell must have had more to drink than his partner because Dion was doing okay.

"Man, I can't wait to get all up in this!" Dion slurred. He held on to Carmel's ass for dear life as he walked behind her. Carmel cringed at the feel of him touching her.

Moochie had followed them from the club and was now watching everything from his car. He couldn't wait to get his hands on them two cowards. He needed them to be asleep for a long time while he set things up. Sena had specific instructions on how she wanted them when she arrived. He didn't mind doing as he was told. That was what he had done for Kidd for years, so it was natural for him. He had no misunderstandings of what he was: a killer, and a very good one at that. He wasn't a mastermind or anything of that nature. But you could just point him in the direction of a person who needed to be killed, no questions asked, just let him know how you wanted it done, or he could be quite creative himself. Even though Moochie did whatever he was told, he knew he was the reason they were all millionaires. Kidd may have started it, but he helped keep it going. He made sure Kidd didn't have to lift a finger unless he wanted to participate.

The trio disappeared behind the door of the motel room. Moochie liked their choice. It was one of those hotels that paid by the hour and they parked right in front of the door.

As they walked into the room, Carmel pushed Tyrell onto the bed and instructed Dion to lie next to him.

"Damn, you gon' do us both at the same damn time?" Dion asked as he got undressed and lay down on the bed, letting his dick get the best of him. He hadn't noticed that his friend was almost knocked out and Carmel hoped he wouldn't catch on.

Carmel needed his drugs to start kicking in before she actually had to do something sexual with him. He was uglier than an ass crack, and she wanted no part of him. She undressed Tyrell and Dion, making sure to throw his clothes across the room so he couldn't get to them. Once she got Tyrell undressed, she stepped back and looked at

Dion and almost threw up at the sight of him. He had hair all over his fat body, and it was nappy hair, at that. She put on a fake smile and began to slowly undress, dancing to her own beat.

"Damn, you sexy as a muthafucka! Hurry that shit up."

Carmel could see one side of his face starting to droop, so she knew that in just a few more minutes, he would be out like Tyrell. "Yeah, daddy, I'm hurrying. I'm gon' show you the time of your life, believe that." She moved fluidly like a snake as she turned around so he could watch her ass cheeks vibrate.

"Ay, man, you watching this shit?" Dion asked, elbowing Tyrell. When Tyrell didn't respond, he sat up a little too fast, and everything around him started to spin.

"Yo, bitch, what the fuck did you do?" Dion tried to stand up but fell flat on his face, snoring. He was out, and that was her cue.

Carmel opened the door and waved Moochie in. He wasn't hard to miss. He was sitting right outside next to the car they had pulled up in, waiting in a black van. She gathered her belongings and got dressed as he entered the room. She looked up, and his presence filled the room. She almost forgot what they were there for.

"Get his keys," Moochie said, breaking her out of the fantasy that had started to play in her head.

"Uhhh, okay." She was nervous. Moochie looked like a deranged maniac. His eyes darted around the room, assessing the situation.

"Your money is in their car." He hadn't even looked her way. He was ready to get started, but he needed her to go. "Ay, let me holla at'chu for a minute." He stopped Carmel in her tracks as she headed for the door. He walked up to her with a fast pace, grabbed her by the collar, and pushed her up against the wall. Tears instantly flooded from her eyes. But Moochie didn't give a fuck. He had to get his point across. "Open ya mouth," he instructed.

"Please don't kill me! I won't say anything!" she cried.

"Open ya fuckin' mouth now!" he said between gritted teeth.

Moochie was no longer handsome to Carmel. He was the devil in the flesh, and she started to wish she hadn't participated. She prayed to God that he wouldn't kill her. She only wanted the money so she could stop stripping and get her and her son to a better situation. But she did as she was told and he slid his gun into her mouth slowly and deliberately.

"I'm gon' say this one time. If you tell anybody about what happened here, I will kill everything you love down to your dog." Moochie was only inches away from her face, and she could smell the Bubblicious he had been chewing.

Carmel nodded her head up and down. Moochie looked in her eyes a little longer to see if he saw any signs that he needed to kill her. He had never killed a woman, but he wasn't going to jail for anyone. Once he was sure, he let her go.

"Do what you want with the truck. They won't need it again in this lifetime."

Carmel quickly wiped her eyes and ran out of the room, thanking God for her life. She was on her way to get her son. They weren't even going to pack a bag. She was going to drive that truck until the wheels fell off.

Moochie looked around the room and was disgusted at what he saw. He never understood how niggas fell victim to a woman's ways. It was entirely too easy for her to set them up, but their dumbness was his gain.

Moochie wrapped a sheet around each of them, totally disregarding their nakedness. That would just be one thing he wouldn't have to do. Sena wanted them naked and chained to the floor of the basement. He had already set everything up in one of the old warehouses that they owned and used to do their torture sessions in. After he got them situated in the car, he went back in to make sure everything looked the same way it had before they got there. After making sure everything was perfect, he headed off to make sure everything was ready for Sena.

Skillet sat waiting patiently for Carl to exit the bar. Tonight was the night for them to be finished with all this revenge mess and he was glad for it. Shay said she was ready to get Carl and Sena was ready to get the men who had done her wrong. It felt kind of weird to be getting a victim for his lady. He was used to helping Moochie collect victims for Kidd. But this was something that wasn't sitting well with him. He went along with it because he'd rather be involved in it than let Shay go out and get herself hurt.

Skillet was broken from his thoughts when he heard the loud music coming from the open doors of the bar. A drunken Carl wobbled out of the doors, yelling something inside at one of his drinking buddies. He ducked down in Carl's back seat so he wouldn't see him. Carl got to the car and right before he got in, he threw up everywhere, all over the car and himself. Skillet could hear all the fluid splashing everywhere, and it was making him sick to his stomach. It took everything in him not to start throwing up with Carl. He jumped when he saw a big splatter of vomit hit his window. Carl was too drunk to notice the movement the car had just made. Skillet had to hold his nose and mouth because he could smell the fumes of the vomit seeping through the cracks in the windows.

Carl got in, fell into the seat, and slumped down as if he was about to take a nap. Skillet thought the throw up smell was horrible, but that didn't have anything on Carl's body odor. Now that was something that had to be witnessed. He couldn't have described the odor if his life depended on it. It was mixed somewhere between a thousand onions and a garbage dump site.

Once Carl got comfortable in his seat, Skillet jumped into action. He pulled out the bottle of chloroform, poured it into a napkin, and placed it on Carl's face. He pressed so hard he thought that he would surely crush Carl's face. Once Carl was out, he got out of the back seat, opened the door, pushed Carl over to the passenger's side, and made it look like he was just sleeping.

Chapter 25

Vengeance Is a Bitch in Heels

Moochie had finished his part. Now he was waiting on Skillet to get Carl ready and set up.

When he got home, Sena was in the kitchen fixing herself a bowl of Fruity Pebbles. She was worried sick about Moochie. That was the only time she couldn't sleep, and she found herself eating all night long. She was sexy in just a thong, oiled up with her hair pulled up in a sloppy ponytail. He licked his lips at the sight before him. Her body was banging, and he loved every inch of her. The baby fat had fallen in all the right places. He wouldn't have minded getting a quickie in, but he needed her mind to be in the right place. He didn't want her tired or thinking about anything else but the task at hand, because once she busted a nut it was a wrap and she would be out for the count. So he bit his bottom lip to keep the sexual thoughts from roaming around in his head.

Sena had heard him when he came in the door. She exhaled deeply. She was overjoyed with the fact that he had made it home. She continued to eat her bowl of cereal, anticipating his arrival into the kitchen. She heard him walking up behind her and began to melt as she felt his arms wrapping around her waist.

"Hey babe," she said with a mouth full of cereal.

"What's up?" Moochie kissed her on the back of her neck.

"Waiting on you to get home so I can get a good night's rest." Sena turned around so that she was looking at him. She could never get enough of looking at him. He was the air in her lungs, the beat of her heart, and she couldn't wait to spend the rest of her life with him.

Moochie smiled at her because he knew that's why she was up. "Well, I hope you had some coffee, 'cause it's about to be a long night." It was two-thirty in the morning, and he knew they weren't going to sleep anytime soon.

Sena searched his eyes for an answer and could see the concern in his eyes, so she already knew what he was talking about. But she was ready for whatever. It was her turn to unleash the beast within.

When Skillet was finished with his part, he went back home to pick up Shay.

She was lying in a ball in the corner of the bed, sleeping. She looked at peace, and he hated to wake her up, but this was something that she wanted to do. He sat down on the bed next to her and shook her gently.

"What's up? Is everything all right?" Shay looked up at him.

"Yeah." He paused for a minute. "We ready," he said, looking her in the eyes to see her reaction.

Shay was game and got up to put on some clothes. No more words needed to be said. She had been waiting on this day since she was fifteen years old.

Tyrell opened his eyes. He looked around and found himself chained to a cold, dirty cement floor next to his boy Dion and an old naked man. Upon closer inspection, he saw that they were all naked and chained to the floor. He tried to speak, but he couldn't open his mouth. Moochie had used his signature Gorilla Glue on their mouths.

"Mmmm, mmmm!" Tyrell yelled from behind his glued lips, but no one would wake up. So he shook the chains, trying to make noise, and he tried to pull his arms through the handcuffs. No matter how hard he tried, he couldn't get loose or wake the other two men up.

Tyrell took in his surroundings. They were in a dingy basement. It had a spoiled smell about itself with a faint smell of bleach. Then it hit him smack dead in the face when he looked up on the wall and saw a sixty-inch projection screen playing the video of him and his boys invading Moochie's home. He knew they had fucked up royally. The tape alone was enough to make a sane man go crazy. When Tyrell had found out Sonny was dead, he thought shit couldn't get any worse. But now he saw that he hadn't even felt a piece of the pain that was coming to him.

After the home invasion, Tyrell did a little background check on Moochie, and what little info he came up with made him want to leave the country. But he figured no one knew it was them who had gone into Moochie's home and killed his woman. He never wanted to kill Sena, but she went crazy and started shooting at them, so they were forced to strike back. He knew that wouldn't matter in the least bit. They should have never been there in the first place. Hell, they didn't even get paid, no street credibility or nothing because really no one even knew about Moochie and Kidd and their underground beef with the Jacksons.

Tyrell could have kicked himself for not taking into consideration that Moochie might have a home surveillance system. He watched the video about twenty times before he heard footsteps coming down the basement stairs. He started to fidget, not knowing what was about to take place.

Moochie walked in. He stopped and paused and looked at the screen behind him. The video was on the part when ol' boy was stomping Sena in the stomach. He shook his head and then looked back at the men assembled in the room. The sight of them made him want to start killing, but he held his feelings in check. He'd gotten a glimpse of what Sena had in store for them, and he couldn't wait to watch. Only one was awake at the moment, but he was about to change that. Carl could stay asleep until the girls came downstairs, but he would surely wake up once he heard the screaming that was about to take place.

Moochie walked over to Dion and nudged him in the head with the barrel of his gun. He wouldn't wake up after a few more nudges. Moochie got fed up and came down hard with the butt of the gun across the bridge of Dion's nose.

"Wake the fuck up!" Moochie yelled.

Moochie watched as the dude woke up in a full panic. He looked around the room as a fierce pain shot through his face. The blood started to run to the back of his throat, and he began to choke because he had nowhere to spit the blood out. Moochie noticed he was about to choke to death and he couldn't have that, so pulled out a little pocketknife, flipped it open, and commenced to cutting Dion's lips open. He cut through the soft flesh of his lips, not caring really about the effect it was having on the man.

Dion was shaking and trying to get away from Moochie, but Moochie pushed him back so that he was lying down, put his knee in his chest and finished what he was doing. Carl had finally woken up, and he and Tyrell watched in horror. The man's screams were so loud that they were sure the screams could be heard down the street and around the corner. Dion writhed around in pain. Never in his life had he felt such pain. He just didn't know the party was just beginning.

Carl looked around frantically, trying to figure out where he was and how he had gotten there. He didn't know anyone there, so he didn't know what they wanted him for.

Moochie stood back up and watched Dion spit up and cough up blood as he took in deep breaths.

"Don't get used to doing that. You won't be breathing much longer." Moochie went and stood under the projection screen. He twirled the knife around in his hand. He wasn't a man of many words when he was in kill mode.

Skillet walked in and looked around at the mayhem. He thought Moochie had already started working on the men, but he could see nothing really happened yet. He looked over at Carl and disgust instantly showed on his face, remembering how funky the man was when he had to capture him.

"I need you all to look up at the screen above my head. Now, for some odd reason, you niggas chose to invade my privacy and then had the audacity to fuck with my wife. Now I don't know what info you all got on me, but there must have been a major miscommunication because someone surely set you niggas up for failure. Now, you, on the end"—Moochie pointed the knife at Carl—"you had nothing to do with them. Someone else has been waiting a long time to get you, so we just added you to the party." He was talking to them as if they were holding a little conversation and they weren't sitting there chained up, naked, and about to die. Carl was so drunk half the time that he couldn't even remember if he had seen these two men before.

"Are you watching what you did to my wife?" Moochie asked calmly. But everyone in the room could feel the heat coming from him.

"Man, I don't know what you talking about," Dion said as he spat more blood out of his mouth.

"You hear this nigga?" Moochie looked over to Skillet. "You don't know what I'm talking about, huh? Is that not you?" He turned to the screen. "You like stomping women, I see."

"Man, that was a misunderstanding," Dion pleaded.

"You muthafucking right that was a misunderstanding!" Moochie's voice vibrated the basement walls.

He rushed over to Dion and stuck the knife to his throat. He wanted to slice his throat, but once again he had to hold his feelings in check. He had to keep telling himself that God had answered his prayers and he would live by what he had promised God. But it was hard. He was itching to jump back into beast mode. "I told you before you must have misunderstood the info you got on me to think you could fuck with my family and I wouldn't find you." He jammed the knife into Dion's eye just short enough not to kill him.

Dion screamed out in agony.

"Bitch nigga! You muthafuckas fucked with the wrong family this time!" Moochie yelled as he breathed heavily in and out, trying to gain control of his emotions. Moochie was inching his way into the killer beast that he once was, and soon there wouldn't be any way of controlling him.

Moochie backed up off Dion and looked at Tyrell. He then turned and walked toward him, still twirling the knife in hands. All of a sudden everyone could hear water running. Everyone looked around and found the source. Tyrell had pissed on himself. Tears were running down his face. This wasn't part of the game he wanted to play. He just wanted the money. But he failed to realize that there was more to the game than just getting money.

"Now you pissing your pants, but you the boss, ain't you? Wait a minute, shut that muthafucka up!" Moochie said, looking at nobody in particular, but Skillet knew he was talking to him. Dion wouldn't stop screaming. "So you are the brains of the operation, from what I could see? I mean, while y'all was trying to kill my wife? You see, I say trying because she is alive and well and she has a little lesson she wants to teach y'all on how to treat a lady." He smirked. "Baby, come on down; they ready for you."

The sound of heels click-clacking on the stairwell resonated throughout the basement. The men waited with anxiety building in their hearts with every step she took. Sena took slow, deliberate steps coming downstairs. The sledgehammer she was carrying was a little heavy, but it wasn't anything she couldn't handle. Once Sena's steps stopped, another set of heels came click-clacking down the stairs. Shay too was toting a sledgehammer. When she reached Sena, they walked in together. Once they entered they struck a Charlie's Angels' pose, then broke into laughter.

"Damn, I always wanted to do that shit," Sena boasted.

"I know, right? Me too." They laughed at their own little joke, not giving the men their attention just yet.

Moochie laughed at them. He thought they were funny. Skillet, on the other hand, just shook his head. After a little laughter, the room grew eerily silent.

"You want to go first, sis?" Sena looked to Shay.

"Noooo, you go first," Shay insisted.

"Nah, I'm gon' be awhile." Sena waved her off.

"Okay, maybe I'll take you up on that offer. I want to watch you work. Mine will be short-lived." Shay looked over at Carl, who was shaking his head so hard that it looked like it would snap off at any moment.

"I hate to ruin y'all moment, but if somebody don't start screaming or bleeding soon, I'm gon' jump in and start shooting," Moochie interrupted them.

"Huh, okay." Sena put one hand up so she was hiding her mouth from Moochie. "He's a bit touchy this morning, I see," she whispered to the men.

"Okay, how about you do something then I'll do something?" Shay said as she looked at the three men assembled before her.

"Um, hmm, yeah, that's the plan."

Moochie was getting irritated. The men were still breathing, and he didn't like that at all. He was all for Sena getting her revenge, but she had better do it before he took over and chopped them up into itty bitty pieces while they were still alive.

Both women turned to look at him, but neither said anything. They could see that Moochie was getting very impatient.

Shay walked over and stood in front of Carl. She turned to Skillet. "Hey, babe, can you come do something about his mouth? I can't hear him, and it seems as though he's trying to speak to me."

Just as Moochie did earlier, Skillet put his knee into Carl's chest to hold him down while he cut his lips open. Carl's body jumped all over the floor. As Skillet cut into his skin, his whole body rose up off the ground with Skillet on top of him. Skillet had to punch him in the throat to make him lay down so he could finish. But Carl wasn't just going to lie there and let someone slice on his face, so in return, Skillet cut damn near half his face off. Shay wanted his mouth open; she just got a little more, that's all. Skillet got up and walked back to where he had been standing before she had called him over. The way the men in the room were screaming and writhing around, you would have thought that the torture had begun.

Shay put on some latex gloves and walked back over to where Carl lay crying, trying to get his hand to touch his face. If only he could see it. The pain was excruciating. If he had been able to see it, the pain probably would have doubled.

"So you like to fuck little girls, huh?" Shay said as she grabbed his dick and tried her best to lay it on the floor flat. It was so little and short that she was having trouble getting a good grip.

"Plaasss. Don do t'is." His words were coming out like gibberish mainly due to the fact that the bottom and top half of his face were no longer connected.

"You don't get to beg no more. My sister begged you to stop touching her. I cried for years after you made my mother leave me. I was tortured by a sick muthafucka for a long time 'til opportunity came knocking and I filled that muthafucka up with hot lead. But he got off a little easier than you're about to." Shay looked back at Sena standing right behind her. She was ready to jump in whenever Shay needed her. "Can you hand me the glue? This nigga dick so little I can't do what I want right now." She laughed at him. "And this nigga trying to share this baby dick with people. Is that why you like little girls? Because it's too little for a grown woman?" she asked as she rubbed glue all over his flaccid dick and began to smash it to the floor so it would be glued to the floor. She held it in place for a few second so it would stay put. She had to stretch it to its limits to get it to go that far. "You can go, sis. This might take awhile."

Sena said no words. She just walked over picked up her sledgehammer, standing carefully because she still had problems with her balance. She swung the hammer, connecting with Dion's left knee. "Take the tape off, I want to hear him scream!" As soon as the tape was lifted, his screams erupted throughout the basement.

"Ain't this the leg you stomped me with?"

Sena watched as he fought with the shackles and screamed and cried. He had slobber running all over his body. Some looked on in amazement while others were horrified. Sena looked back at the screen. "Damn, that was the wrong leg. You stomped my baby out of me with this leg, didn't you?" She swung the hammer again, landing on his right ankle. Dion blacked out from the pain, but she was prepared for that. He wasn't getting off that easy. "Babe, wake him back up."

Moochie walked over and did a hard sternum rub that would have woken the dead. Dion woke up screaming. The pain that was radiating through his body was so horrible that he prayed for death to come soon.

"Thank you, babe." Sena directed her attention back to Dion. "You know I was pregnant when y'all decided to fuck up my world, right?" She swung again and hit his kneecap. "You like to stomp women? I know your momma taught you to keep your feet to yourself." Sena swung again, hitting his shin.

Everyone in the room jumped every time they heard Dion's bones being crushed under the pressure of the sledgehammer. Sena swung the hammer like she was playing golf and hit him right in the dick. Everyman in the room closed or tried to close their legs at the sight of that hammer slamming into Dion's genitals. Sena had blacked out. She hadn't even noticed the man wasn't moving anymore. She hit everywhere she could, breaking every bone in his body. It was a gruesome mess, and now everyone looked on in horror. Even Moochie wanted to stop her. The man was damn near flat as a pancake.

Moochie walked up behind Sena slowly and grabbed her arm before she could swing again. She had blood all over her. She looked at Moochie and started crying. He held her while she cried. He knew why she was crying. She hadn't cried since the incident happened. She had saved it all until she got them back for herself and her unborn child. She finally got her revenge. That was all she had dreamed about. The rage that was flowing through her body like an electrical current was now subsiding.

"Are you sure you want to do this?" Skillet asked as he walked up to Shay.

"Yeah, I'm sure. I just want to fuck him up a li'l; then you can do whatever with him." She shrugged her shoulders at him. She had dreams of smashing Carl's dick with the sledgehammer. So when Sena said what she was going to do to the guy that had beat her up, Shay jumped on the bandwagon.

While everyone was looking at Sena, Shay took the opportunity to do what she wanted to do. Sena had really thrown her off guard the way she went in on ol' boy. She knew deep down she could never be like Sena; she didn't have that kind of heart. There was no way in the world she could have done something like that. But she was going to make Carl suffer. Shay swung the hammer down in what seemed like slow motion.

Carl yelled, "Nooo!" The sight of his dick exploding made him have a heart attack, and he died instantly. He was an old drunk, and his body would have given out on him eventually anyway, Shay figured.

Everyone jumped and looked as Shay stood over Carl's dead body, studying him. She watched as his chest stopped going up and down. Shay had wanted to see him take his last breath for years, but for some reason, it didn't make her feel better. But she was glad he couldn't harm her family anymore. That was enough satisfaction for her.

Sena noticed that Tyrell was still alive. She snatched the gun off Moochie's hip, pulled the trigger, and put all fourteen bullets in the middle of his face. She handed Moochie back the gun and walked back up the basement steps, closing the door on this chapter of her life. She knew Moochie had made the promise that he wouldn't kill anyone anymore, so she did it for him. She knew her soul was tarnished and she was all right with that. She and Moochie would burn in hell together one day.

"I, Sena Johnson, take you, Deshawn Brown, to be my lawfully wedded husband, my constant friend, my faithful partner and my love from this day forward. In

the presence of God, our family, and friends, I promise
to love you unconditionally, to honor and respect you, to
laugh with you and cry with you, and to cherish you for as
long as we both shall live."

Sena stood on a beautiful beach in Fiji saying her
wedding vows to the man of her dreams. She couldn't
believe she would be getting her happily ever after
with everything they had been through. She imagined
Valencia was standing next to her as her maid of honor.
She stared into Moochie's eyes as she spoke each word
and knew deep down in the bottom of her heart that he
was sent to her from God and she would love him forever.

"I, Deshawn Brown, take you, Sena Johnson, to be my
friend, my lover, the mother of my children, and my wife,
to respect you in your successes and in your failures, to
care for you in sickness and in health, to nurture you,
and to grow with you throughout the seasons of life. I
give you my hand, my heart, and my love, from this day
forward for as long as we both shall live."

Moochie found himself getting choked up because he
never imagined getting married without his family being
there. But he could feel their presence all around. He
looked around at his baby girl standing next to Sena in a
matching dress to her mother's. She looked so beautiful.
Only a few attended the wedding: Skillet, Shay, Momma
Rogers, Raylene, Kelly, and baby Kayla. He felt the love
radiating all around him and felt at peace with what he
was doing.

He knew he had an angel up in heaven looking after
them and he promised to do right for the rest of his life.